Barry Hines was born at Hoyland
Common, near Barnsley. He went to Ecclesfield Grammar School, where his main achievement was to be selected to play for the England Schools' football team. On leaving school, he worked as an apprentice mining surveyor and played football for Barnsley (mainly in the 'A' Team), before entering Loughborough Training College to study Physical Education. Barry Hines taught for several years in London and South Yorkshire before becoming a full-time novelist and television playwright.

The Blinder (1966) was his first novel: it was followed by *Kes* (published in 1968 as *A Kestrel for a Knave*), which became an immediate bestseller and was made into a popular film; *First Signs* (1972); *The Gamekeeper* (1975); *The Price of Coal* (1979) and *Looks and Smiles* (1981) which has also been filmed: it won the Prize for Contemporary Cinema at the Cannes Film Festival in 1981, and was shown on Central Television in 1982.

Unfinished Business

BARRY HINES

PENGUIN BOOKS

Penguin Books Ltd, Harmondsworth, Middlesex, England
Viking Penguin Inc., 40 West 23rd Street, New York, New York 10010, U.S.A.
Penguin Books Australia Ltd, Ringwood, Victoria, Australia
Penguin Books Canada Ltd, 2801 John Street, Markham, Ontario, Canada L3R 1B4
Penguin Books (N.Z.) Ltd, 182–190 Wairau Road Auckland 10, New Zealand

First published by Michael Joseph Ltd 1983
Published in Penguin Books 1985
Reprinted 1987

Copyright © Barry Hines, 1983
All rights reserved

Made and printed in Great Britain by
Richard Clay Ltd, Bungay, Suffolk
Filmset in Palatino (Linotron 202)

W HEN PHIL saw that all the houses in Morley Street had been knocked down, he turned off the main road and drove slowly between the piles of rubble. He stopped the car and got out, but he wasn't sure if this was where the house had stood or not. All the familiar landmarks had disappeared: lamp posts, corner shops and the covered entries which had punctuated the terraces. The street seemed wider now that all the houses had been demolished. It was lighter too, like a room with the curtains and furniture removed.

Phil stood there, trying to reconstruct the street which he had grown up in. He remembered all the families who had lived there and, as he scanned the heaps of sooty bricks, he found it difficult to believe that so many people had lived in such a small space.

'Thank God for progress,' he said, as he got back into the car and returned to the main road to continue his journey home.

Phil thought about his mother as he drove down Linnet Close. He imagined her sitting beside him looking out approvingly at the modern detached houses and dormer bungalows, the neat front gardens and caravans on the drives. She would have been proud of him. 'You've come a long way from Morley Street,' she would have said. Phil would have agreed with her.

He had to drive carefully as he turned in through the gateway. The narrow drive was his only serious criticism of the house. His friends on the road agreed with him. They were always grumbling about their wives' scraping their cars against the gateposts on their way in and out.

Phil stood by the car and inspected the front lawn; he had been

5

troubled with worm casts recently. No more had appeared since he went to work, so he plucked all the dead heads off a rose bush then went into the house.

Lucy was standing at the sink peeling potatoes. She turned round and smiled and Phil walked across the kitchen and kissed her on the cheek. He was just about to ask her where the children were, when he looked through the window and saw them playing in the garden. Tracey was sitting quietly on the swing on the lawn. She was singing to herself and tapping her toes in time on the flagstone which Phil had set into the turf underneath the seat. Mathew left the path and pedalled towards her on his tricycle which, judging by the engine-like roar of his voice, had been transformed into something more powerful and exciting. The roar increased and, just when it looked as if he was going to hit Tracey head on, he turned his handlebars and veered away. Tracey squealed and kicked out at him, but she was too late, and he pedalled furiously away in the direction of the vegetable patch.

Phil grinned and shook his head. 'The little bugger.' He knock- ed on the window, then walked across to the open door and stood on the step.

'Mathew! Be careful. It's dangerous riding at her like that. You might hurt her.'

Mathew began to circle the lawn. He smiled at Phil every time he passed him, as if he was riding on a merry-go-round at the fair.

'I'm a racing driver, daddy.'

'You'll be racing upstairs to bed if you don't behave yourself.'

Tracey stood up on the swing and pulled it into jerky motion.

'He says he's going to run over me, daddy, like that cat that we saw at the side of the road near my grandma's.'

Phil shook his head in mock censure.

'Don't be cruel, Mathew. It's not nice to say things like that. You wouldn't be laughing if something like that happened to Snowy, would you?'

Mathew stopped smiling and his lips began to quiver and turn down at the ends. He stopped in front of the rabbit hutch, which stood against the fence next to the garden shed, and stepped down off his tricycle. Snowy came to the front of the cage and Mathew touched his cleft nose through the wire netting, then stroked his furry face for comfort.

Phil went back into the kitchen and sat down at the table. A place had been laid for him, and the condiments were grouped

6

neatly in the centre of the clean formica top. Lucy dropped a handful of chips into the boiling fat and looked up at the wall clock.

'You're late, aren't you?' She hurriedly replaced the lid on the pan, then closed the middle door to keep the smell out of the rest of the house. 'I thought your dinner was going to spoil.'

Phil picked up the newspaper from one of the dining chairs and glanced at the front page.

'I gave George a lift home. His car's gone in for a service.'

He was just about to open the newspaper, when he remembered something and looked round at Lucy.

'After I'd dropped him off, I took a short cut through Derwent Square and came past Morley Street. Do you know what they've done?'

Lucy picked up a teacloth and opened the oven door without asking him.

'They've knocked all the houses down.'

'Have they?' She was more concerned with the state of the lamb casserole than with Morley Street. 'I didn't even know they were empty. I haven't been round there for ages now.'

'I haven't, I was amazed. There's still some folks living in Gregory Street by the looks of it, but it's terrible round there now. Half the houses are boarded up, some are derelict. It's a right dump . . .' He looked smugly round his own kitchen with its fitted units, split-level cooker and cork-tiled floor which he had laid himself. 'Fancy living in conditions like that in this day and age. It's primitive.'

Lucy placed the casserole on the table, then, after wiping her hands on her pinafore, she took down a sheet of notepaper from the shelf above the worktop and handed it to Phil.

'What is it?'

'My A-level results.'

She stood behind him and watched him read them.

'An "A" and a "B". Is that good?'

He passed her the paper over his shoulder without turning round. Lucy snatched it off him.

'Of course it is. I couldn't have done much better, could I?'

Realising from her sarcastic tone that he had offended her, Phil turned round to make amends. But before he could speak, his eyes settled on the chip pan on the cooker and his thoughts turned to more basic considerations.

'Them chips are not burning, are they, Lucy?'

She could have hit him with the pan.

'I don't know. Why don't you get up and have a look?'

Phil looked so angry that if he had got up it would have been to see to her, not the chips.

'What, when I've been at work all day?'

Lucy thought of the obvious retort, but she knew that she would only invite sarcasm if she said it. As far as Phil was concerned, she had stopped working eight years ago when she was expecting Tracey. Bringing up children did not count as work. Not *real* work anyway. Real work was done outside the home, for wages. And now that Mathew had started school and she had some time to herself again, she knew that, whatever arguments she put forward, Phil would remain convinced that her life was one long holiday. 'It must be like winning the pools,' he had once said. 'You just get up in a morning and potter about all day.'

Lucy served his dinner in silence. But she made her feelings plain by the vicious way that she stabbed the chops, and the clatter she made when she spooned out the vegetables. She banged down the plate in front of Phil with such force that two chips jumped onto the table.

Phil picked them up and ate them. He was still angry too, but he was too hungry to start an argument which might spoil his dinner. Just as he was about to start eating, Tracey and Mathew came in from the garden, sidled across to the table and stood either side of him staring at his plate. Cutlery poised, Phil glanced down from one to the other.

'Now then, what do you two want?'

He tried to sound severe, but they were too familiar with the performance to be deceived. Tracey moved closer and leaned against him brazenly like a hungry cat.

'Can I have a chip, daddy?'

Mathew, whose chin was resting on the table top, kept his eyes on the food.

'Can I have one too?'

Phil clicked his tongue in mock exasperation, but Lucy, who seemed genuinely annoyed by their begging, moved quickly to the table and tried to pull them away.

'No, you can't. You've had your teas. Now go outside and play and let your daddy get on with his.' She was tempted to add that he had been at work all day, but decided against it in case he thought she was being provocative.

8

She was just about to smack Mathew's hand to make him let go of the table leg, when Phil said, 'Leave him, Lucy. Get them a little plate each; they can have one or two.'

Before Lucy could object, Tracey ran across to the sink and picked up two side-plates off a clean pile on the draining board. She placed them on the table and Phil scraped a few chips onto each one. He counted them to make sure that they both had the same number or there would have been another argument. Lucy looked on disapprovingly. Phil spread the remainder of his chips to disguise the loss, then grinned at her.

'It'll do me good, anyway. You're always saying I could do with losing a bit of weight.'

But Lucy refused to be mollified and, without looking at him or replying, she left the kitchen, taking her examination results with her.

Phil tried to appease her again later that evening after he had cleaned the car, and Lucy had bathed the children and put them to bed. They were sitting in the through-lounge, which had a picture window at each end and was partially divided by a plaster archway. Phil was stretched out on the settee watching television in one half of the room, while Lucy was sitting at the dining table reading a novel in the other.

Looking through the archway when the advertisements ended, Phil said, 'Why don't you come and sit over here? It can't be very comfortable sitting like that.'

She had pushed the book towards the centre of the table to catch the light from the overhanging lamp Leaning towards it, she looked like a plant straining towards the sunlight. Without looking up, she said, 'I'm all right here, thanks.'

'I'll turn the tele off if you like.'

'It doesn't matter.'

Phil stood up and switched it off anyway. Lucy looked across at him.

'I thought you liked that programme.'

'I used to, but it's gone off lately.'

Phil stood with his back to the gas fire, hands spread instinctively behind him even though the room was warm and the fire was turned off. It was dark outside and Phil was attracted by the glow of the television set in the house across the road. He wondered what they were watching. He hoped it was the serial which he had just switched off, so that he could ask his friend Bob

9

what had happened. Still looking through the window, he said, 'If Bob and Sue's television was as big as ours, I'd be able to watch it from here.'

Then, as if to highlight the grandeur of his own set, he switched on the lamp standing on top of it.

'Do you know, when I was down Morley Street today, I couldn't believe that I'd ever lived there. Christ, what a dump. I don't know how my mother and dad stood it all them years.'

Lucy looked up from her book again.

'They'd no choice, had they?'

Phil picked up a beer can from the coffee table in front of the settee. The table took up most of the space on the hearth and Lucy usually kept it in a corner out of the way during the daytime. She had never cared for it, even though it had come free with the three-piece suite, but Phil said that it finished off the room and he liked the motif of vintage cars on the tiled surface.

'Our kids don't know how lucky they are,' he said, shaking the can to liven up the drop of beer inside and looking about the room with obvious satisfaction. 'It's a completely different world to what we were brought up in.'

'Different perhaps, but not necessarily better.'

'What do you mean?'

'Well, when we grew up we could at least be sure of getting a job.'

'I know, but it's only temporary. Things'll pick up. They always do.'

'We'll have to wait and see about that, won't we?'

As she was turning back to her novel, Phil said, 'Anyway, what are you going to do now that you've passed your exams, enrol again in the autumn and take some more?'

Lucy replaced her bookmark and closed the book as deliberately as if she was pressing a flower.

'I've been thinking of applying to university.'

She tried to sound casual, as if such thoughts were commonplace, but her true feelings were revealed by her stillness and the intense way in which she appeared to be studying the picture on the cover of her book. Phil just stared at her, and after a while the force of his gaze made her look up. It was like the reverse of the game in which children stare each other out. Phil had stared Lucy in.

'What do you mean, go to university? Which university?'

10

'The university here, in the city. I could go as a day student. If they'd have me, that is.'

'And how long have you had that idea? You've never said anything about it before.'

'I was waiting for my results. There was no point in saying anything until I knew how I'd got on.'

'You could have said something though . . .'

Phil picked up a fresh can of beer from the table and opened it with a sharp pull of the ring, like someone necking a small animal. He stood there, drinking quickly and saying nothing, then he flopped down in an armchair and began to roll the can between his hands.

'Don't be like that, Phil. I'm only thinking about it.'

'And what about me? Don't I come into it? It does affect me as well, you know.'

'I know it does. We shall have to talk it over. I'm not sure about it myself yet.'

She was just about to stand up and go and sit with him, when he said, 'The best thing you can do is forget all about it. It's a ridiculous idea.'

Lucy stayed where she was.

'Why is it?'

'Well, because you're too old, for a start.'

Lucy was so angry that for a few moments she did not know what to say.

'Too old? Don't talk stupid. How can you be too old to study?'

'You'll feel out of it amongst all them kids. You're old enough to be their mother.'

Lucy grasped the volume of George Eliot on the table. It was only a paperback edition but it would have hurt if it had found its mark with the bound edge.

'What, at twenty-nine? I think it's you that could do with going to university to learn some maths.'

'Don't be so smart. You know what I mean.'

'What's age got to do with it, anyway? There were pensioners taking courses at night school.'

'That's different though, isn't it? They've nothing better to do with their time.'

'And have I?'

'Of course you have. You've a house to run and a family to look after, for a start.'

'Do you call that better?'

11

Lucy shocked herself when she said it. But she had been hurt and she wanted to hurt back. It was Phil's turn to be angry now.

'Yes, I do! Don't we mean anything to you then, me and the kids?'

'Of course you do! You're the most important part of my life, you and our Tracey and Mathew.'

Speaking their names suddenly made her cry. She felt in the pocket of her skirt for a handkerchief, then hurried into the kitchen wiping her cheeks. Phil listened to her blowing her nose, then there was silence for a few minutes before she returned clutching a wad of tissues and sat down on the arm of the settee. Phil ignored her and continued to stare stubbornly at the blank television screen. Lucy knew that if she did not speak first, the rest of the evening would be spent in silence. And probably the next. His record sulk had lasted for four days.

'It's not enough for me being at home all day now, Phil. I want to do something else.'

'Well, why don't you try and get a little job then?'

'Doing what?'

'I don't know. You could do with something part-time like Christine. She says it's ideal. It gives her a bit of pin money and she's home in time for the kids coming home from school.'

'I don't want to work in a shop, Phil.'

'Why don't you try and get back into office work then? You'd only have to brush up on your typing . . .'

'I had enough of offices before we married.'

'I know, but it would come in handy. In fact, I was only thinking at work today that if the orders keep coming in . . .' He leaned forward and touched the leg of the coffee table. '. . . and you could get a job, we might be able to afford a little car for you next year. It'd make your life a lot easier, not having to rely on the buses every time you went out.'

Lucy fought hard to conceal her irritation. First a little job, now a little car. What did he think she was, a midget?

'I don't think I'm really interested in a job at the moment, Phil.'

'No, you wouldn't be, would you?' Now that his plans for her had been rejected, he became sullen again. 'You'd sooner mess about, I suppose.'

'What do you mean, mess about?'

She squeezed the damp tissues in her hand so hard that they turned into pulp.

'Well, what good will it do you, going to university?'

12

Lucy hesitated. It was a difficult question to answer at this stage.

'I was thinking of doing an English degree.'

'And what use will that be? They're sacking teachers left, right and centre just now.'

'Who says I want to be a teacher?'

'What else can you be with an English degree? I mean, it's not even useful; not like computer studies, or science, or something like that.'

'Look Phil, I'm only thinking about it . . .'

'And what was that other subject that you took, Sociology? That's even more useless. What can you do with that?'

'I don't know, but I enjoyed it. Isn't that enough?'

Phil was too exasperated to sit still any longer and he heaved himself out of the chair as if he was escaping from chains.

'I wish you'd never started bloody night school. There'd have been none of this then.'

'But you encouraged me to go, Phil. You said it would do me good.'

'I thought it'd be a change for you, that's all, get you out of the house a bit. I wouldn't have let you go if I'd known it was going to lead to this though, I can tell you.'

'It hasn't led to anything yet. It's only an idea. I just wanted to know what you thought about it, that's all.'

'Well, you know now, don't you?'

He glanced at himself in the mirror above the mantelpiece, then began to button up his cardigan.

'Where are you going?'

'I'm going out for a drink.'

'It's a bit late, isn't it?'

Phil left the room without replying and banged the kitchen door on his way out. The walls vibrated with the impact and Lucy instinctively cocked her head and listened for any disturbance upstairs. Tracey had always been a light sleeper, and Lucy knew that if she did wake up, she would probably have to read to her before she settled down again. She willed her to stay asleep. She was not in the mood for reading just now.

The car door slammed. After it had left the drive, the car accelerated away from the house as if destined for Monte Carlo rather than the Malt Shovel at the end of the road. Lucy listened to it fade and disappear, then sat on the settee and stared at the unlit fire. It was too warm to turn on the heat, so she switched on the 'coal effect' and tried to comfort herself with the glow from the plastic coals.

Lucy looked up the university telephone number after breakfast the following morning, but she kept putting off the call. She convinced herself that she had a few jobs to do first. She would feel more relaxed then. It would give her time to compose herself and think about what she was going to say.

She washed up the breakfast pots first, then shoved a load of dirty clothes into the washing machine. She made the beds, tidied up the children's rooms, then dusted and hoovered the carpet in the lounge. Should she telephone now, or wait until she had had coffee? But would she enjoy her coffee break with the question on her mind? Perhaps it would be better to get it over with . . . She went into the kitchen and decided to make out her shopping list first. She would do it then: definitely. After she had made out her shopping list *and* had a cup of coffee. She would feel refreshed then and more composed. Yes, that was the best plan, that was what she would do. She had made up her mind now . . . or perhaps she could do the shopping first and then make the call . . .

Lucy filled the kettle, switched on the radio and picked up a newspaper from the table. The headline read: PHEW! ANOTHER SCORCHER!, and the story of record temperatures in various regions was illustrated by a photograph of a girl in a bikini sitting astride a donkey sucking a stick of rock. Phil grumbled about the hot weather every time he came home from work. He said that the heat inside the fabrication shop was intolerable. He also said that it had come too soon and was forced to break before they went on holiday. The other story on the front page concerned an escaped parakeet terrorising small children in Swindon. Army marksmen were being called out, it said.

The kettle had just boiled when Lucy's neighbour Judith knocked on the kitchen door. She had come to show Lucy her new mail-order catalogue. Lucy invited her in, and over coffee, Judith told her what she was going to buy from the catalogue, that her husband was in line for promotion and what she was going to cook for his tea. She told Lucy another anecdote about their holiday in Portugal and asked her if she had seen the photographs yet. She thought that the dog had got out last night and it was still on heat. She hoped that the Afghan up the road hadn't been out too. Joanne wasn't well. She had a cold. Fancy, in this

14

weather too. It must be that bug that was going round. French Flu or something, wasn't it? Tony had seen Mike Parks in a pub in town with another woman. She had heard that his wife was leaving him and they were putting their house up for sale. She was thinking of buying some new curtains for Maxine's bedroom. Her sister was expecting another baby. Helen Rawson said they were getting a new car but they were putting their caravan up for sale. The greenfly were ruining their roses. Tony had tried everything. He was thinking of writing to *Gardeners' Question Time* about it. Her mother had once had her name read out on the radio, on *Housewives' Choice*. She couldn't remember what record she had asked for though. Had she tried that new furniture polish yet? Marvellous! She was thinking of slimming, but what was the point now that she'd been on holiday? Her aunty Joan had died suddenly. She'd been in town shopping, the day before. They didn't know whether to cremate her or bury her. Did she know that John Hartley had been made redundant? Had she seen that film on the tele last night . . . ?

Lucy telephoned the university as soon as Judith had gone home. She explained her circumstances to the switchboard operator, who then asked her what subject she was thinking of studying. 'English.' 'Language or Literature?' Lucy hesitated. 'Literature, I think.' 'Hold on please.' Her call was transferred to the Literature Department, where she repeated her story to a secretary.

'Well, there's no one here at the moment, I'm afraid. Everyone's on holiday. I think the best thing would be for me to take down all the details and give them to Professor Jupp when he gets back . . . He won't be there, I'm afraid. He's away in the Greek Islands somewhere . . . No, I think everyone's away at the moment. But there's no point in seeing anyone else anyway. Professor Jupp will have to see your application first . . . I'm not sure. At the end of the month, I think. But he's sure to ring in as soon as he gets back . . . No, I don't think so. Now, if I could just take down what you've told me . . .' Lucy repeated the information for the third time. 'And now your address and telephone number please . . . Thank you. I think it might be a good idea if I sent you along an application form as well . . . Yes, I'm sure Professor Jupp will be in touch as soon as he returns. Goodbye.'

Her tone was husky and encouraging. It was a professional farewell. A man would have been flattered by it. Lucy was devastated. She stood there, holding the receiver. Surely there was something else she could say, something else she could do. But what? She stared at the doodle she had drawn on the telephone pad during her conversation with the secretary. It looked like a cobweb with thick, strong strands. Quietly she replaced the receiver.

What an anticlimax it had been. But what had she expected, immediate admission on the strength of one telephone call? She felt that somehow she had made a fool of herself, and blushed as she imagined the secretaries in the Literature Department office making fun of her. 'This woman just phoned up enquiring about a place in October. She seemed surprised when there was nobody here. Honestly, some people have no idea . . .' Lucy rushed back into the kitchen and slammed the door as if they were laughing at her in the hall.

Lucy did not mention the telephone call to Phil and he did not raise the subject again either. Days passed. Nothing more was said and, as Lucy became increasingly involved in the preparations for their annual holiday, Phil was convinced that she had given up the idea of going to university.

He was wrong about the weather too. It remained fine for the whole of their fortnight in Torquay. Phil was jubilant. There was nothing worse than going back to work after a rain-spoiled holiday and everybody gloating about it. One of the welders was so unlucky with the weather that the others waited until he had booked his holidays so they could avoid the same dates.

They had rented a holiday flat in the town. It had looked cold and uncomfortable at first with its unfamiliar furniture and bare surfaces, but once they had unpacked and spread their own belongings around, it soon looked like home.

They spent most days on the beach. Then, in the evenings, after Lucy had cooked a meal, they walked along the promenade, or visited a pub and sat outside while the children played in the garden.

Lucy enjoyed it on the beach. She had time to relax and think while Phil played with the children. He organised all the ball games and castle building, and Lucy joined in sometimes when they needed her to make up a team; but she was happiest sitting in a deckchair looking after the clothes and equipment, and having the towels ready for the children when they ran back glistening and triumphant from the sea.

She read and dozed and watched other people from behind her

16

sunglasses. She sometimes thought about university, but more dispassionately now. It seemed less important here, three hundred miles from home, with the sun in her face, a book in her lap and her feet excavating the warm sand. There was no point in getting worked up about it. It was probably too late to go this year anyway. Her best plan would be to take another subject at evening class and apply for next October. Yes, that would be much more sensible. That would give Phil more time to get used to the idea too. She had sprung it on him too soon. He would come round to it in the end. After all, he had allowed her to go to evening classes when she had wanted to do that.

Lucy watched him playing with Tracey and Mathew in the sea. He was standing up to his waist in the water and the children were taking turns to climb onto his shoulders and jump off. Lucy smiled. That was her family playing out there in the waves: those two boisterous children and that patient man with the sore back. Perhaps Phil was right. Perhaps she ought to forget about university and look for a job. And even if she couldn't find one, she knew that he wouldn't mind. He liked her to be at home, to take and collect the children from school, to keep the house clean and to have his dinner ready for him when he came home from work. And wasn't that enough? Was it really worth disrupting the family just to pursue a selfish whim?

She watched Mathew crouched at the water's edge drawing patterns in the smooth wet sand. Every time a strong wave came in, it erased them and he had to start again. Lucy wanted to run down the beach and hug him. She wanted to pick him up and press his cheek against hers. Yes! It was enough. She had been wrong. Her first duty was to her family. University could wait.

She was just about to get up out of her deckchair and join the others when she noticed a woman in a white bikini walking out of the sea. She passed close to Mathew (even he looked up at her), continued calmly up the beach and stopped at a small pile of belongings a few yards away. She picked up her towel, and Lucy could see that other people were watching her too as she shook it loose and leisurely began to pat herself dry. Lucy marvelled at her self-assurance. Whenever *she* came out of the sea, she couldn't wait to get back to her towel, and she always dried herself on her knees crouching down.

Lucy tried to work out how old she was. Middle twenties? Twenty-five, twenty-six perhaps. That was only three years younger than herself. It did not seem possible! Lucy was sure that *she* looked ten years older, at least. She noticed the younger woman's firm thighs and flat stomach, and when she looked over her sunglasses to see how brown she really was, her suntan was just as impressive in the daylight.

Lucy looked down at her own loose flesh and wished she was wearing a bathing costume. As she breathed in and hitched up her bikini pants, she noticed how worn and faded the material was. Every year she intended to buy a new one. Every year she took her old one out of the drawer and stuffed it into the case.

The woman in the white bikini (Lucy's model looked twice as big as hers), spread out her towel and lay down. As she stretched her arms, Lucy noticed that she wasn't wearing a wedding ring. So what? A lot of married women didn't wear wedding rings these days. Not that she knew any personally, but she had been told. And why should she wear a ring? Most men didn't. In that case, why was she wearing hers? Lucy felt her own wedding ring and tried to twist it round; the heat had swollen her finger and it would not move. But she knew that the other woman wasn't married. She didn't *look* married. Lucy knew that she looked married. She felt married. Even when she was on her own.

Lucy was fascinated. There she was, a single woman, with a canvas bag and a few clothes. She looked round at her family's possessions. It would take them fifteen minutes to pack up when they decided to leave. The other woman would be gone in seconds. Lucy wondered where she would go to when she left the beach. One thing was certain, she wouldn't be calling for groceries at a supermarket, then cooking a meal for four in a back-street furnished flat. She would be staying in a seafront hotel: single room with private bath. She would go back and soak for a long time, then go out to a restaurant. Meet someone perhaps. Dinner for two . . . Tracey dashed up the beach and created a minor sandstorm as she skidded to a halt in front of Lucy's deckchair.

'We're going to play piggy-in-the-middle, mummy! You come and play!'

Lucy cautiously opened her eyes and spat out some sand.

'Can't you play without me, love? I'm having a rest.'

Tracey took the plastic football out of the pit which they had dug for it in the sand.

'No, mummy. You're on my side and Mathew's playing with my daddy.'

Lucy looked past her and saw Phil beckoning to her from the

sea. His swimming trunks were old too. She also noticed how thick his waist was, and how stocky he had grown.

'Come on then.'

Lucy placed her book under her deckchair and Tracey pulled her to her feet. She pulled down her bikini over her buttocks, then, feeling awkward and self-conscious, ran hand in hand with Tracey down to the sea.

When she returned ten minutes later, out of breath and dripping wet, the woman had gone, and another family had taken her space.

As soon as they arrived home from their holiday, Tracey and Mathew ran round the back of the house to say hello to the rabbit. They had brought him a pound of carrots for a present, and they had a little squabble in front of the hutch to decide who should give him the first one. Phil unstrapped the roof rack while Lucy, carrying a basketful of empty flasks and sandwich boxes, unlocked the front door.

She put down the basket and picked up the scattering of letters from the doormat. They consisted mainly of circulars and official-looking brown envelopes addressed to Phil; but there was one for her and she opened it straightaway and read it.

She was still standing there when Phil struggled into the hall grunting under the weight of two large suitcases. Without looking up from the letter, Lucy moved to one side to let him pass. Phil was furious. He banged down the cases and glared at her in disgust. It had been a long, tiring drive, the roads had been busy, the children fractious, and now, with a carful of luggage still to unload and the cases to unpack, all Lucy could find to do was stand there reading letters. At least she could have put the kettle on first!

'It must be important, that's all I can say.'

'It's just a note from the university, that's all.'

She tried to sound casual as she folded the letter and replaced it in the envelope.

'The university? What have they written to you for?'

Lucy crossed the hall and opened the kitchen door. The air smelled cool and stale and for an instant everything looked unfamiliar.

'I telephoned to enquire about courses.'

'What courses? You never said anything about it to me.

'I did. Just before we went away.'

19

'I can't remember.'

'You were watching snooker or darts or something. You probably never heard me.'

Keeping her back to him as much as possible, and her eyes averted, Lucy tried to divert Phil's attention from the letter with an impressive display of domestic devotion. She opened the window, switched on the refrigerator and freezer, filled the kettle and fetched in the milk from the back doorstep. But Phil was still suspicious. Surely he would have remembered. On the other hand, if he had been watching darts (especially if he had been out for a drink first), he might not have been listening.

'What do they say?'

Lucy smiled at his use of the plural. He made it sound like a reply from the hospital or the income-tax office.

'Nothing much.'

Phil picked up the envelope from the kitchen table and took out the letter. Lucy felt indignant that he had not asked her if he could read it; that he took it for granted that her business was his business too. She felt like snatching it out of his hand. Instead, she left the house by the front door and went out to the car.

She was unloading the boot when Phil emerged seconds later brandishing the letter.

'What's all this about then?'

Lucy picked up Mathew's bucket of seashells and placed them on the drive next to Tracey's wellington boots. Phil stood behind her waiting for an answer, but when she took no notice of him and took out a bunch of dried seaweed and a crab's shell, he read out a few sentences to attract her attention.

Lucy was immediately struck by the formality of the language and how incongruous it sounded coming from Phil. He sounded like a policeman giving evidence in court. Lucy opened a paper-bag and took out some crusts.

'It's just a general reply, that's all.'

'It sounds more than that to me. It mentions here about you going for an interview.'

'There's nothing wrong with that, is there? Anyway, there's no chance of me going this year. It's too late for that now.'

'Well, I think we ought to have another talk about it before you decide to go anywhere.'

Lucy began to break up the crusts and throw them onto the front lawn. Phil looked on aghast, all other considerations dispelled by her brazen act of vandalism.

'What are you doing?'

'Well, nobody else is going to eat them now, are they? I might as well give them to the birds.'

She continued to litter the grass with stale bread.

'You could at least have done it round the back. It looks a right mess.'

Untidiness distressed him. He felt the same way about rusty tools and dirty cars.

'It doesn't matter, does it? They'll have eaten it in no time.'

Then, as if to support her contention, a sparrow flew down from the gutter and carried away the first scrap of bread.

Their argument was cut short by Judith, their next-door neighbour, knocking and waving at an upstairs window. Moments later, she hurried outside to welcome them back.

Had they had a nice time? Had the weather been good? It had been marvellous here. Last Sunday had been the hottest day for ten years. She had been in every day to check that everything was all right. She had watered the plants only yesterday. Tony had watered the tomatoes. She had put the milk out of the sun. David Brazier had been knocked off his bike. It wasn't serious though . . .

By the time she had brought them up to date with the local news, and Phil and Lucy had unloaded the car, the front lawn was clear again.

When Lucy called Professor Jupp at his home the following Monday to arrange an interview, a boy answered the telephone. He had to shout above the noise of a dog barking ferociously close by, and when Professor Jupp finally heard him and came to the telephone, he shouted to someone called Marion to 'please come and remove this infernal hound!' If Lucy had not been so nervous, she would have laughed at the farce taking place at the other end of the line. The hound was removed, still barking, and Professor Jupp explained to Lucy that it appeared to have a strong objection to the cat sitting on the mantelpiece.

As they talked, Lucy could hear someone practising a violin in another room. She wrote down the arrangements on the telephone pad, then ripped off the top sheet in case Phil saw it when he came home from work. She had decided not to say anything to him about the interview. It was unlikely that anything would come of it anyway, so there was no point in causing unnecessary trouble.

*

Lucy had never been to the university before. She had been past it many times on her way to and from town, but she had never stopped there. She had had no reason to. She enjoyed stating her destination when she got on the bus. 'The university, please,' she said, glancing up at the conductor to see if he was impressed. But he wound out her ticket with the same indifference that he had shown for the last request, which had been for Central Avenue.

Lucy stood and looked round at the buildings for a few moments when she reached the university. They stretched along both sides of the road, and their styles ranged from red-brick Victorian, through 1930s' municipal Greek (complete with Doric columns and wide steps), to the sheer steel and glass constructions of modern times. 'The English Literature Department is on the tenth floor of the Albert Schweitzer Tower,' Professor Jupp had informed her on the telephone. 'It is the tallest and most hideous building on the campus, and will assail your eyes as soon as you alight from the bus.'

Lucy recognised it straightaway; it was the building in front of her across the road. But she did not think it was hideous: she liked the simple shape and the gleaming walls of tinted glass. She crossed the busy road by the subway, the walls of which were covered with ragged posters, political slogans and puzzling items of graffiti which she did not understand: STOLEN PETS. MORTUARY IN WAX. VICTORIAN OUTCASTS. Whatever did they mean? She was still trying to work it out as she walked up the ramp at the other side of the road.

The paved areas between the university buildings had been planted with flowerbeds and shrubs; and a stand of birch trees, reflected in the ground-floor windows of the Schweitzer Tower, gave the impression that the landscaping had been continued inside.

Lucy entered the foyer, where she was confronted by two open-fronted lift-shafts containing moving compartments: one travelling up, the other down. She stared at it fearfully. Surely she wasn't supposed to ride in this? Stepping on escalators was dangerous enough without extending the ordeal to vertical ascent. She did not like the grinding noise it made either. What if she managed to jump on, but daren't get off and went right up to the top? What would happen to her then? Would she be mangled to a pulp in the machinery? Or just thrown onto her head, and come down the other side in an unconscious heap, on exhibition at every floor? Wasn't there an ordinary lift? Or even stairs? She was just going to find out when a man's head appeared at floor level in the lift before her. He grew to full size, then stepped casually out into the foyer. Lucy hesitated. It looked easy enough. And there was nobody about if she did make a fool of herself and fall down. Anyway, she had to do it. This was her first test. If she could not even master the transport arrangements, she might as well pack up and go home now.

She approached the edge of the lift-shaft, waited for the floor of the next compartment to rise level – and let it go past. Right then, the next one. She looked round to see if anyone was watching her, but the only other person in the foyer was a porter, and he was busy checking the labels on some parcels near the door. Right, this time then . . . Next time then. Definitely this time. One, two three. Go! She leaped as if into a speeding train, stumbled forward and banged against the metal walls. The porter looked round at the clatter, but all he saw was the bottom half of a woman dressed in a checked skirt and high heels disappearing upwards. Lucy brushed her velvet jacket with her hand and pulled it straight. Thank goodness it was the holidays and there were no students around to witness her launching. The humiliation would have been devastating.

As the floors went by, she began to enjoy it. She thought of Tracey and Mathew. They would have loved it. It would have been like a free ride at the fair. She smiled as she imagined their excited faces and heard their squeals as they jumped in and out. Phil would have been interested in the lift too. He would have stood and watched the compartments clanking by for a while, then probably approached the porter and discussed with him how it worked.

She stepped out confidently at the tenth floor, then stood there wondering where to go. The corridor was deserted, but she could hear the faint clatter of a typewriter in the distance so she started towards it. As she walked along the corridor, she read the nameplates on the doors, and was impressed by the number of doctors on the staff. One of them was called Pybus. For a moment she thought it said Pyrex. She also noticed how few women were on the staff too.

The door of the Literature Department office was half open. Lucy knocked and looked in. The secretary did not hear her for the sound of the typewriter, and she reached the end of a line before looking up.

'Hello. Can I help you?'

23

'Yes, I've got an appointment with Professor Jupp.'

'What's your name, please?'

'Mrs Downs. Lucy Downs.'

'Ah yes.' She stood up and walked round the desk. 'Professor Jupp is expecting you.'

She knocked on an adjoining door, a voice called, 'Come!' and the secretary showed Lucy into Professor Jupp's office.

After their bizarre telephone conversation, Lucy had expected to meet an eccentric-looking man, with unruly grey hair perhaps, and wearing a crumpled tweed suit. The sort of man you would guess to be a professor if you saw him in the street. Instead, she shook hands with a man with short back and sides, wearing corduroy trousers and a short-sleeved shirt. His face and arms were deeply tanned from his holiday in Greece. Lucy remembered the suntanned woman on the beach at Torquay . . .

'Nice to meet you, Mrs Downs. Please take a seat. I'd better not offer you a chair in case my meaning is misconstrued. It has been known to happen at interviews.'

Smiling diffidently at what she presumed to be a joke, Lucy sat down in one of a pair of armchairs set at a coffee table in the centre of the room. Professor Jupp remained standing, facing her.

'Would you care for a sherry, Mrs Downs?'

Lucy was flustered by the invitation. She hesitated. What if she gave the wrong answer and it prejudiced her chances?

'Or I could get you a coffee, if you prefer it?'

'No. No. A sherry would come in, er . . . rather pleasantly, thank you.'

Come in rather pleasantly! Lucy slowly repeated it to herself as Professor Jupp crossed the room to a glass-fronted bookcase standing against the wall. What sort of answer was that? Why hadn't she just said 'yes please' as she would have done to anyone else? She blushed at what he must be thinking about her: what he would tell his family when he got home.

Professor Jupp opened the bookcase doors and slid two bottles to the front of a shelf. Most of the furniture in the room was standard issue, but the bookcase, faded Indian carpet and mahogany knee-hole desk were obviously his own. The desk was so big that Lucy wondered how they had managed to get it all the way up here. What if the floor collapsed and it fell through? Would it come to rest in the office below? Or keep going until it reached the basement?

'Sweet or dry, Mrs Downs?'

24

Lucy was again taken by surprise.

'Oh, er, sweet, please.'

He filled her glass, then, Lucy noticed with dismay, his own from the other bottle. Not another faux pas, she hoped, as Professor Jupp crossed the room and handed her the darker glass of sherry.

'Good health,' he said, raising his glass and taking a sip before sitting down opposite Lucy and settling back in his chair. Lucy took a sip too, but remained upright in her seat.

'Well, Mrs Downs, perhaps you could begin by telling me a little bit about yourself. All I know of you is from your letter and application form, which, if I remember correctly, catalogues very impressive Advanced-level results . . .'

He sat up and looked towards his desk as if he meant to go and fetch the form. But, as he surveyed the disorderly spread of papers on its surface, he changed his mind and sat back again.

'I suppose the most obvious question to start with is, why do you want to go to university now, when you could have made it much easier for yourself by staying on at school and going from there?'

Lucy cleared her throat and crossed her legs. She noticed Professor Jupp glance down at them, but resisted twitching at her skirt as the gesture might have seemed too pointed.

'I never really thought about stopping on. I just wanted to leave school as soon as I could and earn some money.'

'But what about your parents, didn't they encourage you? They must have known you had potential.'

'They didn't encourage me or discourage me. They said it was up to me what I did.'

'But the school must have given you some guidance.'

'They did. Mr Parkhouse, the headmaster, said it was criminal that I was leaving. He sent for my dad to try to persuade him to make me stop on.'

'He obviously failed.'

'My dad said I was old enough to make up my own mind what I did.'

'He appears to have shown remarkable confidence in your maturity. Do you think he was right?'

Lucy hesitated and picked up her glass from the table.

'No, not now. But I don't suppose he ever thought about me going to university. He just took it for granted that I'd leave and get a job, like most children did where I come from.'

Lucy was ashamed of herself. It sounded like a betrayal. She made him sound ignorant and unconcerned. But he wasn't like that at all. He was a kindly man. He had been a good father and she loved him. She resented Professor Jupp probing her past. What did he know about it anyway? She couldn't imagine his father calling to see the headmaster on a ramshackle bicycle on his way home from work. (Lucy remembered how embarrassed she had been when she had seen him in the corridor in his overalls.) His father would have *been* the headmaster: the person sitting behind the desk, rather than the one in front of it on the edge of his chair. Like Lucy was sitting now, the only difference being that she was holding a glass of sherry instead of a flat cap.

'If not then, Mrs Downs, why now, when your domestic circumstances make it so much more difficult?'

Lucy studied his trousers while she thought about it. She hadn't seen such a pair of thick corduroys for years. And with turnups too. Someone she knew used to wear trousers like that. Who was it?

'Well, I think I'm really ready for it now. I really feel I want to do something different. Whereas, if I'd stopped on at school and gone on to university then, I'd have been doing it for a job qualification more than anything else.'

'And what will you be doing it for now?'

Lucy had a sip of sherry before she replied.

'Because I want to.' It sounded like a child's answer. 'I feel as if I've been asleep for a long time and I'm just beginning to wake up.'

Professor Jupp smiled at her and tapped his finger ends together. It looked like miniature applause.

'Why have you chosen English Literature? Did you enjoy literature at school?'

Lucy leaned forward to pick up her glass again, then changed her mind. She did not want to finish her drink before Professor Jupp, in case he formed the wrong impression of her.

'Not particularly. I started reading seriously when the children were little. I used to get so bored sometimes that if I hadn't have done something else, I'd have gone mad.'

'Literature as therapy, eh, Mrs Downs? I'm sure T. L. Stanger would approve of that.'

Lucy smiled (knowingly she hoped, T. L. *Who*?), and remembered those precious interludes when the children were asleep, and instead of tidying up their toys, or washing clothes, or

26

tackling a basketful of ironing, she had opened a novel and read, oblivious of the time, until a cry from upstairs brought her back home, and she realised with mounting panic that Phil would be home from work soon, and she hadn't even thought about his dinner.

'How old are your children, Mrs Downs?'

'Eight and six.'

'So they're both at school then?'

'Yes. I suppose it was when Mathew started school and I had a bit of free time to myself at last that I first started thinking about taking a course of some kind.'

'And what about your husband? What's his attitude to all this? Is he sympathetic . . . ? What I'm trying to get at is, would you be able to cope with a full-time course of study in addition to your existing domestic commitments?'

Lucy finished her drink and licked her lower lip. Professor Jupp mistook this sign of tension for enjoyment, and offered to refill her glass. Lucy declined politely, even though she would have liked him to.

'Yes. I think so.'

'That's good. It's vital that both partners are in full accord in a matter like this, or it can lead to the most appalling discord.'

Suddenly, Lucy wanted a cigarette, even though she hadn't smoked for years.

'I suppose it'll take him a bit of time to get used to the idea. But he'll come round to it in the end, I'm sure of that.'

'You're fortunate to have such a sympathetic partner, Mrs Downs. Not all husbands adopt such a positive attitude, I can assure you. By the way, what does your husband do?'

'He's a welder. The charge-hand welder,' she added hastily, hoping that his recent promotion would enhance his status (and hers).

'Ah!' He made Lucy's revelation sound significant and she began to worry in case Phil's job might somehow prejudice her chances.

'Now then, Mrs Downs, perhaps you could tell me what books you studied at Advanced level?'

Lucy was still wishing that Phil was a doctor or a bank manager and she almost missed what he said.

'We did Shakespeare – *Measure for Measure* and *The Winter's Tale*. Pope – *The Rape of the Lock*. Wordsworth . . . Hardy – *Tess of the D'Urbervilles*. Dickens . . .'

27

'How did you get on with Hardy?'

He finished off his sherry, then twisted the stem of his glass between his finger and thumb while he waited for an answer. Sunlight, striking the remaining drop of liquid in the bowl, made it look as if it was being kindled by friction.

'Well, I did all right in the exam, but I didn't enjoy the book very much. It was too gloomy, too . . . fatalistic. There was no hope in it.'

'Some people might argue that it's not the function of the novelist to provide hope, that that task is best left to the propagandist or politician.'

'I'm not sure what the function of the novelist is.' She immediately wished she hadn't said it. If she was hoping to study English Literature at university, perhaps she ought to know. Professor Jupp's silence seemed to indicate that he thought so too. 'Well, different writers have different intentions, I suppose. Some are just content to entertain the reader, and some want to go further and put over certain points of view. They try to influence the way that you think and make you see things in a different light.'

Lucy was distracted slightly by Professor Jupp's habit of nodding at everything she said. He reminded her of the nodding dog on the shelf in the back window of their car.

'I once read somewhere that great writers were like prophets. It said that they felt the tremors before the earth quaked.'

Lucy decided to forgo a triumphal pause and press on in case Professor Jupp asked her where the quotation came from (*Reader's Digest*), and to name one of the great writers (she couldn't remember).

'I found Hardy too pessimistic. It's like religion. Everybody has their place and there's nothing you can do about it.'

Professor Jupp moved his fingers slowly round the rim of his glass and stared into the empty bowl.

'Hardy's not to everyone's taste, I agree.'

Lucy wondered if Hardy was to Professor Jupp's taste. He did not say. He continued to deliberate over the glass before carefully placing it diagonally across the table from Lucy's. With an ashtray between them, it looked as if he had completed a winning line at noughts and crosses.

'I presume you would want to read for an Honours degree, Mrs Downs?'

Lucy wasn't sure what an Honours degree was, but she

liked the sound of it and said she would. Anyway, she could always ask Mrs Boyd when she started evening classes again in September.

'Well, we do in fact have a couple of unexpected vacancies due to students who were accepted provisionally failing to achieve their required A-level grades. In view of this, and if it is acceptable to you, Mrs Downs, I would like to offer one of those places to you.'

Lucy just stared at him. Professor Jupp began to smile at her incredulous expression.

'Do you mean for this year?'

'That's right. It's short notice, I'm afraid, and I'm not sure what the position will be regarding a grant, local-authority finances being what they are.'

'That would be marvellous. Even if I don't get a grant, I'll manage it somehow.'

'I hope so. I think you've earned a second chance.'

Lucy put her hand to her mouth. Her eyes shone. She looked as if she had won the pools.

'I can't believe it really.'

Professor Jupp wondered what state his handkerchief was in, in case she started to cry.

'That's settled then.'

He picked up the empty glasses from the table and stood up.

'Perhaps I can persuade you to have another sherry now? I think a little celebration is in order.'

Lucy looked up at him and smiled.

'Yes, I'd love one, thank you very much.'

On her way out, Lucy stepped on and off the paternoster lift as if she had been riding it for years, and as she walked back to the bus stop, she remembered who used to wear thick corduroy trousers like Professor Jupp's: it was Mr Catchpole, the eccentric History master at school, who sometimes taught from a chair on top of his desk and pronounced Trafalgar *Trafal-gar*.

'If you don't get a grant, I'm not keeping you, Lucy.'

'You never have kept me, Phil. I just haven't been paid for the last nine years, that's all.'

'Don't be so clever. You know what I mean.'

'Yes, I do, and I resent it as well. Because if I'd have been paid hourly like you, I'd have earned a fortune in overtime.'

'And what if I get put on short time, or made redundant?'

'I thought you said you'd plenty of work on?'

'We have, for the next month or two. There's no knowing what'll happen after that though.'

'We'd just have to manage, wouldn't we? Other people do.'

'Yes, and other people's wives would put their families first and try to get a job to tide them over.'

'Well, if I get a grant there'll be no problem. You'll be able to stop at home, and I'll be able to keep you for a change.'

'Very funny, I must say.'

Later, in bed, they lay apart with their backs to each other, both aware that the other was awake, but neither of them speaking. Lucy was thinking about her interview. She kept running it through and smiling to herself in the dark. She watched herself shaking hands with Professor Jupp . . . saw him pouring sherry . . . overheard fragments of their conversation . . . But all the time, she was aware of Phil lying there sulking. She wanted to turn over and reach out to reassure him, but she didn't. She was afraid that he might take it as a sign of weakness and start dissuading her again.

Phil listened to the clock. He was afraid to look at the time in case it was later than he thought. Lucy was wrong about his mood. He wasn't sulking: he was worrying. He felt apprehensive and threatened by what she was doing. He was trying to be reasonable and to understand her needs, but every time they talked about it he finished up losing his temper. He wanted to turn over and reach out to Lucy for reassurance. But he didn't. He was afraid that she might take it as a sign of weakness and think that he had given in.

Two cats started wailing and screeching underneath the bedroom window. It was a chilling sound, like someone being tortured. Lucy was relieved that they weren't at the back of the house, or they might have wakened the children and frightened them.

Phil used this diversion as an excuse to speak.

'Bloody things. Somebody ought to throw a bucket of water over them.'

'What's the matter, are they keeping you awake?'

'They're not helping any.'

'Do you want me to go down and make you a cup of tea?'

'No, I'll be all right.'

Lucy smiled at his martyred tone and turned over.

'You're worrying too much, Phil. It'll not make that much difference. It'll only be like going out to work.'

She put her arm round him and moved closer to his back.

'You're determined to go through with it, aren't you, Lucy?'

'I want to give it a try, Phil. I've set my mind on it now.'

He knew then that there was no more to be said. No matter how much he objected, pleaded, argued, threatened, raged or sulked, there was nothing he could do now to make her change her mind. He was going to have to put up with it. And it was a relief, in a way, to have reached that decision. It was like receiving the result of a diagnosis: it might not be good news, but it was better than the turmoil of not knowing.

Phil turned over and pulled Lucy to him.

'I hope it's not going to make any difference to us, that's all, Lucy.'

'Of course it won't. I wouldn't do anything to spoil it between you and me, Phil, you know that.'

She kissed him urgently on the face and mouth and Phil responded to her unexpected ardour by pushing her onto her back and rolling on top of her. There was no preliminary coaxing or caressing or gentle exploration; he just prised open her thighs with his knee and thrust his way inside her. Lucy tried to relax and work up to the explosion in her head, the shouts and moans, the tearful release. But she was too slow, Phil would not wait for her, and, when she heard him grunt and felt his grip tighten, all she could do was hold on to him while he banged his hips against hers and enjoyed his gasping, spurting pleasure.

Lucy lay patiently under his dead weight waiting for him to get off. She stroked his damp hair, and when he finally withdrew, the pillow was also damp where he had pressed his face into it.

'Do you feel better now?'

He grazed her cheek with his whiskers as he nodded.

'Go to sleep now then, or you'll never get up in the morning.'

Phil turned over and Lucy lay there listening to his breathing slow down and deepen as he went to sleep. She stayed awake, as she had done many times before, but this time, instead of seeking consolation in her home and children, she tried to relieve her frustration by thinking about her interview and her new life at university.

When Lucy told Phil that she had received a grant from the education authority, he just carried on with his dinner. He did

31

not even ask her how much it was worth. He never asked her anything about university now: it was her business. He might have accepted her decision, but he did not approve of it.

And he showed his disapproval in various cutting ways, like refusing to read any of her university correspondence or, if the children asked him a question when Lucy was present, telling them to ask her, as 'she was the brains in the family'. And sometimes, when they were out with friends, he made them laugh by calling her 'Brain of Britain' or 'Mastermind'.

Phil found a staunch ally in Lucy's mother, who visited most weeks to see the children. She always waited until Phil came home from work before starting her tirade. It usually went something like this:

'I can't understand you at all, Lucy, wanting to go back to schooling at your age. What's the point? Why make things harder for yourself? If you'd wanted to go to university, you should have stopped on at school and gone at the proper time like everybody else. And don't say we stopped you, because we didn't. It was your decision. Mr Parkhouse begged and prayed you to stop on but you wouldn't take any notice. That's when you should have done it, then, all them years ago when you were single, not now, when you've a husband and children to consider. You can't study and do full justice to your home and family, it's impossible. And if you think that I'm traipsing across town every day to look after the kids when they come home from school, you've another think coming. You can make other arrangements. I suppose they'll finish up with latchkeys round their necks like you read about in the papers. There's too much of that going on, if you ask me. There's no wonder that we're in the state that we're in and kids are running riot everywhere. Sheer irresponsibility, that's what it is, and the sooner you get these daft ideas out of your head and settle yourself down, the better it'll be for everybody concerned . . .'

Lucy only argued with her the first time. After that, she just ignored her and allowed her to carry on. Phil made it obvious whose side he was on, just by keeping quiet.

But Lucy felt too sanguine to be intimidated by either of them, and during the weeks leading up to the start of term, she tried to forestall any criticism by being extra diligent about the house. She always had Phil's dinner ready for him when he arrived home from work. The living room was always tidy so that he had nothing to grumble about when he sat down afterwards. She put

the children to bed early and she always allowed him first choice
of television programmes. She even mowed the back lawn one
afternoon and weeded the borders. But not the front lawn. That
was sacred ground, only Phil was allowed to cut that. Sometimes,
when Lucy saw him on his hands and knees searching for weeds,
she longed for an invasion of moles, or a visit by spade-wielding
vandals during the night.

One evening when Lucy was bathing the children, Tracey asked
her what university was. 'It's like a school for grown-ups,' Lucy
told her, and one Saturday morning, before the new term started,
she took them on the bus (Phil was using the car), and showed
them round the campus to try to make it more real for them.

'It's a big school, mummy,' Tracey said, as she stood gazing up
at the Schweitzer Tower.

Lucy took them inside, and once she had persuaded them onto
the paternoster lift, she could not get them off again. Clinging to
her skirt and squealing with excitement, they rode past the English
floor to the top of the building, then down the other side to the
foyer, where Lucy held their hands and with a one, two, three
helped them to jump off.

Phil was underneath the car when they arrived home. Tracey
and Mathew could not wait to tell him their news, so they knelt
down and shouted to him what they had seen and done at
mummy's university. Lucy grinned as she walked past his legs
which were sticking out from under the bonnet. There was a
comical resignation about the splayed angle of his boots, and
she could imagine his face as he lay there trapped, waiting
patiently for them to finish so that he could continue draining
the sump.

Phil tried every excuse he could think of to avoid going with Lucy
to buy her books. Why didn't she go on the bus? Because they
would be too heavy to carry on her own, she told him. (He did not
believe her until she showed him her booklist.) In that case (the
supreme sacrifice this), she could borrow the car and he would
stop at home and look after the kids. But the kids did not want to
stay at home. They wanted to go to the bookshop with their
mum. Perfect, Phil thought. You three go in the car and I'll stop at
home on my own. But Lucy would have none of it. She wanted
him there to supervise the children so that she could concentrate
on buying her books.

Phil was trapped. 'What a waste of a Saturday,' he said, slowly shaking his head.

Lucy looked at the signs indicating the various departments, then took Tracey and Mathew by the hand and led them towards the children's section at the far end of the shop. It was an attractive, welcoming area with posters on the walls above the shelves, mobiles hanging from the ceiling and tables stacked with vivid-coloured picture books. Lucy looked through some of these books with the children, while Phil stood back looking ill at ease, like he did in dress shops when Lucy was in the fitting rooms trying on new clothes. She told the children to have a good look round, and if they behaved themselves, she would buy them a book after she had bought hers.

'I want this one,' Mathew said, opening a pop-up book and raising ghosts and monsters every time he turned a page.

Lucy looked at the price. 'I think you'll have to write to Father Christmas for that one.' She turned to Phil who was studying an alphabet wall-frieze. 'Are you stopping here then?'

'I might as well. It's just about my level this, picture books and ABCs.'

He said it loud enough to make an assistant glance round at him and smile. Phil smiled back, and even though Lucy knew that he was being sarcastic she was still angry because she felt that he had demeaned himself in front of the girl.

'I'm going upstairs, Phil, if you want me.'

As Lucy climbed the stairs to the education department, she experienced that same mixture of fear and excitement that she had felt as she approached the Schweitzer Tower on the morning of her interview. She wanted to turn back, but her feet kept moving forward.

It was quieter and more sedate upstairs, and the few people at the shelves looked as if they were browsing rather than buying. Lucy went to the English Literature section first, took out her list, then started to look on the shelves for the set books: Gardner, H. (ed.), *The Metaphysical Poets* . . . Spenser, E., *Poetical Works* . . . Jonson, B., *The Alchemist* . . . Marlowe, *Dr Faustus* . . . Shakespeare, *Hamlet*, *A Midsummer Night's Dream* . . . Donne, J., *Complete English Poems* . . . As Lucy took the books from the shelves, she opened them at random and read parts of prefaces, exchanges of dialogue and odd lines of poetry. She wanted to read more. She picked out books that weren't on her list and she wanted to buy them too. She wanted to buy them all. She felt greedy, like when she was buying clothes sometimes. One dress wasn't enough. She wanted the whole rail.

She took her books to the counter, then returned for the novels: Austen, J., *Emma, Persuasion, Sense and Sensibility* . . . Fielding, H., *Tom Jones* . . . Richardson, S., *Pamela* (vol. 1) . . . Then on to English Language: Sweet's *Anglo-Saxon Primer* . . . Sweet's *Anglo-Saxon Reader* . . . Robinson, F. N. (ed.), *The Works of Geoffrey Chaucer* . . .

As Lucy turned round with her second pile of books, she was surprised to see Phil standing at the shelves in the metallurgy section. Proudly, she approached him, hoping that he would turn round and see her carrying her books. When had she once felt like this before . . . ? Yes! That was it! When Tracey had been born, and she had arrived home from hospital carrying her in a white shawl, and her parents and Phil's parents had come out of the house to greet them.

But Phil was too engrossed in his book to notice her, and although Lucy stood behind him for several seconds, she had to speak to him to make him turn round.

'Hello. What are you doing up here?'

'Just having a look round to see what all you brainy people get up to.'

Lucy ignored his sarcasm and pretended to adjust her pile of books, in the hope that some of the titles might catch his eye and impress him. But Phil just thought they were too heavy for her and offered to hold them. Lucy shook her head and clutched the books protectively as if he had threatened to steal them.

'It's all right, thanks. I'll put them on the counter with my others.'

When she returned, she said, 'Do you think the kids'll be all right down there on their own?'

Phil looked up slowly from his book.

'Of course they'll be all right. I've told them to behave themselves, and they know where I am if they get fed up.'

'I know, but you know what they're like. I wouldn't want them to run out into the street or anything like that.'

'What's up, are you trying to get rid of me or something?'

'Don't be silly.' But her reply was too emphatic to be convincing, and she tried to hide her embarrassment at being caught out by pretending to show interest in Phil's book.

'What are you reading?'

Phil turned it round to show her.

'What's it about?'

'Metal stresses.'

'Do you understand it?'

Phil looked at her scornfully, but Lucy was still staring vacantly at the diagrams and formulas and did not see the expression on his face.

'I ought to. I have to deal with it every day at work.'

He closed the book and slid it back into place between *Light Alloys* and *Tool Steels*.

'If you hurry up, I'll help you to carry your books downstairs.'

Lucy did not want to hurry up. She wanted him to go away and leave her to choose her books on her own. She wanted to savour the experience. But Phil thought that he was doing her a favour, and as he accompanied her along the shelves, he said, 'They ought to provide baskets like they do in supermarkets.'

Tracey and Mathew helped Lucy to carry the books into the house, while Phil went to close the greenhouse door. 'There might be a touch of frost tonight,' he said. Lucy told the children to put the books on the dining-room table, then, before going into the kitchen to prepare the tea, she unwrapped them all so that she could see them when she walked in and out of the room. As soon as they were all on show, she wanted to sample them again and start reading. She picked up the copy of *Persuasion*, smoothed her hand across the glossy cover, then flicked over the pages and inhaled the draught. But no, not yet. She had more pressing business now, like frying eggs and sausages. She would wait until she was on her own. It would be something to look forward to.

While Lucy prepared the meal, Phil waited for the football results on television, and Tracey and Mathew lay on the carpet in front of the fire and looked through their new books. Tracey had chosen a story about a boy who had been squashed when his bulletin board fell on him, and all the tricks he could get up to now that he was flat. Mathew's book was about three kittens called Inky, Binky and Boo who lived on a farm, and their struggle to find something to eat when they woke up one morning and found that their mother had disappeared. He asked Tracey to read it to him, but when she stumbled over some of the words he became irritated, snatched the book from her and took it to Phil. But Phil was busy checking his football coupon and he told

Mathew to go and ask his mum. Lucy said that she was busy too and that he would have to wait until after tea. But when she saw his bottom lip begin to quiver and the tears come to his eyes, she put down the knives and forks, sat him on her knee at the table, and with the pans sizzling and hissing on the cooker behind her, read him the story from beginning to end.

When Lucy opened the lounge door to tell them that the tea was ready, Phil was standing at the table looking at one of her books. She immediately felt resentful. She wanted to tell him to put it down, and she hoped that he had washed his hands after messing about in the greenhouse. Phil held up the book towards her.

'What's this, then?'

Lucy walked across to the table, and on the pretext of wanting to read the title, took the book from him. It was called *The British Political System* by S. Beer.

'It's for my Politics course.'

She kept hold of the book after she had told him.

'What politics? I thought you were doing English.'

'I am. In the first year you do Literature and Language plus another subject. So I thought I'd give Politics a try.'

'What for? You don't know anything about politics.'

'Well, that's as good a reason as any for having a go at it, isn't it?' Her reply was sharp enough to distract the children from the television. 'Anyway, you want to talk. I know more about it than you.'

'Don't talk silly.'

Mathew lost interest in the argument and was drawn back to the cartoon on television, but Tracey continued to watch them anxiously. She had become increasingly aware of the tension between them in the last few weeks and it worried her. She knew that it had something to do with the university, and that her daddy did not like it. But she could not understand why. She thought it was lovely and her mummy had promised to take her again.

'I'm not talking silly. You didn't even vote in the last general election, that's how interested you are.'

'There was nobody worth voting for, that's why. That doesn't mean to say that I'm not interested though.'

'Who's the present Home Secretary then?'

'What's that got to do with it?'

He picked up another book from the table and opened it, as if

37

he was hoping to find the answer inside. Lucy could not help smiling. It was her copy of *Beowulf*. When Phil looked up, he thought she was gloating because he did not know the answer.

'I suppose you know then?'

'Of course I do.'

(Only because she had just heard him being interviewed on the radio in the kitchen. She did not tell Phil this though.)

Phil closed the book and put it down. He wanted to ask Lucy what language it was written in, but he was afraid of appearing even more ignorant. He wasn't even sure how to pronounce the title.

'Anyway, bugger the Home Secretary. Let's go and get some tea before it goes cold. That's a lot more important than politics.'

He went into the kitchen, leaving Lucy to deal with Tracey, who had decided that she wasn't hungry, and Mathew, who broke out into a carpet-kicking tantrum when she told him to turn off the television.

Later, when the children were in bed, and Phil was asleep in front of the late-night film on television, Lucy sat at the table and looked through her books at leisure. When she had finished, she picked up her pen and signed each one, carefully and proudly in the top corner of the title page: *Lucy Downs. Lucy Downs. Lucy Downs.* These were her books now.

For a moment, it was just like any other morning. Lucy heard the letter box creak (would the boy push the newspaper right through, or leave it trapped there to let in the draught?). She heard . . . Then she remembered! It was the first day of term! Today she was starting university! From now on, she was a proper, full-time student. How could she have forgotten when she had still been awake at two o'clock, thinking and worrying and wondering if she would ever go to sleep? She curled up and hugged herself, and when she opened her eyes, Mathew was standing at the side of the bed.

'Hello, love, I didn't hear you come in.'

She lifted up the covers, and as Mathew climbed in beside her, he said, 'You were smiling in your sleep, mummy.'

Lucy kissed his warm cheek and cuddled him up to her, and, as he lay with his head against her breast, he was too far down to see that she was smiling again.

Lucy stood in the foyer of the Schweitzer Tower and looked at the timetable: English Lang. lect. th. G.4. She knew that all the lecture theatres were on the ground floor, so all she had to do was walk along the corridor. She looked up at the wall clock above the porter's lodge, then checked her watch. It was a quarter to ten. Her first lecture began at ten o'clock, so she decided to wait for a few minutes before moving off.

The foyer was as crowded as a department store at Christmas, and Lucy stepped back against the window to avoid the crush. Some of the students were obviously as new and nervous as she was. They moved through the crowd tentatively, as if they did not belong there, or stood frowning over timetables looking confused and forlorn. The sight of these students reassured Lucy; at least she wasn't the only one feeling terrified. Other students, returning to continue their studies, greeted each other with hugs, slaps and kisses, then stood around in raucous groups recounting adventures from their long vacation. They seemed to have travelled all over the world. Lucy did not hear anyone mention Torquay. There was an abundance of denim, even down to shoes in some cases, and Lucy felt overdressed in her velvet jacket and skirt. She looked more like a secretary than a student.

She looked at the clock again, then at her watch. Even that seemed to be the wrong style. It was a dress watch, more suitable for occasional evening wear than everyday use. It was time to go. The thought of being late for her first lecture, and all those faces turning towards her as she opened the door, made her hurry across the foyer, her high heels clicking on the terrazzo floor in contrast to the squeak and pad of the ubiquitous track-shoes.

Lucy chose a row halfway up the lecture theatre and sat down near the end of the bench. The girl sitting next to her turned and smiled briefly. Lucy smiled back. They were waiting-room smiles: apprehensive and comforting at the same time. Lucy glanced at the girl again when she wasn't looking, then looked round at the students behind her. They all looked so young! Lucy did a quick calculation. No, she wasn't old enough to be their mother as Phil had suggested, but she certainly felt it. She took her new notepad out of her bag and placed it on the shelf in front of her. Had Phil been right then? Had she made a mistake? Perhaps she would have been better with a 'little' job more suitable to the family's needs. She thought about Tracey and Mathew, imagined them at school. How she missed them. And how she missed Phil too. Suddenly, she felt hopelessly out of place, a misfit, an elderly intruder. And the glossy cover of her notepad did not help. It was too clean, too conspicuously new. Even her ballpoint pen was new! She slid it underneath the pad and looked at her neighbour's stationery. Her notepad looked used. The corners were bent and doodles decorated the cover. But how could it be? They hadn't even started yet! Lucy noticed the girl's clothes: T-shirt, faded jeans and an army-surplus shoulder bag with badges pinned to the flap. It was her first day too and she did not know anyone either, but how Lucy envied her. At least she *looked* like a student, and she wasn't *really* starting from scratch. She had had a break after school, that was all, and was now continuing her education somewhere else. She looked at home sitting there. From classroom to lecture theatre; it was a natural step. Lucy wondered if that's where she ought to be, at home, drinking coffee with Judith, or walking across the road to Sue's Tupperware party. Talking about children, food, new kitchen appliances, subjects she was familiar with, instead of sitting here with a crowd of teenagers waiting for an English Language lecture to begin.

She was seriously considering walking out, when Dr Hobday entered the room and everyone went quiet. He walked across to the table at the front, put down his notes, then turned to face the audience.

'Good morning, ladies and gentlemen. Welcome.'

The formality of his greeting depressed Lucy even more. To be addressed as 'lady' at eighteen was a novelty, but to fit the description only emphasised the gap between them and made her feel older still. It was like being called 'madam' in a shop.

Dr Hobday rested against the edge of the table and crossed his ankles, revealing hairy green socks. Brown brogues and a tweed suit completed his country outfit, and with his legs stretched out before him he looked as if he was sitting on a shooting stick.

Lucy listened with increasing anxiety as he outlined the year's work, which included an introduction to the literature of medieval England, a comparison between Elizabethan English and the language as it is used today, and a study of the grammatical structure of contemporary language . . . She began to encircle the heading on the top sheet of her pad. Would she be up to it? Was she too old to be tackling new subjects at this level . . . ? There would be nine essays to be completed by the third, sixth and tenth Wednesday of each term. After they had been marked, they would be discussed in seminars . . . *Discussed!* Writing them would be hard enough, but the prospect of having to talk about them made her even more nervous and she obliterated the heading with heavy scribble.

She was saved from further self-doubt by a student entering the room. Everyone turned towards him and the boy remained in the doorway, transfixed by their common stare. Dr Hobday smiled at him encouragingly and, after a long pause, the boy said, 'Excuse me, is this Ancient Civilisation?'

Dr Hobday stood up and buttoned his jacket before replying.

'In my case it would be foolish to deny it. However, I'm certain the young people before me would object to being categorised as such.'

Everyone laughed and the boy hurriedly apologised and left the room. On the inside of the door, the handle moved slowly upward as he carefully closed the door behind him.

Lucy continued to smile long after the interruption had been forgotten by the other students. Dr Hobday had included her amongst the young people. She felt better already. Of course she could cope! She hadn't come this far to give up now. If they could do it, so could she. Her stroke through the defacement on her notepad was so decisive that the girl sitting next to her glanced across at the noise.

Lucy made a new heading, underlined it firmly, then settled back and listened attentively to what Dr Hobday was saying. The next time her pen touched the paper it was to make her first note.

It was warm enough to sit outside at lunchtime, so Lucy found an empty bench in front of the student-union building. She had brought her own food, and when she took out her flask and sandwich box (bought at one of Sue's Tupperware parties), it was like meeting old friends. They reminded her of home and family and made her feel less lonely. She closed her eyes and tilted her face to the sun. It was summer heat, but the crop of berries on a nearby rowan tree and the quiet song of a robin in its branches were reminders of the true season and harbingers of harsher days ahead.

As Lucy unscrewed the flask top, she remembered when she had last used it: on the beach at Torquay. It had been warm there too. She remembered Phil and the children playing in the sea, the

41

suntanned girl on the beach . . . Where was she now? It all seemed so long ago, part of a different life almost.

The robin dropped down from the branches of the rowan tree and began to hop around in front of the bench searching for food. Lucy opened her sandwiches and broke off a crust. It might be autumn for him, but it felt more like springtime to her. She looked at her timetable. At two o'clock she had an English Literature tutorial with Dr Pybus. The rest of the afternoon was free. She could go home then.

But she went into town first, and bought herself a new pair of jeans which were tighter than the ones she usually wore. They would be a good incentive to slim, she told herself on the bus home, as she opened the bag and peeped inside.

The student who had mistaken English Language for Ancient Civilisation was not the only one to make an error during the hectic, opening days of the new term. The place was full of students looking lost, looking at timetables, and looking at numbers on doors. Lucy was one of them. She often found herself on the wrong corridor and occasionally even in the wrong building. One afternoon, she found herself in the Zoology Department, peering into a laboratory at a group of white-coated students surrounding a rabbit on a bench. It certainly looked like Practical Criticism of some description, but definitely not the sort that she was seeking.

At first, Lucy thought she would never find her way around. She imagined herself walking the corridors for ever, seeking mythical lectures in imaginary rooms. But gradually, after the first few days, she discovered that her timetable was not part of a malicious plot to confuse her after all, and that a pattern of work established itself and her time took shape.

When she had lectures beginning at nine o'clock, she had to leave Tracey and Mathew with Judith next door, who took them to school with her own children. Lucy always felt uncomfortable when she said goodbye to them in Judith's house. The parting kisses and reassurances seemed excessive in someone else's kitchen, and there was something reproachful about the way that Judith fussed over them and offered them biscuits and drinks, as if they hadn't been given any breakfast before they came out.

One evening, when Phil and Lucy were out drinking with a group of friends, Judith said, 'It's not that you're cleverer than the rest of us, Lucy, you're just more determined, that's all.'

Lucy did not know what to say and the women moved on to talking about their children, and how advanced they were for their ages. Their husbands were standing in a separate group at the bar. Occasionally, one of them would come to the table and enquire if anyone would like another drink. Lucy was glad that Phil had not heard what Judith had said, or it would have given him the chance to start grumbling again. Only he would have been more direct than Judith. He would have called her stubborn and selfish, and his friends would have winked at each other and teased him and said that he was losing his grip.

Phil was finding it difficult to adjust to Lucy not being at home as much. He liked to come in from work to a warm house and the smell of his dinner cooking when he opened the door. Now, he often arrived home to a cold house and a note on the kitchen table. Lucy always prepared the meal for him. She even left instructions how long it should be cooked and at what heat, but Phil refused to be mollified. Cooking wasn't his job. He had finished his work for the day and now he was having to do Lucy's as well.

Sometimes, particularly after a hard shift when he was exhausted, he refused to get his own dinner ready and waited for Lucy to come home. When she complained that she was tired too, he scoffed at her and said how could she be, when all she had done was sit about all day. He did not regard what Lucy did as work, and when, one evening, he picked up her timetable from the kitchen table, all his suspicions were confirmed.

'Bloody hell,' he said, counting all the blank squares, 'you've got more free time than lessons.'

Lucy looked up from her essay. She was working in the kitchen because the television was on in the lounge.

'It's not free time. You work on your own then.'

'Look at this! All Wednesday afternoon off. It's hardly worth your while going in.'

'Everybody has Wednesday afternoon off.'

'Everybody!' The thought of a weekly half-day holiday in addition to such sparse-looking commitments shocked him. 'I've heard of being on short time, but this is ridiculous.'

Lucy looked up at the wall clock. She was impatient to resume work. She wanted to make a good start before she went to bed.

'It's supposed to be games afternoon. All universities have it. It's a tradition.'

'Do you mean like at school, PE and that?'

43

'No. You don't have to do it. It's for the teams, football and hockey and that. They play other universities.'

Phil placed the timetable back on the table and laughed.

'What's the matter with you?'

'I'm just thinking of you playing games.'

He walked across to the sink and Lucy twisted round in her seat so quickly that she looked as if she had been turned mechanically.

'And what's funny about that?'

Phil filled the kettle and did not reply, but even though he had his back to her, Lucy could see that he was still laughing by the way that his ears kept moving up and down.

Similar thoughts had amused her too when she had read the university handbook and glanced through the long list of clubs and activities available to students. She couldn't really imagine herself caving or learning lacrosse, and the prospect of hang-gliding had made her giggle. But she didn't tell Phil this. She didn't mind making fun of herself, but she wasn't having him laughing at her, especially as he was a stone overweight and looked as if he could have done with a bit of physical activity himself.

But Lucy suspected that Phil was referring to more than just her athletic defects. She was right. Moments later, he said, 'You'd look all right running around a hockey field at your age, wouldn't you?'

'Why would I? They have women's hockey teams, don't they? And what about all them people you see out jogging? They do it at all ages.'

As Phil turned round from the sink, Lucy turned her back on him to register her annoyance. Still grinning, he came up behind her.

'You'd be carrying top-weight if you started jogging, I know that much.' He reached over her and squeezed her breasts. 'They'd look like two cats fighting in a sack.'

Lucy wasn't sure whether to laugh, elbow him in the stomach or allow him to carry on. She decided to sit there and enjoy it. It might relax her a little. She was anxious about her essay. She had intended to start it earlier but the children wouldn't settle down. Mathew said he wasn't tired: there was a noise outside. He wanted his mummy to sing him a song. Tracey wanted another story. She had tummy ache. She didn't like school any more.

Perhaps if they had a quick one on the settee it would calm her down and relieve the tension in her neck. Phil might go to bed then and leave her on her own for a couple of hours. She was just about to press her head against him and reach back, when he took his hands away and walked across to the cupboard.

'Would you like a cup of coffee?'

I know what I would like, she thought. Instead, she said, 'Yes, please.'

She watched Phil open the cupboard doors and take out the coffee jar and mugs. It was years since they had made love downstairs. It seemed like years since they had made love in bed! And when they did, it was always under the covers with the light switched off. She remembered Christine Evans, who used to tell them lewd stories at work. According to her, her husband used to 'give it her' all over the house: on the settee, on the rug, on the stairs, and occasionally, even on the kitchen table. The bedroom was never mentioned.

Lucy stared at her manuscript and gently stroked the table top. Was he still giving it her now? She smiled: she hoped he was.

As Phil leaned over to put down her coffee, he read the essay title on the top sheet: *Consider how relevant and helpful is the term 'metaphysical' to the understanding of the poetry of Donne or Herbert or any of their successors and imitators.*

Metaphysical. Metaphysical, Phil kept repeating to himself, as he walked through into the lounge to find Lucy's dictionary. He read the definition several times, but every time he looked away he forgot what it said. He tried again, but his attention wandered and his eyes moved up the page . . . metaphoric . . . metamorphosis . . . metallurgy. At least he knew what that meant.

Phil sat on the floor with his back against the wall and opened his lunchbox. There was no canteen, so the men ate where they worked, amongst drills, lathes, stacks of metal sheets and welding sets. A few of the men went to a pub across the road, but Phil never bothered. They only had half an hour for lunch, so, by the time they arrived there and got served, it was nearly time to come back.

Phil opened his first sandwich to see what Lucy had packed up for him. There was a second, smaller packet in the box containing a slice of fruit cake, and tucked snugly into the corner, an apple. His lunch looked appetising just by the way it was packed, and there was no indication in those neat, firm sandwiches that they had been cut at two o'clock in the morning when Lucy had been desperate to go to bed.

Phil was sitting in his usual place in the corner of the fabrication shop with two of his mates, Colin and Roy. Most of the men had regular places and groups, like members of common rooms and gentlemen's clubs.

As Phil bit into his first sandwich, Colin winked across at Roy and grinned.

'I suppose you have to cut your own snap now, Phil, now that Lucy's busy studying?' Phil could not speak immediately because his mouth was full. 'I wouldn't have that, would you, Roy?'

Phil swallowed hurriedly to get his answer in.

'What would you do then, bloody starve?'

But he spoke too quickly, some crumbs went down his windpipe and he began to cough. The others started to laugh, and Roy leaned across and thumped him on the back so hard that dust came out of his overalls and his body reverberated dully like a punchbag.

'Bloody hell, Phil, I know you've made them sandwiches yourself but surely they're not that bad, are they?'

Colin and Roy could not stop laughing. Phil could not speak and he unscrewed his flask and poured himself some tea to try to clear his throat. Sipping the hot drink with his eyes still wet from coughing, he looked like someone recovering from bad news.

'You can laugh. You can't expect her to do everything at home now that she's studying as well.'

Roy unfolded a newspaper and turned straight to an inside page.

'Fucking hell, I wouldn't mind studying her.'

He turned the paper round and showed Phil and Colin a photograph of a bare-breasted woman wearing a short grass skirt and holding a coconut in each hand.

'I don't know where they find them. There's none like that down our street, I can tell you.'

He sat there on the oily concrete floor, chewing his pork pie and staring lustfully at the woman's tanned thigh parting the strands of her skirt. A flake of pastry fell onto her breasts. Roy licked his fingertip, then touched it off and ate it.

'Just imagine coming home to her every night. I wouldn't let her out of my sight if she was mine. There'd be every fucker and his grandad sniffing around as soon as your back was turned.'

One of the works' cats walked up to them miaowing, with its tail stuck up like a question mark. It arched its back and quivered all over as it rubbed up against Phil's leg. He scratched it between the ears and wondered what Lucy was doing now. Having a lecture: or her dinner perhaps? But where? He did not know. He had no idea what she did when she was at university. Perhaps every fucker and his grandad was sniffing around her at this very moment. And why not? She still looked smart when she was dressed up. He had often noticed men looking at her when they went out together.

He looked at the photograph in Roy's newspaper again and imagined Lucy topless in a grass skirt . . . No, she was a bit too floppy for that sort of thing now. A few years ago perhaps, before she had had the children. Anyway, why would anybody want to be sniffing around her when there were all those young girls about? He picked a scrap of ham out of his sandwich and threw it down for the cat.

Colin took a carton of yoghurt out of his lunchbox and began to pick at the lid.

'What's Lucy studying at university, Phil?'

'English Literature.'

'What, Shakespeare and that?'

'I suppose she must be, I've seen *Hamlet* lying around the house.'

Colin worked patiently round the rim of the yoghurt carton, lifting the tin foil.

'I was in a play once at school. I was a bell. I had four words to say: ding-dong, ding-dong.'

Roy looked up from the newspaper. He had turned straight from the pin-up to the sport.

'I bet that took a lot of learning, didn't it?'

Phil unwrapped his slice of battenburg cake and peeled the marzipan from round the edge. (He always saved that until last.)

'I haven't got a clue what she does most of the time. She was writing an essay on a poet called Donne last night.'

Colin slowly peeled the lid off the carton and placed it on the floor for the cat to lick.

'Don who?'

'I've no idea.'

'It's not Don Jackson who works in the machine shop, is it?'

When they had finished laughing, Phil said, 'I doubt it. Still, knowing him, he could probably manage a few verses on the back of the bog door.'

He took the apple out of his lunchbox and polished it vigorously on his overalls.

47

'She must be clever your Lucy, Phil.'

'She is. She leaves me standing, I can tell you.'

He sounded as if he was proud of her, but the vicious way that he bit into the apple revealed his ambivalent feelings on the matter. Roy watched him take a second bite.

'What's up, Phil, still hungry?'

Phil stared moodily at an oil stain between his boots and did not reply. The hooter sounded for the end of lunch. Roy folded up his newspaper and stood up.

'To be or not to be. That's the fucking question, isn't it, Phil?'

Lucy received B– for her essay on Donne. Dave Pybus, her Literature tutor, wrote at the bottom: 'Perceptive and well argued. Perhaps not enough emphasis placed on the originality of Donne's work. Remember Jonson did say of him that he was "the first poet in the world in some things".'

At the end of the seminar, when Lucy was putting away her books, Dave said, 'Did I detect a hint of cynicism in your attitude to Donne's love poetry, Lucy?'

Lucy threaded the sheets of foolscap onto the rings of her file and clicked them shut.

'Not cynicism. Scepticism perhaps.'

The other students squeezed past her and left the room. Dave tapped cigarette ash into a dirty polystyrene cup on his desk.

'"I wonder by my troth, what thou and I did, till we lov'd?" Don't you think that's beautiful?'

By speaking the lines straight at her, he embarrassed Lucy and made her blush.

'Yes, I suppose so.' She hesitated and stared at the books on the shelves behind him. 'I find Donne too clever. He's a bit too contrived for my taste.' She hesitated again as if afraid to go any further with her criticism. 'I prefer Marvell myself.' ('Captain Marvell!' Phil had shouted, when he had read the name on the cover. 'I didn't know he wrote poetry as well.')

Dave dropped his cigarette into the coffee dregs and looked at his watch.

'I suppose we'd better be going. I'm back on again at two.'

He stood up and lifted his jacket from the back of his chair. Lucy stood up too, and for a few seconds the only sounds in the room were the swish and rustle of material as they put on their coats.

'Right then.'

48

Dave picked up his keys and threw the cup into the wastepaper bin. Lucy heard coffee slop against the side and wondered if it would seep through onto the carpet.

As they were walking along the corridor towards the lift, Dave said, 'Would you like to come for a drink?'

Lucy felt herself blushing again. She looked at her watch, tried desperately to think of all the things she had to do, all the places she had to go. In the end all she could say was, 'I'm sorry, but I've got to go home.'

She could have thrown herself down the lift shaft. What a feeble excuse! What a big soft baby she must have sounded! The lift arrived before she could think of a more plausible reason, and she could not say anything on the way down because they were separated by other people.

Lucy thought that Dave had forgotten all about the invitation as they crossed the foyer, but when he reached the door, he stopped and touched her sleeve.

'I've arranged to meet a couple of students in the union bar, why don't you come along and meet them?'

Lucy paused for the sake of decorum, then smiled and nodded.

'All right then. Just a quick one.'

Her conscience was clear now. The change from a private meeting to a social gathering made the invitation acceptable.

But why should it? she asked herself as they entered the union building and walked down the stairs to the bar. What was wrong with going with him on her own? What did she think was going to happen at one o'clock in the afternoon, in broad daylight in a crowded bar? Guilt, that's what it was. She felt guilty because she was with another man. But there was more to it than that. She felt uncomfortable too. She did not know what to say to him. She tried to remember the last time she had been out with another man, even innocently like this . . . She wasn't sure, probably before she was married. She was angry at having to admit it, angry for feeling shy, and angry that she was watching her feet instead of looking people in the face as she entered the bar.

So this was the reward for all those years of devoted motherhood, was it? Shattered confidence and nothing to say. She had even begun to speak like a child at one time. She once asked Phil if he wanted a chucky egg for his tea.

'What would you like to drink?'

A double Scotch, she felt like saying.

'I'll have an orange juice, please.'

She expected him to ask her if she would prefer anything stronger, but he did not seem surprised by her request, and he ordered it along with a pint of bitter for himself.

'Would you like something to eat?'

Dave bent down and examined the rolls inside a transparent container on the counter. As he moved his head around trying to see what they contained, he looked as if he was peering into an aquarium.

'The choice is rather limited, I'm afraid. There appears to be two ham heavily outnumbered by sweaty-looking cheese.'

Lucy fancied cheese, but she could hardly order one now after what he had said about them.

'I'll have ham, please.'

'Right.' Dave lifted up the front of the plastic case. 'You take the drinks and I'll bring the food.'

Lucy looked round for a place, then picked up the glasses from the bar and carried them across to a table by the window. It was littered with the refuse of previous occupants, and before she sat down, Lucy stacked the dirty glasses, placed all the crisp and nut packets in the ashtray, and wiped the top clean with a tissue. She did it automatically. She had been well trained for it over the years.

Dave put down the plates beside the glasses and sat down next to Lucy on the padded bench which stretched round the room. As he picked up his roll, Lucy noticed that he had chosen cheese. Sweaty or not, he had made the right decision she decided as she sneaked a look at the slice of fatty ham inside hers.

'Did you notice any mustard on the bar?'

'No, I didn't. But I'll go and ask if you like. What would you like, English or French?'

Lucy hesitated. She didn't really care. They always had English at home. She decided to live dangerously.

'I'll have French, please.'

She felt pleased with herself and sipped her orange juice triumphantly, hoping that Dave had mistaken her indifference for deliberation.

He returned from the bar carrying a familiar-looking yellow jar and a knife.

'They've only got English, I'm afraid.'

Lucy accepted the privation bravely.

'Never mind, it'll do.'

'They've probably banned the French. There's a very strong

50

anti-European feeling amongst the students at the moment. Were you at the debate the other evening?'

At it? She didn't even know about it.

'No, I was working.'

She tried to make it sound like a question of priorities.

'The vote was overwhelmingly in favour of leaving the Common Market.'

Lucy unscrewed the mustard jar hoping desperately that he would change the subject. She didn't know anything about the Common Market. She hadn't even bothered voting in the referendum.

'Serves us jolly well right, that's all I can say. Anyone with an iota of sense could predict what would happen when we went in.'

Lucy tried to work out if abstaining was less culpable than voting in favour of entry. She decided there was nothing in it, and tried to think of something else to talk about before her ignorance was revealed.

'I'm afraid I can't get to much in the evenings. There's always such a lot to do at home.'

'Yes, I suppose there is if you're married. Where is it you live?'

'Hartford.'

'That's out near Crossways somewhere, isn't it?'

'That's right. It's a couple of miles further on . . .'

But before she could tell him what time she started out in a morning, and how long it took on the bus, he said, 'I don't know it out there at all.'

He made it sound like another planet, and when he looked past her and waved to someone across the room, Lucy realised that he did not want to know either. She sat back and ate her roll. There wasn't much to know about Hartford anyway: it was just a small village surrounded by modern housing estates. But it had seemed like paradise when they first moved there; so clean and fresh after the city back-street where they had lived before. Their house was right on the edge of the countryside and they could see fields and woods from the kitchen window. Now they had to go upstairs and look across the roofs of newer houses in order to see any open land. They were going to take up country pursuits. They planned long moorland hikes and imagined cosy evenings beside log fires in remote hotels. But it never worked out. There was always so much to do in the house at weekends. Then Tracey was born . . . But they did drive out to a garden centre sometimes, to buy fertiliser and bedding-out plants.

Lucy watched the couple at the next table. The boy was trying to tuck some loose strands of hair behind the girl's ear while she tried to distract him by kissing his face. They kept laughing and dodging about, and every time they raised their arms to counter each other's moves their bare midriffs appeared between their sweaters and jeans. Lucy wondered if it had ever been like that between her and Phil. Would they finish up making trips to the garden centre too? She had a sip of orange and hoped not.

'How are you finding the course, then? Have you settled in all right?'

Lucy turned back to Dave, who seemed to have edged closer on the seat.

'Yes, thanks. It's hard work but I'm enjoying it.'

'I don't know how you fit it all in. Do you have children?'

'Yes, two.'

She announced them as if they were campaign medals, and would have gone on to give their sex, names, age and brief biographies if Dave had allowed her.

'What does your husband do?'

'He's the foreman in an engineering works.'

'It sounds like a good job.'

Lucy thought so too. It was a pity that it wasn't true though. Phil was the charge-hand welder in the fabrication shop, which wasn't quite the same thing. Why hadn't she told him the truth? What was wrong with being a welder?

Dave noticed the tears in her eyes and touched her arm.

'Are you all right?'

Lucy fanned her mouth with her hand and finished off her drink.

'I must have put too much mustard on my roll, it's made my eyes run.'

Noticing that Dave's glass was empty, and wanting to change the subject, she said, 'Would you like another drink?'

Dave looked at his watch.

'Yes. All right. I've just time for a quick one, I think.'

Lucy reached into her bag for her purse, expecting that this action would set in motion the weary ritual of gallant protestation on his part, followed by demure compliance on hers. But she was wrong. All he did was slide his empty glass across the table.

'I'll have a pint, please.'

Lucy swallowed hard. Not only had he not offered to pay for the drinks (she would have refused of course), but he expected her to go and fetch them as well! She picked up the glasses and stood up.

'What kind is it, bitter?'

'Yes. Ask for Watson's. All the others are keg.'

She was so convinced that everybody was staring at her as she crossed the room that she started to sweat. She sneaked a quick look back when she reached the safety of the bar, and if she had caused a sensation, it had soon subsided, judging by the speed that people had resumed their conversations and regained their concentration on the pool tables and space-invader machines. Idiot, she thought, noticing all the other girls queuing up with her.

It was years since she had bought drinks at a bar. Phil disapproved of it: he thought it was common. Their first meeting had been in a pub, one Saturday night in town. She was with a girl friend, he was with a gang. They kept looking at each other across the room, and when he went to the lavatory, she went too, hoping that they would meet up when they came out. But when she returned the boys had gone and someone else had taken their seats. She wanted to run after them. She wanted to cry. She would never see him again. She would be miserable for the rest of her life . . .

But when they went back the following week, he was there again. He recognised her. She smiled back. They contrived to meet at the bar. He bought her a drink . . .

Lucy rehearsed the order. A pint of . . . ? What had Dave said? She looked round to try and attract his attention, but he was standing at the jukebox choosing records. It did not take him long, and he pressed the selection buttons quickly and decisively, as if he knew exactly what he wanted to hear. He was joined by two students, and it was obvious from the way that they leaned over the jukebox and kept pointing inside that they were discussing the music.

Lucy watched them. Dave looked like a student himself. She tried to guess his age. Late twenties? Thirty perhaps; like Phil. Then why did he seem so much younger? Perhaps it was because he still dressed like a student, mixed with them a lot and obviously enjoyed the same kind of music. Lucy didn't. It was too loud for a start. She looked round the room. It wasn't like being in a pub. It was more like a cross between a youth club and a disco.

She recognised the name of the beer on the handle of the pump and ordered a pint and a half. (What would Phil have thought of her, buying herself a glass of beer? You couldn't get much commoner than that!) She fancied a whisky really, but a short would have seemed inappropriate in the circumstances. While she was waiting to be served, she did not lean against the bar like the rest of the students, but stood up straight with her purse ready, as if she was at the butcher's buying a joint of meat.

As she walked back across the room with the drinks, she caught a whiff of herself. Dave was still talking at the jukebox, so she put down the glasses, picked up her bag and went out to the cloakroom along the corridor.

It smelled strongly of disinfectant, and the white-tiled walls and neon lighting reminded her of visiting Phil's mother in hospital before she died. She locked herself in a cubicle, took a bottle of perfume out of her bag and, after a quick squirt under her arms and up her skirt, her confidence was restored. She unlocked the door and walked across to the wash basins to examine herself in a mirror. She was dismayed by what she saw. Getting up with Mathew, who had been sick in the night, had left her pale, with dark streaks under her eyes (Phil had refused to help, he had to go to work in the morning, he said), and although she realised that it might appear bizarre to the younger students to be applying cosmetics on a Monday lunchtime, she no longer had the insouciance of a nineteen-year-old and she took out her make-up bag and brightened her cheeks and lips.

She returned to the bar feeling refreshed and more relaxed, and as she sat down she wondered if Dave would notice any difference in her. Turning towards him, she said, 'Are you married?'

It was the first question she had asked him since they had left his room.

'Sort of.'

Lucy laughed. It was the first time she had done that too.

'What do you mean?'

'I'm separated. Do you remember the Duane Allman song "Happily Married Man"?' (She didn't.) '"I ain't seen my wife for two or three years. I'm a happily married man."' He lit a cigarette. 'That about sums it up.'

Lucy laughed again, but uneasily this time. She had never heard anyone talk about the break-up of a marriage in such an irreverent way before. Separation and divorce were usually treated solemnly, like death or physical deformity in a newborn child. Dave sensed her discomfort.

'Don't worry about it. The feeling is mutual, I can assure you.'

Lucy had a drink of beer and pulled a face. If this was the best one, what were the *others* like?

'What does she do, your wife?'

'She works in television. Research for documentary programmes mainly.'

'Have you got any children?'

'Not that I'm aware of.'

His flippant manner encouraged Lucy to be bolder than she would normally have been with someone she hardly knew.

'What happened?'

Dave turned on her sharply. 'Nothing happened. We both decided it was for the best.' Lucy blushed at the rebuff. It was like a growl from a dog warning her that she had gone far enough. The jukebox went quiet too and the sudden silence seemed to emphasise the tension between them. But the change in Dave's mood was as brief as the interval between the records, and as soon as the music started up again he began to tap his foot and accompany the singer.

'Beautiful. Do you like it?'

Lucy listened while Dave moved around on the seat beside her. She hoped that he wasn't going to go too far and start dancing.

'I don't know. I haven't heard it before.'

'Really?'

He stared at her in disbelief, shook his head and covered his face in despair: all of which seemed rather excessive on behalf of a pop record, Lucy thought. He was elevating her ignorance of music to monstrous proportions, as if she had missed the news of a nuclear disaster, or the assassination of the President of the United States.

'I don't have much time to listen to music these days. I'm too busy.'

It did not sound like much of an excuse, but it was true. Dave continued to shuffle around and he did not speak again until the record had ended.

'Do you ever listen to live music?'

Lucy paused, then shook her head slowly as if the question had needed some thought.

'No, not really.'

'There are some really good bands play in the pubs in town. If you fancy going any time, let me know.'

He said it casually, but Lucy could feel him watching her, and she had a drink to stop herself meeting his eye. What did he mean? Was he inviting her out? Surely not. Not when he knew she was married with children. She must have got it wrong. She was imagining things. But he was still looking at her as if he was waiting for an answer . . . It was time to leave.

She put down her glass and looked at her watch. She feigned surprise at how late it was and said she must go. She had to go to the library, then into town to buy Tracey two new T-shirts for PE. Her old ones were too small now. She was growing so quickly that it was hard to keep pace. Dave said that he had to go too: he had a lecture in five minutes. Lucy waited for him to drink up, and they left the bar, saying little on the way out and parting immediately at the bottom of the steps.

Lucy glanced round when she reached the corner of the building, but Dave had disappeared. She was relieved in a way; she would have hated him to have caught her looking back. It would have been nice if he had been looking though, and they could have waved.

On the bus home, Lucy realised that she hadn't met the other students whom Dave had said he was meeting in the bar. Perhaps he had meant the two boys at the jukebox? No, that was obviously a chance encounter. And why would he arrange to meet someone just to talk about records? Perhaps they hadn't turned up? In that case, why hadn't he mentioned it . . . ? Surely he hadn't made it up just to get her to go for a drink on her own? She didn't know whether to be flattered or shocked at the idea. It was a ridiculous suggestion, but what other explanation could there be? She did not know, and as she gazed unseeing through the window, she almost missed her stop trying to think of one.

That evening, while Phil was in the kitchen fitting a new plug onto the iron, and the children were playing upstairs, Lucy knelt by the record player in the lounge and looked through their record collection. They had bought most of them when they were courting and newly married. The more recent additions were all collections of fairy stories and nursery rhymes. Lucy took out Phil's favourite Elvis Presley album and smiled. This was the one that Tracey had scratched with a fork when she was a baby. Glancing instinctively towards the door, as she had done all those years ago when she had snatched it from Tracey, she slid the record from its sleeve. There they were, those ruinous scratches, shining like silver threads as she angled the record to catch the light. Phil had been furious when he discovered the damage. He suspected Tracey straightaway, but Lucy said that it couldn't have been her because she hadn't seen her, and if she had done it on her own she wouldn't have been able to slot the record back into its cover. She said that it must have got damaged when they moved. He'd said himself how clumsy the removal men were. This made Phil even more angry and he told her not to talk so bloody stupid. What did she think they'd been doing, playing it in the back of the van . . . ? Even now, six years later, he still did not know how his favourite record had been spoiled.

Lucy put it back and slowly worked her way through the pile. Where were they now, all these largely forgotten groups and singers . . . ? Probably married with children most of them, like herself. She picked out a record with a photograph of an outdoor concert on the cover. Lucy had been there. She was on that photograph somewhere. She had pored over it many times trying to find herself, but the faces were too small and numerous to be identified. She had gone with her friend Andrea. It was the only open-air rock concert she had ever been to. They had hitchhiked. It was the only time she had done that too, although they had told their parents they were going on the train. It had rained most of the time. A couple had let them sleep in their tent and Lucy had lain awake listening to them fucking in a sleeping bag. She was excited all weekend and it didn't matter if she got wet, or walked around ankle-deep in mud. There were camp fires to sit around and new people to talk to, and as she sat in the darkness engulfed by the music, she closed her eyes and planned to move out and find a flat on her own. She was going to move to London. She was going to hitchhike round the world like the student she had been talking to . . .

On Monday morning, she was back at work as usual.

Lucy was still studying the record cover when Phil came in from the kitchen carrying two books clamped roughly together in one hand. He dropped them noisily onto the table, making Lucy start and look round.

'Bloody books. They're all over the house. You can't move for them.'

Lucy had decided to play the record for old times' sake while she did the ironing, but she forgot all about it now.

'Stop exaggerating, Phil.'

'It's true! It's like living in a bookshop. They're in the kitchen. In here. Upstairs . . .'

He made them sound like a plague of mice.

'Look, I can't do everything, you know.'

She stood up and walked across to the table to remove her books. They had stayed together when Phil had dropped them, and she picked up the copy of Chaucer to see what was underneath.

'You should have thought of that before you started university.'

'I did.'

'Well, you can't grumble then, can you?'

He was looking for trouble, but Lucy had too much work to do to waste her energy arguing. She placed the books on the pile on the windowsill, then went into the kitchen to fetch the iron. As she was coiling the flex, she noticed another pile of books on the worktop near the sink and two loose-leaf files on the refrigerator. She tried to even the score by finding fault with the new plug. But there was no chance of that, and she knew it. Phil never made a bad job of anything he did. Then she noticed the old cracked plug on the table. At least he could have thrown that away! But she could not delude herself: she knew why it was there. It was destined for the garage, where Phil hoarded all the other junk which he swore would come in handy one day.

Lucy carried the iron through to the lounge, then made two more journeys for the ironing board and the clothes basket. She contemplated the tangled heap of washing spilling over the sides of the basket and tried to work out how long it would take her to do it all. At least she could make a start before she put the children to bed. Then do a bit more perhaps before she tackled Plato? No, she would have to leave the rest for another time. It was a long section on Justice, and it had to be read by the morning.

Lucy noticed that the leg of Mathew's dungarees draped over the rim of the clothes basket had a hole in it. (There were so many garments in the basket that some of them looked as if they were trying to climb out.) Lucy picked up the dungarees and inspected the torn knee. That was another job to be done: and quickly too, before it got any worse. She threw them back into the basket, and as she pulled open the legs of the ironing board, the sudden screech of metal seemed to express her frustration for her. Phil looked round from the television.

'That sounds as if it could do with a drop of oil on it.'

He turned back to the sports quiz. Lucy set up the ironing board behind him so that she could watch the television while she worked; but, as she wasn't interested in sport, she was soon bored by that too.

'Is there anything else on, Phil?'

He answered the question on television (correctly) before answering Lucy's.

'I don't know. Anyway, I'm watching this.'

'That's typical of you.'

Lucy adjusted the dial on the iron.

'What do you mean?'

'You think you own that television.'

She picked up a pair of Phil's overalls out of the basket and spread them out on the ironing board. She resented ironing these more than anything else. She disliked the colour for a start – it reminded her of her old school uniform – and the material was so stiff and heavy that it made her arms ache.

Phil was so incensed by Lucy's remark that he turned round and missed the next question. Lucy didn't. She knew the answer too for a change: Arthur Ashe. His name had always intrigued her. He sounded more like an elderly uncle than a black American tennis player. Phil said, 'Don't talk so silly. You can't just come into the room in the middle of a programme and expect me to turn it over.'

'It wouldn't have mattered when I came in, you'd still have watched it. You'd never dream of asking me what I want on.'

'How can I? You never watch it.'

'That's not the point. It's the principle of the thing.' She rearranged the overalls and stretched an arm out on the board. 'Anyway, I don't get much time to watch it, do I?'

'That's your fault, isn't it?'

Lucy stopped working and glared at him, but her psychic powers were no match for the powers of the tube and Phil did not turn round.

'I'd have more time if you'd help a bit more instead of expecting me to do everything.'

He turned round then.

'Help a bit! Don't I do enough as it is?' His surprise soon turned to anger. 'Who's just put that plug on the iron? Who does the garden? Who looks after the car? Jesus Christ! There's not much more I could do, is there?'

He sat back and folded his arms, and coincidental applause on the television seemed to acknowledge his endeavour. But Lucy was not deterred and she replaced the iron on the asbestos square so that she could concentrate on the argument.

'I know that, but they're all jobs that you enjoy doing. You like messing about with the car, and gardening and mending things; they're your hobbies. I mean, you can hardly call washing and ironing and cleaning-up, hobbies, can you? They're just plain boring.'

'What, shoving a pile of clothes in the machine and taking them out an hour later; do you call that boring?'

Lucy squeezed the handle of the iron so hard that her finger ends turned red.

'And what do you think I'm doing while they're washing, sitting with my feet up drinking cups of tea?'

'I don't know what you're doing. But if you can't cope it's your own fault. I warned you what would happen.'

'Who says I can't cope?'

Snatching up the iron, she looked capable of tackling the overalls of the entire workforce of Bowes Engineering Ltd.

'You, by the sound of it. I'll tell you what I'll do though; I'll put a few things in the washer, while you dig the vegetable patch over.'

'Right then. And I'll start going to university in the car, and you can go to work on the bus.'

That took the smirk off his face.

'Don't talk daft. How could I get to work at that time in the morning on the bus?'

'You managed it when we lived in Carlisle Street. You haven't always had a car, you know.'

She realised immediately that she had excluded herself from ownership. She always thought of the car belonging to Phil. No doubt he always thought that the vacuum cleaner belonged to her.

'I'd no choice then though, had I? I had to go on the bus.'

'And whenever have I had a choice?'

'Look, you don't expect me to go on the bus at half past six in the morning, do you, and you use the car at nine o'clock? That's a stupid argument.'

'The time has nothing to do with it. If we both left the house together, you'd still expect to use the car, wouldn't you?'

Phil turned back to the television and appeared to ignore the question. Then, with a grin on his face: 'I'd be able to give you a lift in then.'

Lucy folded the finished overalls and placed them on the table.

'Give me a lift to the bus stop more like.'

Phil looked round angrily, but before he could speak, pande-monium broke out upstairs. A door banged, Tracey laughed and Mathew began screaming and shouting for his mummy.

Instinctively, Lucy replaced the iron and turned towards the door. Then, changing her mind, she bent down and began deliberately to sort through the clothes in the basket.

The uproar continued. Lucy wondered how long she could ignore it. She knew that it would end in tears if it went on much longer, then she would be expected to sort it out. She imagined the mess in the bedrooms: she would be expected to clear that up too. She began to sing to herself to try to cut out the noise. Phil did not seem to have heard it. Lucy wanted to shout at him, to tell him to go and see to them, but she did not want to give him the satisfaction of appearing concerned. She turned up the song in her head and mouthed the words in silent desperation as she ran the iron across a tablecloth. She decided that if Phil hadn't moved by the time she had finished it, she would have to go herself . . . No, she wouldn't! Bugger him . . . ! She added the tablecloth to the pile of finished articles and picked out a pillow case . . .

Eventually, when she was on the point of screaming, and ready to shove the ironing board over in despair, Phil turned round. But it was the close-range thumping of the iron which had distracted him rather than the rumpus upstairs. He was about to ask Lucy if she could work more quietly as he was missing some of the questions, when there was a bump overhead which shook the light fitting. Someone had either fallen off the bed or knocked something over. Lucy wondered which it was. Phil glanced at the ceiling. He appeared to be looking for cracks.

'They're making some row up there, aren't they?'

Lucy paused, waiting for the inevitable question. But just as Phil was about to ask it, he noticed Lucy's expression and changed his mind. There was another crash, followed by a yell. Again Lucy ignored it. So, with an exaggerated uncrossing of his legs and a melodramatic sigh, Phil heaved himself out of the chair and left the room. He sounded like a giant going upstairs.

Lucy smiled and took one of Phil's shirts out of the basket. She immediately put it back again and reached for one of Mathew's T-shirts. Normally, she would have enjoyed ironing it. She liked the soft cotton and neat shape. It reminded her of when he was a baby, and sometimes, when she had finished one, she would hold the warm material to her cheek. But not just now. She picked out one of her own blouses instead and straightened it out on the ironing board. Upstairs, Phil was shouting at the children and they were both crying. Lucy checked that the dial on the iron was set at the right temperature, then stroked it gently down the front of the blouse and pointed it deftly round the tiny mother-of-pearl buttons.

Lucy decided to have a bath before starting on Plato. She needed to relax for a while after ironing and putting the children to bed. The water was hot and soothing and she lay with her eyes closed overlooked by plastic toys. It was quiet in the house. She was tired. She wanted to get out of the bath and go straight to bed. Just walk across the landing and climb in between the sheets. Perhaps she could get up early and do her work before she went in in the morning? But she knew there was no chance of doing that. She would have to get up in the middle of the night to beat Phil and the children getting up.

She stood up and reached for the towel spread out on the radiator. It was warm and soft and she pressed it to her face to smell the detergent. The other towels were still damp from the children's bath, but even if they had been dry she would still have used a clean one. It was a treat, a little luxury.

After she had dried herself, she examined herself in the full-length wall mirror. She bared her teeth, then leaned closer and moved her fingers lightly across her cheeks. They looked blotchy (she blamed the heat for that), and she could feel spots underneath the skin. Perhaps she was going to break out in a nervous rash? She smiled. That would have been her mother's diagnosis. According to her, most ailments were caused by nerves. Were those new wrinkles around her eyes? And was she developing a double chin? She stretched her neck and bent her head back, patted and pinched the flesh and tried to look at herself in profile. No, she was still firm enough there. Anyway, why all this fuss tonight? Anybody would think she was going on the razzle instead of downstairs to tackle Plato.

She stepped back to get a better look at her body and legs, then twisted round and strained to see her buttocks. A pale triangle was still visible where her bikini had fitted, and she thought of the woman in the white bikini on the beach at Torquay. She imagined that Dave's wife would look something like her: glamorous, independent, with an interesting job. She would live in a smart flat. Wear attractive clothes. A different outfit every day. Take taxis. Go out for meals . . . Where was she now? Not in Linnet Close, or anywhere like it, Lucy thought, as she pulled on her dressing gown. And she won't have a face like a cherry either and sagging tits. She stuck her tongue out at her reflection, then switched off the light and went downstairs.

Before she left the house the following morning, Lucy measured the alcove by the fireplace and decided that three shelves would be enough for her books. She ordered the wood and a dozen house bricks at a do-it-yourself shop near the university, and the assistant said that they would deliver the material the next day.

Lucy wasn't at home when they brought it. Phil was. 'What's this?' he said as they unloaded the van. 'You must have got the wrong address.' The driver showed him the delivery note, and as there was no one else on the road with that name, he concluded that Lucy must have ordered it. But what for? He signed the note. And why hadn't she told him? Tracey and Mathew were as curious as he was, and when the van had gone, they helped him to carry the timber into the kitchen. He would not let them bring the bricks inside though, and when they wanted to play with them on the patio he said no, they were too heavy, they might drop them and trap their toes.

It did not take Phil long to work out what the lengths of wood were for, especially after the recent argument about Lucy's books being all over the house. But he was still puzzled about the bricks. What did she want him to build? When Mathew asked him what his mummy had bought them for, he said, 'To throw at me.'

Mathew laughed, but he did not look particularly happy at the idea. Phil picked up one of the shelves and squinted along one edge as if he was aiming a rifle. It was slightly warped, and when he examined the surface, he was unhappy at the profusion of knots. The other two shelves were the same and he was angry because he hadn't chosen the wood himself.

Lucy had forgotten all about the order. She had been working in the library all afternoon translating an extract from *The Canterbury Tales*, and she was still thinking about it when she arrived home:

> 'I have heer with my cosyn Palamon
> Had strif and rancour many a day agon
> For love of yow, and for my jalousye .

But she was pleased that the shelves had arrived, and as soon as she had kissed the children and taken off her coat, she picked one up and sniffed the raw wood. She asked Phil where the bricks were, and after he had told her, he said, 'Why didn't you tell me you'd ordered that stuff?'

He sounded peevish as if he thought that Lucy had done it to spite him.

'I forgot.'

'Forgot!'

He could not believe it. How could anybody forget about a dozen bricks and three lengths of 8" × 1"? Whenever he ordered any building materials, he thought about what he was going to make all day at work. He was always planning improvements to the house and garden. It was a release from the constant racket and pressures of his job.

Lucy banged the refrigerator door hard enough to make the milk bottles rattle inside. Phil did not like the way she was holding the packet of butter. She was grasping it like a stone.

'It's not surprising that I forget things, is it, all the different jobs that I have to do?'

Phil had spent his day on one job; he had been doing longitudinal welds. The work was slow and tedious and his eyes still ached from the hours of concentration.

'What are the bricks for?'

Lucy looked round from the cooker to see if he was being sarcastic, but he was setting the table and she could not see his face.

'To stand the shelves on, what do you think?'

It was Phil's turn to look round now, but he was too late, she had turned back to the grill.

'What, just standing on loose bricks? I'm not having that, it'll look terrible.'

'What do you mean, *you're* not having it? They're my shelves, you know.'

'Yes, and they're going to look a right mess as well, by the sounds of it.'

'Why are they? A lot of people make bookshelves like that now.'

'Who?'

Lucy tried to think of someone while she opened a tin of peas. She was still thinking when the lid fell inside.

'Some of the lecturers have them built like that in their rooms at university.'

She could feel Phil watching her as she tried to pull out the lid.

'They would, wouldn't they?'

'What do you mean?'

'You're going to cut your finger on that if you're not careful.'

He started to get up from the table, but Lucy tipped the tin over a pan and the pressure of the contents forced out the lid. Phil sat back wondering if the jagged edge had chipped the non-stick coating.

'It's what you'd expect of university professors. They're a load of old crackpots, aren't they?'

'Why, how many do you know?'

'What about him in the paper the other day, who's walking from Land's End to John O'Groats for charity?'

'What about him? There's all sorts of people go on charity walks.'

'Not on *stilts* though. Silly old bugger. He must have been about ninety as well.'

'What's his age got to do with it?'

'He wouldn't be walking to John O'Groats if he'd to do my job every day, I can tell you. He'd be too knackered. The only place he'd be bothered about walking to was bed.'

'Honestly, Phil, anybody would think you were the only one who did any work. And they're not all old, you know. A lot of the lecturers are no older than us. In fact I bet Dave Pybus is younger.'

'Who's he, Dave Pybus?'

'I've told you about him before.' (Had she?) 'He's my Literature tutor.'

Lucy could see that Phil was going to insult Dave even though he did not know him. She did not give him a chance.

'He must be brilliant to get a job like that at his age.'

Phil frowned and redirected his dissatisfaction at the cooker.

'I hope you're not burning that fish, Lucy.'

She ignored him and concealed her satisfaction by turning away and taking a plate out of the cupboard.

After tea, Tracey and Mathew helped Lucy to build the shelves. Lucy stood two bricks on their sides at each end of the alcove and the children laid a shelf across them. She made the next two spaces two bricks wide, and when the children had placed the top

65

shelf in position, they all stood back and inspected their work. Lucy called Phil in from the garage.

'What do you think of them?'

With barely a glance at the shelves, Phil touched one of the spare bricks with his foot.

'What are you going to do with these, use them as bookmarks?'

Lucy could not help laughing at him. With his mouth turned down at the corners, he looked like Mathew when he was sulking. Lucy was too pleased with herself to be disappointed by his lack of enthusiasm and she linked his arm and kissed him on the cheek.

'No, I'm going to wrap them up and give them to you for a Christmas present.'

Phil managed a grudging smile and felt the shelves to test their firmness.

'They look better than I thought, I must admit. They could do with a couple of coats of polyurethane though, to put a bit of body in the wood.'

Tracey and Mathew could not wait that long and they ran upstairs to fetch their books. They claimed the bottom shelf, one end each with a gap in the middle. Mathew complained because Tracey's row was longer than his and Lucy tried to explain that this was because she was older. But he refused to be mollified and Tracey agreed to lend him some of hers to make their totals equal.

Lucy had intended to wait until the children were in bed before adding her books, but they insisted that she did it now. They helped her to collect them and arrange them in subjects, and when they were all in place they almost filled the remaining two shelves.

It was a good job that Phil had no books to put on, or they would have needed another shelf straightaway.

Lucy was looking at some timetable changes on the notice board, when she noticed a Drama Club poster advertising for people to help with props, costume and sound on their next production. Anyone interested should contact Dave Pybus in room 104.

Lucy was interested, and she went to see Dave at five o'clock after her last lecture. She felt uneasy as she walked along the corridor towards his room. She knew that Phil and the children would be expecting her soon, but she wasn't sure how long the notice had been up, and she wanted to put her name down for something before it was too late.

66

She paused outside the door then knocked quietly with her ear close to the nameplate. There was no reply, then, just as she was about to knock again, a voice called out and she opened the door cautiously and went in. Anyone watching her from along the corridor would have thought she was on a secret mission.

Dave was sitting staring out of the window with a pen in his mouth and a pile of manuscripts on the desk in front of him. Still preoccupied, he turned slowly towards the door; but when he saw Lucy, he smiled at her in such an intimate way that she blushed. It was as if he had woken up in bed beside her after making love. He stood up and pulled a chair close to his desk.

Lucy sat down, trying hard to convince herself that he was as hospitable as this to everybody, and that he was particularly glad of a visitor just now, to relieve the boredom of marking.

'Would you like a drink?'

Lucy hesitated and looked at her watch.

'It'll not take a minute. I've already had the kettle on.'

As he bent down and plugged it into a socket on the skirting board, she felt his breath on her legs.

'Now then, what can I do for you?'

He pulled his chair round to face her and leaned foward.

'Well, I saw the poster this morning about the play which the Drama Group are putting on, and it said that you were looking for people to help . . .'

'That's right. What would you like to do?'

'I'm not sure. I don't know much about it really.'

'Well, if you're thinking of acting, the parts are already cast, I'm afraid.'

She shook her head and smiled at the improbability of the notion. Inspired by the film *The Red Shoes,* her mother had once dreamed of her becoming a ballet dancer. But when she enquired about the cost of dancing lessons, she decided that Lucy was the wrong build for it after all.

'No, nothing as grand as that. I was wondering if there was anything I could do behind the scenes?'

She glanced down as the kettle began to rumble. If it had been on already, why was it taking so long to boil?

'I'm sure there is. Have you worked on a production before?'

Lucy shook her head.

'Do you go to the theatre much?'

He reached across to the windowsill and picked up two cups.

67

Lucy was glad that he was looking away from her when she answered.

'Sometimes.'

Once, in fact. And that was to see a production of *Measure for Measure*, which she had been studying for A-level English. Phil went to the theatre more than she did. He went every year to watch the world snooker championships at the Crucible in Sheffield. 'I never seem to get much time these days, what with essays, and housework and the kids . . .'

She was ashamed of herself. Why didn't she tell him the truth? Why not come straight out with it and tell him that she hadn't been interested in the theatre until recently. That her parents weren't interested, her husband wasn't interested and none of her friends were interested. That theatre-going had never been part of her life. Why not tell him this, instead of trying to justify herself with a catalogue of domestic excuses?

'I watch plays on television though,' she said, as if somehow this was a legitimate excuse for staying at home.

'Well, the best plays are often on television these days. Not that I see many myself, I must admit. I always seem to be doing other things in the evenings.'

He took a box of coffee filters out of a drawer in his desk and fitted one inside a plastic cone.

'Will coffee be all right? I'm afraid I've run out of tea.'

Lucy could smell the coffee as soon as he began to spoon it out of the packet into the filter. The aroma was even stronger when he poured boiling water over it.

'Working on a play tends to be very time-consuming you know, particularly during the run-up to opening night. If you've got heavy domestic commitments in addition to your work, then I think you ought to think about it seriously before taking anything else on.'

'I have done.'

She sounded so definite about it that Dave did not try to dissuade her any more, and for a few seconds there was a silence between them, punctuated by the trickle of coffee through the filter. Dave sniffed at the spout of a milk carton.

'Milk?'

'Yes, please.'

He picked up a bag of sugar. Lucy shook her head.

'No, thanks.'

She could not understand why he did not use instant coffee

and powdered milk, instead of going through this performance every time he made a drink. She would have kept the sugar in a jar too; it wouldn't have been scattered all over the windowsill then. She wanted to fetch a damp cloth and wipe it clean.

'Why the sudden interest then?'

Lucy had a sip of coffee to give herself time to consider. It could have been hotter, but it was delicious, she had to give him that.

'Well, it's not all that sudden.' She had another drink. She was halfway down the cup already. 'Even though I have got a lot on at home, I don't just want to spend the rest of my time studying, as if I was back at school. I could have done the Open University if I'd wanted to do that. I'd like to get involved in university life in some way apart from work, otherwise I'm not going to get the full benefit from it.'

'That makes sense.' Dave nodded a few times, then looked past her and began to smile. 'I don't know if you've noticed, but we're sitting in the dark.'

Lucy glanced round and smiled with him.

'No, I hadn't. Would you like me to switch the light on?'

'Well, I prefer what's left of the natural light if that's all right with you.'

'I don't mind.'

They looked out across the city, where clusters of lights were appearing in offices and shops, and, in the distance, the factories and steel mills were merging into the darkening sky. Dave said, 'I love this time of the day, when it's quiet and everyone's gone home. It's incredibly peaceful.'

He continued to stare out of the window as if Lucy wasn't there. She glanced at her watch. She ought to be going. It might be a peaceful time for him, but he didn't have a meal to cook as soon as he got in and a family to look after. She felt guilty just sitting there drinking coffee when there was so much to do at home.

But, guilty or not, she still did not move. Dave was right; it was peaceful here, with the murmur of distant traffic, the pewter-coloured light by the window, and darkness gathering in the far corners of the room. If only . . .

Dave finished his coffee and looked round.

'Sorry, I was getting carried away again.'

Lucy thought he looked sad. Or was it just the shadows etched in the contours of his face?

'What were you thinking about?'

'Oh, nothing much. Just reminiscing . . . There was a pub in London I used to go to, near the British Museum. I sometimes met people there. We'd have a few drinks and make plans for the evening. It was a magical time. The day behind you, the whole night ahead . . .'

Lucy tried to imagine it. She did not know any pubs in London so she had to make up one of her own. She could see Dave at the bar with his friends. Some of them women. (One of them was his wife perhaps?) They were laughing, assured, relaxed. And where was she while they were deciding where to go next? That was easy. She was at home with two babies to look after. A day's work behind her, a night's work ahead.

Dave stood up and took down a book from his shelves.

'You'd better take a copy of the play. Do you know it?'

Lucy read the title and shook her head.

'It's a little obvious in parts, but worth doing, I think.'

Lucy slipped the book into her bag and stood up.

'I'll read it straightaway. Do you think you'll be able to find me something to do, then?'

Dave leaned across the desk and studied a calendar on the wall. It was too dark to read the numbers from where Lucy was standing.

'We're having a read-through in the drama studio on Thursday. Why don't you come along to that?'

'What time?'

'The usual, about seven thirty.'

Lucy hesitated, then nodded slowly. But her doubts were obvious even when she smiled. Dave touched her arm.

'Don't worry about it. If you feel it's going to be too much for you, forget it. There'll always be another time.'

He accompanied her to the door and, as Lucy opened it, he said, 'Would you like to come for a drink?'

Lucy stepped outside the room and directed her answer along the corridor.

'No, thank you. I have to go home. I'm late enough as it is.'

'Right, it's back to Jane Austen then.'

'You could do worse.'

'I suppose so. But even her charms wear thin after a dozen essays. Especially as all the students seem to use the same reference books.'

Lucy buttoned up her coat with exaggerated care.

'Sure you won't change your mind?'

70

'Sorry, I can't.'

Still looking downward, she appeared to be answering a child. Or a dwarf.

'I'll see you around then.'

Lucy could feel him looking after her as she walked away, and she had to struggle to resist turning round. Then she heard the door close as he went back inside. She was free! She hurried along the corridor. She wanted to get home. She wanted to see Phil, even though she knew that he would be angry because she was late, and there would be another row when she told him about the play. But she did not care; she still wanted to see him. She wanted to see Tracey and Mathew too. She wanted to hug them and kiss them. How she loved them! All of them. Even Snowy the rabbit. She even loved him too.

She desperately needed to be with them. Now. This minute. To be safe in her own home, with her own family.

Phil finished work at four o'clock and arrived home about half past. He could have been a few minutes earlier, but there was no hurry, he knew that Lucy wouldn't be in. He still hated the days when she stayed late and the house was empty when he arrived home.

He switched off the car engine and closed his eyes. He was exhausted. If Tracey and Mathew had not been due back from Judith's, he would have gone to bed for an hour. His eyes ached and his ears were still ringing from the incessant hammering of metal sheets. They were under severe pressure to complete the ventilation pipes for Oxspring Power Station on time. If they failed, they had been warned that the next contract would be awarded to one of the other subsidiaries of the Falco group of companies. Phil knew little about Falco International, except that they were based in Seattle in the United States. When they had taken over Bowes Engineering, a new general manager had been appointed, but it was soon obvious that he had no real power and major policy decisions were taken elsewhere. Whenever Phil or the works foreman went in to see him with a problem, it always had to be 'referred back'. Phil often argued that there was enough work for two more welders in the fabrication shop. This would have given him more time to check the quality of the work produced, instead of having to spend most of his time on the job himself. But the general manager always said that the company could not afford it. Labour costs had to be kept down to encour-

age investment. Without investment there would be no jobs . . .
It sounded convincing, but Phil still wasn't sure. There *must* be an
alternative, even though he had no idea what it was . . .

Phil had worked at Bowes Engineering since leaving school. He
was a good welder and proud of his skill. But there was too much
uncertainty and unremitting stress for him to enjoy working
there now.

He unlocked the kitchen door and went in. How he loathed the
silence and the sight of the dirty breakfast pots in the sink. He
switched on the light, the radio, the gas fire in the lounge, then
returned to the kitchen and put the kettle on. After he had looked
in the refrigerator to see what Lucy had left for his dinner, he
made a mug of tea and carried it through to the lounge with the
newspaper. 'Mummy's paper', as the children called it. Lucy had
ordered it while she was doing her A levels. The Sociology
teacher had said that a serious newspaper would be helpful as
background reading for the course. Phil looked at the headlines.
It reported a further fall in the pound against the dollar. In the
newspaper that he had bought on his way to work, rumours of
another royal romance had dominated the front page.

For a long time, out of sheer cussedness, he had refused to read
the new paper. It was boring, too big, too many words and not
enough pictures, he said. But eventually, as Lucy spent more and
more time studying in the evenings, and when the television
programmes were particularly bad, he began to read it just for
something to do.

Now he read it regularly, while Lucy only had time to look
through 'the comic', as she disparagingly called the newspaper
that he brought home.

But he was too tired to read for long. The heat from the fire
made him even more drowsy, and after a few minutes his head
dropped and the newspaper subsided around his knees. He
made an effort to revive himself, sat up and started again. But the
words remained intractable and, after he had started the same
paragraph three times without taking in a word, he dropped the
newspaper onto the carpet and lay down on the settee. The faint
clash of metal still rang in his head. He tried to ignore it. He knew
that poking his ears wouldn't clear it. He would have to put up
with it until it faded away.

He fell into a fitful, twitching sleep, in which he relived
incidents from work in turbulent, inconclusive snatches. But he
had only to suffer a short shift this time, because Tracey and

Mathew burst into the kitchen and dashed straight through into the lounge.

Phil groaned, turned away from the noise and pressed his face into a cushion. Perhaps, if he lay very still, they would respect his exhaustion and go away? He tried it. He even held his breath to exaggerate the effect.

It did not work, and judging by their boisterous approach, they appeared to regard his immobility as a challenge.

'Daddy! Daddy! Look what Aunty Judith's given us!'

Hands pulled at him, and when they failed to turn him over (they may as well have tried to turn a log), Mathew climbed on top of him.

'Can I eat mine now, daddy?'

Phil tried to open his eyes, tried to move his lips, tried to think of something to say (but not necessarily in that order), and failed on all three counts.

Tracey made the decision for him.

'No, you can't. He's to wait until he's had his tea, hasn't he, daddy?'

'I'm hungry. I want to eat them now.'

'Well, you can't.'

Thump! The vibrations travelled right through Mathew's body into Phil's.

'Daddy! She's hitting me!'

'You should do as you're told then. Mummy says that you won't want your tea if you eat sweets first.'

Phil turned over and managed to open his eyes. Tracey and Mathew were looking down at him solemnly, as if he had just regained consciousness in hospital.

'Listen, you two, stop making such a racket. I'm tired. I'm trying to have a little rest.'

His plea was totally ignored by Mathew, who shook a little box of sweets in front of his eyes.

'Look what we've got, daddy. Aunty Judith gave us one each.'

His simple pleasure at the gift was irresistible, and Phil was forced to smile, even though he did have to force his head back into the cushion to evade the waving fist.

'Yes, love, I can see it. You'd better save them until after tea though, like our Tracey says. You don't want your mum to be cross with you, do you?'

Mathew stopped shaking the box and inspected it thoughtfully from every angle. No, he didn't, but he looked as if he might have been willing to take the risk. Phil took Tracey's hand and pulled her down onto the settee beside him.

'Now then, tell me what you've been doing today at school?'

Tracey plucked at a button on her cardigan while she tried to remember.

'We did some maths. Then Miss Pallister read us a story. Then . . .' She suddenly looked up as she remembered something *really* important.

'You know our Mathew? He got into trouble with Robert Atkinson for giggling in assembly.'

'He did what?'

Phil was all mock severity as he contemplated Mathew who was sitting on top of him.

'He'll be getting a smacked bum if he doesn't behave himself.'

Tracey hurriedly stood up and stepped away from the settee to avoid the consequences of her betrayal. She was just in time.

'I didn't! I didn't! It was Robert who did it, not me!'

As Mathew started to scramble down to get at her, Phil held him back and tried to jolly him out of his temper by hugging him, and growling, and nuzzling his neck. Then, when Mathew was laughing and squealing, he sat him upright and kissed his cheek.

'Come on, I'll get you some tea, then you can eat your sweets.'

As they were leaving the room, Tracey said: 'What time is my mummy coming home?'

Before Phil could answer, Mathew kicked her on the shin.

'That's for telling lies,' he said.

Phil made them beans on toast. He forgot to stir the beans, and when he scraped them out of the pan, he scratched the non-stick surface with the spoon. They still smelled appetising though, and the children did not seem to care that the sauce had boiled dry and they were stuck together like mashed potato.

The sight of the children eating made Phil even more hungry, and he took Tracey's fork from her and sampled her beans. She waited anxiously for it back. If he took another mouthful like that, she would have none left.

'When are you going to have your tea, daddy?'

Phil had a taste of Mathew's beans then, just to keep matters even.

'When your mum comes home and gets it ready.'

'Will she be coming soon?'

'I hope so, or I shall starve to death.'

Mathew sawed earnestly at his dry toast, but he pressed on too

74

hard and a piece snapped off and flipped onto the table like a tiddlywink. Phil picked it up and ate it. Mathew watched him resentfully.

'If you're hungry, daddy, why don't you make your tea as well?'

Instead of eating ours, Tracey almost added, but decided against it because she could tell that he was getting grumpy again, by the way that he frowned every time he looked at the clock.

'Because I've been working all day, that's why.'

He realised immediately how ridiculous he must have sounded. What sense were two young children supposed to make of an answer like that? To them, it must have seemed like a perfectly good reason for getting on with it. But he felt too frazzled to explain his objections in detail, and in order to avert any more tiresome questions, and because he was too hungry to wait any longer, he decided to take Mathew's advice and prepare his own meal for a change.

'I don't know why your mum doesn't take a bed and sleep at the university,' he said, opening the refrigerator door and surveying the food on the shelves.

Tracey looked across at him with interest.

'Can you sleep there as well, daddy? Is it like a hotel?'

Mathew showed no interest in this exchange: he was eating as fast as he could in case Phil changed his mind and raided his plate again. Phil took a polystyrene tray out of the refrigerator and examined the lamb cutlets under the transparent wrapper. They were so puny that they appeared to be snuggling together for warmth.

'I've seen more meat on a whippet,' Phil grumbled, as he placed them under the grill. He put the chip pan on, then read the heating instructions on a tin of broad beans. As he tipped the frozen chips into the pan and watched them thaw, he shook his head disapprovingly. Chips with frost on. It wasn't natural.

'I eat more frozen food than an eskimo,' he said, opening the refrigerator door again and sliding out a cream cake. Lucy had not taken it out early enough the day before, and it had been so cold that it had made his teeth ache. What a tragedy, he thought, poking the hard sponge, when Lucy could bake such delicious cakes herself. That was the main reason why his mother had liked her, because she was such a good cook. Not up to *her* standard of course, but she knew that Phil would be well looked after. What would she have thought if she had seen him now? Perhaps it was a good thing that she was dead, or the disappointment might have killed her.

He crumpled up the cellophane cake box, then gathered together the polystyrene meat tray, torn clingfilm and polythene chip bag.

'It's more like making a model aeroplane than a bloody meal,' he said, dropping them all into the waste bin.

He burned the cutlets. Tracey brought his attention to the smoke as he was clearing the dirty plates from the table. As he dashed for the grill, the beans obligingly turned themselves off by boiling over and extinguishing the flames underneath the pan. The chips refused to brown, but he couldn't wait any longer because the cutlets were getting cold. So he served them while they were still pale and soggy, and sat down to a meal of overcooked meat, undercooked chips and disintegrating beans.

He was disgusted at the mess on his plate. He was angry with Lucy for not being home to make him a proper meal, but more than that, he was angry with himself for making such a bad job of it. Even though he wasn't interested in cooking, he still liked to do a job well, no matter what it was. He was a practical man. He could build a garage, service a car, lay a concrete drive. And if he could do jobs like that, he ought to be able to cook a simple meal. He was ashamed of himself. He was glad that Lucy was late now. He would have hated her to have walked in just then and witnessed his failure.

The foyer of the Schweitzer Tower was deserted. It was the first time that Lucy had been back in the evening, and the silence seemed strange after the activity of the day. It was like a school when all the pupils have gone home. It reminded her of evening classes.

She walked down the stairs to the drama studio on the lower ground floor, then paused outside and listened. There was no noise from inside so she stood there wondering what to do. Had she got the wrong night? No, she was sure that Dave had said Thursday. Perhaps she was too early? Perhaps the others hadn't arrived yet? There was only one way to find out. She opened the door and went in.

Dave was sitting in the middle of the studio with a girl and two boys. They had arranged their chairs in a circle, and there was an ashtray on the floor between them. Lucy was surprised how bare it was. She had expected a conventional theatre with rows of seats and a curtained stage. Instead of which, she was faced with an open space with chairs stacked round the walls, and a pile of rostra blocks in one corner. Grouped together, and illuminated by a single spotlight, Dave and the three students looked as if they were holding a meeting on a dance floor.

Lucy just stood there, embarrassed and uncertain what to do next. She had opened the door as quietly as she could, but the others had still heard her, and were now peering across the studio to see who had come in. She felt like an intruder. The spotlight seemed to unite them against her, and she felt isolated and vulnerable standing out there in the shadows on her own.

When Dave saw who it was, he stood up and crossed the floor. Lucy was attracted by the loud squeaking of his shoes on the boards. They looked like teddy boys' shoes; real brothel-creepers, with suede uppers and crepe soles. Why was a university lecturer wearing shoes like that? Perhaps it was something to do with the production? But she couldn't see how, as the play was set in 1930. Perhaps they were updating it, like they did with Shakespeare sometimes. The squeaking stopped.

'Hello. Glad you could make it. Come and meet the others.'

Lucy wasn't sure whether she was glad or not. She had lied to Phil about the play. She wasn't absolutely certain herself why she wanted to get involved, so she knew there was no chance of making him understand. He would have been outraged at the idea of her wanting to spend more time out of the house. He was even angry when she arrived home late! There would have been another row. The children would have cried (they were sensitive to the slightest raising of their voices these days), and Lucy would have been made to feel even more irresponsible. So, in the end, she told him that the play was part of her degree course, and that all English students had to do some practical work in Drama in order to cover all aspects of the subject. Phil still didn't like it, but because he thought it was official, he had no choice but to accept her explanation.

Dave stood behind his chair and introduced the students in turn.

'Julie. Chris. Robert. This is Lucy.' No one stood up or shook her hand, but their smiles and casual greetings seemed friendly enough. 'Lucy is going to help Tanya with props and ward-robe.'

It was the first that she had heard about it. But he announced it with such certainty that he made it sound as if she had been included in the production from the start. Lucy was quietly thrilled: it was like being picked for a team.

'Julie's playing Alice. Chris is playing Sam Kirk; and Robert, Arthur Morris. Have you read the play?'

Lucy nodded. Dave paused, and the others looked up at her as if expecting an opinion. If she had one, she kept it to herself, and Dave turned round and pointed up to the lighting box at the back of the studio, where a dim figure could be made out behind the glass panel.

'That's Andrew up there. He can always use a bit of help if you find you haven't enough to do . . .'

'You're right there! Hi, Lucy! Come up and see me some time!'

It was like magic. Lucy did not know what had happened at first, and she was startled and embarrassed to hear her name booming out of nowhere like that. The others laughed and looked up at the control box, and when Lucy realised where the voice had come from, and saw Andrew waving down at them, she waved shyly back. Dave took her arm and directed her towards a door at the front of the studio.

'Let's go and meet Tanya.'

He led her into the props store, where a young woman dressed in dungarees was sitting with her feet up on a table, reading a book and eating an apple. Dave pointed at her in a melodramatic, accusing way.

'Ha-Ha! Skiving on the job, eh? You want to be careful, my girl, or you'll be getting the sack. Millions of people would be glad of your job, do you know that?'

Tanya smiled and bit deeply into the apple. 'Not without wages they wouldn't.' She held out the apple towards them. 'Have a bite, it's delicious. Helen brought a boxful back at the weekend. They're from her parents' orchard.'

Lucy took her lead from Dave. (She quite fancied tasting it after him.) Dave laughed and said he didn't accept bites from strange women. Lucy just smiled and said, 'No, thank you.'

Tanya finished off the apple herself and aimed it at a waste bin in the corner. It missed, and skidded underneath a rail of old clothes.

'I picked up a couple of suits at the CND jumble sale on Saturday. I thought they might come in useful.'

Lucy wasn't sure if Tanya meant for herself or the play. Perhaps she meant both. Dave said, 'This is Lucy, Tanya. She's keen to help on the production. I wonder if you could find her anything to do?'

Lucy noticed how cleverly he had changed his approach. In the studio, he had told the actors straight out what she was going to do, because she was no threat to them. They didn't care what she did, as long as it was backstage. But here, in the props room, it was different. He had to be more circumspect. This was Tanya's department, and if she was going to accept Lucy and work with her, then she had to feel that the decision was hers.

As Tanya swung her legs down from the table, Lucy realised that her red boots were like the ones she had just bought Mathew for school. They even had the same green laces.

'Of course. There's plenty to do. The flats need painting for a start.'

The flats! What flats? According to the script, all the action took place in the kitchen of a terraced house. Anyway, they didn't have flats in villages, at least not in 1930, when the play was set. Perhaps they were updating it after all. Perhaps they were going out and performing it in a block of flats somewhere in the city, like the community theatre groups that she had read about . . . It was all very confusing, and Lucy wondered if she had made a mistake after all. She had not come to get involved in interior decorating; she could get plenty of that at home.

Then she noticed that Tanya and Dave were looking at some scenery stacked against a wall. Tanya said, 'Sunny skies are hardly the right atmosphere for this play, are they?'

So *that* was what Tanya meant by flats. Lucy blushed, and went hot all over as she realised what a fool she had nearly made of herself. She would have been a laughing stock. The whole university would have got to know about it. She imagined herself walking down a corridor, and students whispering to each other and sniggering into their hands . . . It was too humiliating to think about. She concentrated on the flats instead.

They were all painted blue, with occasional white patches for clouds. Leaning against each other gave them a chance perspective, and created the impression of real sky because some of the clouds overlapped. Lucy did not mind painting these; it was scenery, and that made all the difference. It meant *real* theatre, a proper play.

'Right then, I'll leave you to it. Tanya will show you the ropes. Come through when you've finished. The others won't mind.'

Dave went back into the studio, and Lucy and Tanya smiled at each other to span the awkward silence between them. As Tanya closed her book, Lucy cocked her head to try to read the title. Tanya helped her by holding it straight up.

'Have you read it?'

The book was called *The Feminine Mystique*.

Read it? Lucy hadn't even heard of it.

'No, I haven't. Is it good?'

She tried to sound enthusiastic, as if it was merely an oversight that she had not read it already, and that it was the next book on her reading list. But secretly she was annoyed. Inexplicably (because she was older perhaps?), she had taken it for granted that she would have read the book, and that somehow this would have helped to redress the balance of authority between them . . . She felt even more like Tanya's assistant now.

'Good? It's essential reading.' She threw the book onto the table and stood up. 'It's one of the seminal books of the women's movement, I suppose.'

Lucy sneaked a look to see who the author was. She hadn't heard of her either. She felt dejected and confused.

'Would you like a coffee?'

It was as if Tanya had sensed her mood and was trying to comfort her.

'I'd love one.'

She walked across to the sink in the corner and switched on an electric kettle.

'Milk?'

'Yes, please.'

'There's no sugar, I'm afraid.'

She returned with the mugs and placed them on the table. On Lucy's it said: I DON'T WANT TO LEAD THE STUDENT BODY. I JUST WANT TO KISS HER.

Tanya noticed Lucy reading it.

'Disgusting, isn't it? If we weren't already short of cups, I'd smash it.'

She bent down and began to rummage in a large canvas shopping bag, which appeared to be full of books and items of woollen clothing. She came up with a jar of honey and offered it to Lucy.

'Would you like some?'

Lucy was astonished. What, on its own? Or was she going to produce some bread and butter to go with it? She decided to play safe and politely refused.

80

Tanya dug out a blob with a teaspoon and stirred it into her coffee.

'It's good for you, you know. Gives you extra energy. Helps to build you up for the winter.'

Lucy was reminded of her mother. She was always giving her foods to build her up when she was a child. Lucy had been terrified of the idea. She didn't want to be built up. She just wanted to stay the same size as everybody else. As Tanya screwed the lid back onto the jar, Lucy noticed that it was labelled PURE ORGANIC. She wanted to ask Tanya what it meant, and what the difference was between her brand and the one that she bought at the supermarket for the children. But she did not have the courage. She had been humiliated enough for one evening. Tanya said, 'Are you in the English Department?'

'Yes.'

'Really? I don't remember seeing you around. Are you in the first year?'

Lucy hesitated. She was reluctant to admit it at her age. Especially to someone as young and assured as Tanya.

'Yes, I am. What year are you in?'

'This is my fourth year actually. I'm just starting an M.Phil.'

Fourth! That was the end. Lucy could have crowned her with the honey jar. Tanya slowly stirred her coffee and stared at Lucy as she tried to place her. She gave up and tapped the spoon on the rim of the mug.

'It's strange not seeing you around though. Especially as we're in the same department.'

'That's because I'm not around very much. I only come in for lectures. I've got two children, so I have to spend a lot of time at home.'

If she thought she could impress Tanya with the duties of motherhood, she was wrong.

'Are you married as well?'

Lucy was outraged by her impudence. How dare she ask such a question? What sort of woman did she think she was?

'Yes. Of course I am.'

Tanya gave her a pitying look, as if Lucy had told her that she had rabies or cancer of the breast.

'You've really got your work cut out then, haven't you?'

Lucy was bewildered. She had never met anyone before who regarded it as a liability to have a husband and two children. *That* was what she had been brought up to want! She had even

81

managed a child of each sex, even though Phil had been disappointed when the firstborn was a girl.

'What do you mean?'

Tanya seemed surprised that Lucy of all people should ask.

'Well, in most cases when married women go out to work, they end up doing two jobs, their own plus all the domestic chores, while the husband refuses to lift a finger to help . . . like the guy in the play, in fact.' She picked up the playscript from the table.

'Have you read it?'

Lucy nodded.

'God, what a bastard he is.'

Tanya skimmed the book across the table as if she could not bear the man near her, even in printed form.

'So typical as well, out drinking all the time while his wife is stuck at home . . .'

She glared at the book, which had come to rest against an old flat-iron at the edge of the table. The sight of it reminded Tanya of more practical, less emotive aspects of the play.

'The props are interesting though.' She leaned across and picked up the book again. 'I think the mangle should dominate the stage; after all, it's the symbol of her oppression, isn't it?' She consulted the list of props which she had jotted down on the flyleaf of her book. 'Two washing tubs. They shouldn't be too difficult to find. There's going to be a hell of a lot of water splashing around. Dolly . . . ? I don't know what a dolly looks like, do you?'

Lucy wasn't listening. She was thinking about what Tanya had said about the play. Ignoring her question, she said, 'It doesn't say that her husband is out drinking when the two men call to see him.'

Tanya looked up from her script, and stared at Lucy for a few moments while she regained her thoughts.

'No, but that's what it implies, doesn't it? Otherwise, why would she send that boy to every pub in the village to find him?'

'Because Alice says to the men that he sometimes calls for a drink on his way home from work . . . And the boy doesn't find him, does he?'

'No, but there's a reference somewhere in the text where Alice says that he's always out with his mates . . .' She tried to find it, but she was too agitated for a thorough search, and after a few random glances she slapped the book shut.

'Who's side are you on anyway? Surely you don't sympathise with her husband, do you?'

Lucy did not reply immediately. She was thinking about her own husband.

'I'm on Alice's side, obviously. But I think that the issues involved are a lot more complicated than you're trying to make out.'

'You're prevaricating! You do sympathise with him!'

'I do not! I can understand his attitude, though. I know why he behaves like that.'

'That doesn't excuse the way that he treats Alice though, does it? She's nothing but a slave.'

'And what is he? It's no bed of roses getting up at half past four and working in the steel works, you know! Isn't he a slave as well?'

Lucy realised that she was shouting, but she did not care. She was furious with Tanya, who, by the aggressive certainty of her manner, had forced her into defending a position that she would normally have attacked. With her own friends, she would have taken Tanya's line, instead of which she was arguing like Phil. Lucy could have strangled her. Perversely, she carried on.

'Anyway, it's absurd to class all men alike as if they're all anti-women. What about the play? It's obvious to me where the author's sympathies lie, and he's a man, isn't he?'

'Sympathy!' Tanya spat out the word like rotten food. 'Who needs that? It's totally defeatist. What happens to her at the end? She just carries on working. The message is totally fatalistic: nothing can be done. Alice has no choice but to accept a life of drudgery and subjugation.'

Lucy was so exasperated that she found it difficult to contain herself. She glanced rapidly from wall to wall, then at the ceiling, as if seeking a way of escape.

'But she had no choice at that time. What could she have done? Where would she have gone?'

'My grandmother left home in the thirties. She was engaged to a doctor, and she changed her mind and decided to go to university instead. Apparently, it caused quite a rumpus in the family at the time.'

'Yes, and so did my mother. She went into service to work for a doctor in Manchester. Who knows, it might even have been the same one that your grandmother was engaged to.'

Tanya glared at her. Then she smiled. She liked Lucy's spirit. There was more to her than she had first thought.

'Why don't you come along to a university Women's Group meeting some time? You might find it interesting. We meet in the union Wednesday evenings.'

Lucy had no idea what the university Women's Group was, but she was still roused enough not to show it.

'No, thank you. I haven't got the time.'

She felt like adding that it was difficult enough getting out of the house as it was, without taking anything else on. But she decided against it, as she could hardly expect Tanya to be sympathetic to such an admission.

After they had finished their coffee, and worked out what props were still needed, and where they might get them from, Lucy went back into the studio. Dave told her to bring up a chair, and she joined the group in the middle of the room. She took her playscript out of her bag, then sat back and watched.

Chris and Robert were pretending to walk up a street. Occasionally, one of them would turn and peer at a house number. They had their shirt collars turned up and their hands in their pockets, and shoulders hunched as if it was raining. When they reached the right house, they paused, then Christopher knocked on the door. Dave stamped his foot to simulate the sound, but Lucy thought that he did it too loud and destroyed the tension which the boys had built up as they approached the house. Lucy was also surprised by the way that Julie answered the door. She responded to the knocks too readily, she thought, opened the door too wide, and spoke to the men like a receptionist, rather than a harassed housewife doing the weekly wash and preparing her husband's dinner at the same time. She made 'What do you want?' sound like 'Can I help you?'

Lucy opened her book and read the first page. There were no directions on how the scene should be played, but she was convinced that the interpretation she had just seen was misjudged. She wanted to say so, but she thought it might seem impudent, especially as she had never worked on a play before, and she was only involved behind the scenes in this one. She kept quiet, but when Dave lit a cigarette, then stood up and asked them if there were any other ways that Alice might react to the arrival of two strangers at her door, she thought that he was aware of the misinterpretation too. Chris said that she would probably be more suspicious, or at least puzzled. Dave said yes, perhaps Julie had opened the door to them a little too readily. Julie said that Alice might be glad to see the two men, and their unexpected arrival was probably a touch of excitement in her boring life. She might even have thought they were bringing her good news. Like what? Robert wanted to know. Julie could not think of any. Perhaps she thinks they've won the pools, and the two men have come to tell them how much the prize is, Chris suggested. They didn't have the pools in 1930, did they? Julie asked. Dave said he didn't know, but he thought it highly unlikely; but what about further on, after she has invited them into the house, and she mentions that, when she first saw them, she thought they had come from the works; what did she mean by that?

They picked up their books from their chairs. 'Page four,' Dave said. 'Halfway down, just after Alice has asked them if they would like a cup of tea.'

After they had read the relevant lines, several other suggestions were made. Perhaps she thought that they were two of her husband's workmates with a message . . . Perhaps . . .

Lucy could not keep quiet any longer.

'It's obvious what she'd think. She'd think that they'd come to tell her that something had happened to him. That he'd been killed or seriously injured.'

The others turned round, surprised at her intervention. They'd forgotten that she was there. Lucy felt isolated again. But this time she felt as if she was under the spotlight, and it was Dave and the students who were standing in the shadows. She blushed at her own temerity, but she expected the others to be grateful for her contribution after they had thought about it, and to congratulate her on her perception. But she was wrong, and Julie seemed to resent her suggestion.

'It doesn't seem obvious to me. And there's no indication in the script that that's what the author means either.'

But Lucy wasn't going to be put off as easily as that. Especially as she was convinced that she was right.

'He probably thought it was so obvious that he didn't need to elaborate.'

She realised how arrogant this must have sounded, especially coming from her, a complete novice. But Dave took the suggestion seriously, and after further scrutiny of the script and a long draw on his cigarette, he said, 'It's an interesting opinion. Perhaps you would like to elaborate?'

'Well, if your husband works in a dangerous job, it's your main concern. You think about it all the time he's at work. It's something you always dread, the knock on the door, followed by bad news. It happened in our family when my grandfather was badly burned in the steel works. My mother was the same, always looking at the clock when my dad was due home from work, and sending me to the end of the entry to look up the street if he was late . . .'

Lucy suspected that the students were listening more out of politeness than interest (she wasn't sure about Dave), and she remembered Phil's observation about the cricket commentator reading out the day's scorecard, adding that it was for the benefit of people coming in late from the office. He must think nobody works anywhere else, Phil had said. The students probably thought the same thing. What Lucy was describing was as unfamiliar to them as life on Mars.

'Anyway, she's bound to have been frightened, whoever it was. She wouldn't have wanted to go to the door for a start because, if it hadn't been bad news from work, it would probably have been the police, or the bailiffs, or somebody like that. She'd have been suspicious of anybody who knocked and didn't walk straight in. She'd have taken it for granted that it was the authorities in some guise or other.'

It was only after she had finished that Lucy realised how forceful she had been. It must have sounded like a telling-off. The students just stood there, bemused by her intensity. Dave stared at her, nodding slowly.

'OK. It makes sense. I think it's worth a try.'

Lucy realised that Dave had not understood the scene either, and had cleverly concealed his ignorance by drawing the meaning from her.

He told Robert and Chris to come up the street a bit quicker next time – after all, it was pouring with rain. And they had to catch the train back to London at three o'clock, so they wouldn't be hanging about. He also told Julie to do something positive to stop her anticipating the visitors. Such as? Well, why not try a bit of business with Frank's dinner, as he'll expect it to be ready when he gets home from work.

As Robert and Chris approached the house again, Julie tipped an assortment of ingredients into an imaginary bowl and stirred them vigorously. Lucy had to concentrate on the two boys to stop herself laughing. It certainly looked like an interesting dish. She wondered if Julie would give her the recipe afterwards. Mischievously, she wished that Tanya had been watching with her. She would have suggested to her that there was no wonder Frank never came home for his meals on time, if his wife made him dinners like that. She smiled as she imagined Tanya's outraged response. Dave thought she was smiling at him and smiled back, but Lucy was unaware of this, because all she could see was an indignant Tanya, fuming away inside her head.

The opening was more convincing this time. Julie tried to look startled when the knocks came. She hesitated before putting down the bowl, and when she opened the door, she peered out and narrowed her eyes to convey suspicion. But Lucy still didn't believe her. She wasn't frightened enough. She wasn't *feeling* the part. Lucy was, just sitting there watching. She knew how Alice felt.

They all walked across the road to the Cross Keys after the rehearsal. It had been easy for Lucy to accept the invitation in the intimate atmosphere of the studio, amongst new friends and exhilarated by a novel experience. But, as soon as she stepped outside, into the familiar world of cars and buses and ordinary people, her mood changed. She became depressed. It all seemed so dreary after what she had just left.

When they reached the pub, Lucy opened her bag and pretended to look for her purse so that the others would go in first. Dave held the door open for her and she felt a rush of warm air, heard voices and laughter, and saw a glowing fire at the far end of the room.

'I've changed my mind, Dave. I think I'd better go home.'

'Come on. You've time for a quick one, surely.'

He pushed open the door invitingly wide, daring and bullying her to enter, like a doorman at a strip club. Lucy hesitated, then shook her head as abruptly as if she had just taken smelling salts.

'No, I'd better not. I'm not sure how regularly the buses run at this time of night. I don't want to be too late home.'

Somebody inside shouted, 'Were you born in a barn?'

Without looking round, or showing any sign of embarrassment at this rebuke, Dave stepped outside and allowed the door to close behind him.

'Don't worry about that. I'll run you home if you like.'

'You can't do that.'

'Why can't I?'

'Because I don't want to put you about.'

'Put me about!' Dave laughed. 'It'll be a pleasure, I can assure you.'

Lucy looked away, and hoped that the sulphurous glow of the street lamps would neutralise her deepening colour.

'Anyway, you're not going to save any time going by bus. By the time one arrives' – he gave the impression that the chances of this happening were remote – 'and you've travelled out there' – how far did he think Hartford was? – 'you could have had a drink and been taken home by car. It sounds much more sensible to me.'

It didn't to Lucy, but it certainly sounded much more enjoyable. There had to be token resistance though, and she pretended to study her watch.

'Well, all right then. I must leave here by ten o'clock, though. I should be home then by quarter past.'

She knew really that it would be nearer half past, unless Dave drove like a lunatic, but the discrepancy in times was crucial to the necessary deception. Quarter past seemed much earlier. It was close to ten, and still belonged to the body of the evening. Half past marked the climb to eleven, and the encroachment of late night.

'Great.' Dave pushed open the door again and they both went in.

The students were standing in a group near the bar. They had all been served, and when Dave walked past them, Andrew said, 'Where have you been then, hanging about outside so that you wouldn't have to buy us a drink?'

Dave pulled Andrew's cap down over his eyes, and Lucy noticed that Julie was watching her as she laughed.

'What would you like to drink, Lucy?'

She did not care that everyone else was drinking beer. This time, she was going to choose what she really wanted.

'I'll have a whisky, please.'

Dave suggested that they all sat down, and led the way to a table in the corner of the room. Lucy moved her chair round to face the fire, so that she could feel the comforting heat on her face and legs. Dave sat down beside her, but as she stared into the glowing coals, her thoughts wandered, and she forgot all about him and the rest of the group. Anyone looking on would have thought that she was there on her own.

When she returned to them, Tanya was telling a story about an encounter with a man somewhere. '. . . And he finished up by saying that he would have kicked my head in if I hadn't been a woman. Well, that really got me going. I told him that it was a typical, aggressive male attitude wanting to settle an argument with violence rather than reason, but if he did intend getting violent I didn't want any favours from him, and that I refused not to have my head kicked in just because I was a woman.'

Lucy looked at her watch. She had five minutes left. At the bus stop she would have urged them by. Here, by the fire, she wanted time to stand still. She wanted to press the winder on her watch and stop it.

Dave and Lucy left the pub on their own and walked back to the university. The car park in front of the Schweitzer Tower was empty and Lucy panicked, thinking that Dave's car had been stolen. What would she do now? If only she had gone on the bus as she had intended. Did she have enough money for a taxi? Would Dave contact the police? She imagined telephoning Phil:

Hello Phil, it's me.

Where are you?

I'm at the police station in town . . .

Dave had parked his car on a hill at the back of the university library.

'It's a bit reluctant to start sometimes,' he said, holding up a bunch of keys to the street light. 'Every time I go anywhere, I have to study the ordnance survey map first, to make sure they've got hills.'

'You'll have to get a bike instead.'

'I've got one.'

It was in the back of the car, and when Dave unlocked the door, Lucy could not get in because the front wheel was sticking out over the passenger seat.

'Hang on a minute.'

He knelt on the driver's seat and tried to push it back. It would not move. He tried to lift it, but the pedals jammed between the seats and dug into the upholstery. Finally, grunting and cursing quietly, he managed to twist the front wheel out of the way with the handlebars. He looked as if he was wrestling with a recalcitrant ram.

'Right. I'll just move these.'

He threw his briefcase and a pile of books onto the back seat and Lucy climbed in.

'Ignore those things on the floor. Just kick them to one side if they're in the way.'

At first, she thought he meant the pile of papers which formed a shifting, slippery mat. Then her foot touched something else. The floor space was too dark and cramped for her to look down discreetly and determine what it was, so she tried to recognise it by touch . . . It was a shoe. It must be one of Dave's . . . It was a bit light though and, although she had seen him wearing winkle pickers and beetle crushers, she couldn't really imagine him going as far as high heels. Then she touched something else. A garment: something soft and flimsy. She feared the worst and hurriedly removed her foot. And where was the other shoe? Kicked over the back no doubt in a fit of wild passion . . . Lucy backheeled the offending objects under the seat and concentrated on the road ahead.

Lucy felt ill at ease sitting beside a strange man in a strange car, especially at this time of night. She was used to Phil and their family saloon, with its familiar fittings and smells, and smooth-running engine. She did not like the sound of Dave's car at all, and the way that he crouched over the steering wheel like a jockey urging on a tired horse wasn't very reassuring either.

Lucy was so disoriented that even the route home seemed unfamiliar, and when they stopped at some traffic lights and Dave asked her which road they should take, she had to think for a moment before she could answer. She imagined Phil drawing up beside them and looking out at Dave's car. How he would have hated it: the corroding paintwork, the filthy windows, the battered bumper. And how he would have hated Dave for allowing it to get like that. It was beyond Phil's understanding how anyone could own a car and not look after it. He regarded it as a serious offence, like ill-treating children and pets.

The lights changed. As they drove along a wide, tree-lined avenue, Dave said, 'God, I hate the suburbs.'

Lucy looked out at the detached houses with their timbered gable-ends and spacious gardens.

'There are worse places to live.'

'It's so oppressive, though. It gives me claustrophobia.'

Claustrophobia! What, here? Lucy shook her head in amazement and wondered where he had been brought up.

'Did you enjoy it this evening?'

Lucy turned back towards him.

'Yes, very much.'

'Good. I wondered if you'd make it . . . I hoped you would.'

'It was difficult.'

'I'm sure it was.'

They passed a cinema and Dave glanced up to see what was on.

'I've always thought Rex was a curious name for a cinema. It sounds more like a dog.'

The Rex was one of Lucy's landmarks when she travelled home on the bus. She divided the journey into sections to make it seem shorter, and the cinema was the start of the last stretch. Usually, she was pleased to see it. But not tonight.

'We're nearly there now.'

She was expressing her regret, but Dave thought that she was apologising for taking him so far out of his way.

'Pity.'

'I'll try and get the car next time, then I won't have to leave so early.'

But she said it more in hope than expectation, and Dave knew it.

'If it's going to cause trouble, I wouldn't worry about it. It's not worth the hassle.'

Lucy welcomed his reassurance, but she wasn't sure that he was right.

'I wonder what Tanya would say to that?'

'Tanya?' Dave laughed. 'Has she been getting at you already? She's a fanatic, that girl . . . woman, I should say.'

'Perhaps you have to be.'

The car headlights lit up the Hartford sign at the side of the road.

'She's terribly bright, though. She's doing her thesis on the role of women in eighteenth-century painting, with particular reference to Hogarth.'

As they passed the Malt Shovel, Lucy instinctively looked for Phil's car in the car park. He had a favourite place near the wall. Another car was in it tonight.

'You can drop me off anywhere here. I only live down the road.'

'Show me where it is, I'll take you.'

Lucy hesitated. She wanted to get out of the car now and walk home before anyone saw her. As they passed the fish and chip shop, she turned away and pretended to touch up her hair.

'Just past the post office. The first on your right.'

Dave turned into Lapwing Drive and Lucy felt for the door handle, ready to get out.

'Drop me off here, please. This'll do fine.'

'Show me where you live. I'll take you to the door.'

Lucy pointed ahead and seemed about to tell him, then she placed her hand on his arm.

'You'd better not, Dave. I'd like to get out here.'

Dave immediately drew in to the kerb, and they sat in silence for a few moments with the car engine running. Lucy felt horribly exposed, even though there was no one in sight. She knew people who lived on this road. Alan, a drinking pal of Phil's, lived in the house opposite. She couldn't see any curtains moving, but she felt as if she was being watched by the whole street.

'Well, thanks for the lift.'

'Any time. I hope you're not late.'

Lucy checked her watch.

'No. It's worked out perfectly.'

If she arrived home within the next five minutes, Phil would think that she had come home on the bus. There would be no trouble: no questions asked. As she turned to say goodnight, Dave leaned across and kissed her on the mouth. He put his arm around her before she could withdraw, and as she sank back under his weight, she forgot about getting home on time, Phil's wrath, inquisitive neighbours: everything . . .

When she opened her eyes, Dave was smiling down at her.

'I've been wanting to do that for a long time.'

Lucy forced herself upright and jerked her skirt down over her knees.

'Let me go now, Dave. If anybody sees us . . .'

The consequences were too horrifying to contemplate and she scrambled out of the car and slammed the door. The noise made her even more terrified, and she hurried away as if to dissociate herself from it.

She wanted to turn round and wave, but there was someone approaching from the other direction. She crossed the road before they met, in case it was anyone she knew and her expression betrayed her emotions.

Lucy found a table by the windows. She liked this side of the library because it overlooked the park. There was a pond with willow trees and bullrushes and a flock of wild ducks. Lucy never tired of watching them fly in. They came down fast, feet outstretched to slow them down, and after a short glide and a shake of the feathers, they looked as if they had never been away.

Mothers brought their children to feed the ducks, and one afternoon, Lucy had been so outraged when she had seen some boys throwing stones at them that she had forgotten where she was and knocked on the window, like she did at home when Tracey and Mathew were misbehaving in the garden. Students jerked round in alarm. A library assistant appeared briefly at the end of the shelves, and Lucy hurriedly sat down and tried to bury her blushes in her books.

She often tried to invent similes to describe how the branches of the weeping willows trailed in the water. But she never came up with anything that satisfied her. They were always trailing languidly like hands from rowing boats, or spread out across the surface like Ophelia's hair.

It was warm and quiet in the library, and the corridors of shelves and snug alcoves formed secret, whispery retreats. Lucy had not known how to use the library at first. She was frightened of it. Three floors of books and a basement of old journals were too much for her. She had been put off libraries when she was a little girl. She had gone to join the branch library wearing roller skates, and the librarian refused to let her in unless she took them off: choosing books on wheels offended her sense of propriety. Lucy refused and went away without joining. She was averse to libraries for many years after that.

But she had been forced to use the university library when she needed a book on Marlowe for an essay. At first, she tried to find the book on her own. She looked for English Literature on the board outside the lift in the foyer (it was like looking for furniture or bedding in a department store), then went up to the second floor and began to walk along the shelves. English Literature was listed 900–930, but Lucy could not find any shelves numbered higher than 729. Perhaps she had got the wrong floor? She asked a browsing student. She didn't know. Lucy started again. There seemed to be no logic to the numbers on the shelves. 500 . . . 10 . . . 20 . . . 30. She reached the end and turned the corner . . . 603. *603?* She looked around, where was 540? She never found it. It was like standing at a crossroads not knowing which road to take. She asked a library assistant who was shelving returned books from a trolley. The girl pointed vaguely ahead. 'Along there to the end. Turn right and keep going. Next to Architecture, I think.' Lucy never found Architecture. She never found the library assistant again either. She started to sweat. She felt like crying. She wanted to go home. She went back to the foyer, and after a few minutes' wary circling, waiting for an opportune moment when there was no one near enough to overhear, she approached the enquiry desk and told the librarian what she wanted. The librarian pointed to the catalogues; the conventional card catalogue, and the new microfiche readers, which looked like television sets. Lucy panicked at the thought of using one of these, and hoped that the book was listed in the authors' index, somewhere between MAC and MAS. She opened the drawer, flicked through the cards. There it was! What a relief. She wrote down the reference number, and this time, feeling much more confident, took the lift to the second floor.

The missing section had been miraculously restored in her absence and there were six copies of the book waiting to be borrowed. Lucy presented one of them at the desk; the librarian asked her for her ticket. She said she hadn't got one. She felt angry and embarrassed as if being wrongly accused of shoplifting. Was she a student? Yes. The librarian demanded proof. Lucy produced her union card and the librarian, after what seemed like an unnecessarily thorough inspection of her photograph and particulars, sent her across to another desk to register. 'No,' she said, placing her hand firmly on the book when Lucy tried to take it, 'leave that here until you come back.'

After receiving her tickets, there was only the electronic security system and porter's search to negotiate as she went out. At last she had done it. She had borrowed a book! She walked down the steps drained but elated. She now knew how a bank robber must feel after making a successful getaway.

Lucy set out her books on the table, then stared out of the window for a few minutes before starting work. The wind was stripping the last leaves from the trees, and the surface of the pond was dark and choppy. A young couple walked across the grass with their arms around each other. The wind blew the woman's hat off, and they both set off in boisterous pursuit. Lucy strained forward to follow the chase, but they still had not caught the hat when they ran out of sight behind the conservatory.

Lucy read through her last paragraph. She was writing an essay on Anglo-Saxon word-formation and derivation.

A couple of miles away, across the city, Phil and another welder were using the occasional Anglo-Saxon word in an argument about the quality of a weld between two pipe joints. Phil drew his thumb along the silver ridge and shook his head.

'It's a bit rough, isn't it that, Bob?'

'Why, what's wrong with it?'

'It looks as if a pigeon's shit on it.'

'Does it fuck.'

'Harry Rogers could do a better job than that.'

That did it. The first insult was bad enough, but to be compared unfavourably with the worst welder in the shop was intolerable.

'Fucking hell, Phil. It's not that bad, is it?'

'Look at it, Bob. It's as rough as a bear's arse.'

They were having to shout at each other across the pipe, because of the deafening noise from the next bay, where a plater was levelling a steel panel with a seven-pound hammer. A fitter, filing a templet a few yards away, had no idea that they were in dispute.

'There's no fucking wonder it's not perfect, is there? How can anybody do a decent job with the pressure we're having to work under?'

Phil did not have time to answer (he would have had difficulty finding one), because the works foreman came up to him and shouted that he was wanted on the phone. Phil immediately forgot all about the faulty weld.

'Who is it?'

'How the fuck do I know?' he roared at Phil, disgruntled at having to walk the length of the shop to find him. Phil hurried away. Whoever it was, it must be serious. He was hardly ever contacted by telephone at work. None of the men were, except for emergencies. The practice was discouraged. There was no time for casual conversations when there were orders to complete. The last time that Phil had received a telephone call was three years ago when his mother had died.

The telephone was in the foreman's office in the machine shop next door. Phil closed the door behind him to cut out the noise, then picked up the receiver from the desk.

'Hello?'

'Hello. Is that Mr Downs?'

'Yes.'

'This is Mrs Lockwood from Hartford Primary School . . .' There was an open newspaper on the desk. Phil fixed his eyes on one of the headlines while he listened to her. 'Mathew has had a slight accident. He's fallen down in the playground and cut his head . . .'

'Is it bad?'

'Well, it may need a couple of stitches in it.'

'Christ. Where is he now?'

'He's in my office. Don't worry, he's comfortable enough and we've managed to stop the bleeding. He needs to go to the hospital though. Could you come and take him?'

'Me?' He could not have sounded more surprised if he had been selected as the celebrity for *This is Your Life*. 'How can I? I'm at work.'

'Yes, I'm aware of that.' There was a distinct change in Mrs Lockwood's manner due to Phil's response. It was a familiar answer from many parents. They expected the teachers to act as nursemaids as well. 'I'm afraid I can't spare a teacher to take him. It would mean doubling up on a class, which I'm very reluctant to do.'

But she was mistaken in Phil's case. He did not expect a teacher to take Mathew to hospital.

'What about my wife, can't she take him?'

'We can't contact her. That's why we've contacted you. She's not at home and they can't find her at the university.'

'Well, where the hell is she then?'

He made it sound as if Mrs Lockwood was responsible for Lucy's disappearance.

'I've no idea, Mr Downs. But I'm more concerned about Mathew at the moment, and what's going to happen to him.'

Phil stared out of the glass booth into the machine shop, where a steel girder was being lowered to the floor by an overhead crane. It was a delicate manoeuvre, and Phil wanted to go out and help the machinist, who was guiding it down into a narrow gangway between a lathe and a drilling machine.

'I'll take him to the hospital.'

'How long will you be?'

'Tell him I'll come straightaway.'

He did not even stop to have a wash or visit the locker room. He told the foreman what had happened, threw his overalls into the back of the car, and drove off. He felt strange as he passed through the gates on his own, even though he did have a legitimate excuse for leaving work early. It was like playing truant from school.

Phil parked the car at the end of the line of teachers' cars in the playground. He looked back at the registration plates as he walked towards the school and noted with satisfaction that none of their cars were as new as his. He did not stay smug for long, however, because, when he glanced down at himself, he realised how scruffy he looked now that he was away from work. Usually it did not matter. He drove straight home and nobody saw him. Now, dressed in old trousers, torn shirt and oil-stained boots, he looked like a candidate for free dinners. I must look like a tramp, he thought, as he felt the stubble on his chin. He wondered about finding the boys' toilets and having a wash before going to see Mrs Lockwood. He never considered using the staff cloakroom.

As he crossed the playground, he tried to remember who Mathew's teacher was. Phil did not visit the school very often. He had attended an occasional parents' evening and a Summer Fayre, but he left all the details of the children's education to Lucy. He had bad memories of school. Years of boredom, bullying teachers and a continual sense of failure had left him wanting revenge. For years afterwards, he had imagined a scene in which he met an ex-teacher in a pub, and when the teacher recognised him and tried to be matey, Phil smashed him in the teeth.

All that had faded now, but he was still wary of schools, and although this pleasant, low building with its flowerbeds and adjoining field was nothing like the dreary, back-street institutions that he had attended, the old fear returned, and his stomach churned when he pushed open the door.

As he walked along the corridor to the secretary's office, he looked at the children's pictures on the walls and tried to see if Tracey or Mathew had done any of them. He passed the hall, where children were swinging on ropes and climbing up wall bars, then stopped at the secretary's office and knocked on the door. A voice immediately called, 'Come in!' Phil hesitated. He felt like a schoolboy again. If he had been wearing a cap, he would have taken it off.

'Hello. I'm Mr Downs, Mathew's father.'

He was immediately aware of the formality of his introduction. Mathew's *father!* He couldn't remember calling himself that before. It made him sound grave and distinguished, a description totally at odds with his appearance.

'Ah yes.' The secretary was obviously expecting him. 'Just a moment, please, I'll fetch Mrs Lockwood.'

As she stood up and turned towards the door adjoining the headmistress's room, her swivel chair turned with her, and remained in position to receive her when she resumed work. She returned immediately with Mrs Lockwood. If Phil had not known who they were, he would have mistaken the young head-mistress, dressed in tight skirt and high heels, for the secretary, and the elderly secretary, in twinset and flat shoes, for the head.

97

'Hello, Mr Downs.' Mrs Lockwood smiled at him and shook his hand. She was wearing maroon nail polish and a silver ring shaped like a snake. Phil became more conscious than ever of how shabby he must look. 'Please come through. Mathew's in here.'

As he followed Mrs Lockwood into her office, Phil noticed the outline of her bra under her blouse and smelled the perfume on her hair. But, when he saw Mathew in the armchair by the window, he forgot all about her. He looked so forlorn sitting there, holding a square of lint to his eye. His face was sickly pale, and there were dirty rivulets down his cheeks where the tears had run. As soon as he saw Phil, he started to cry again. Phil crouched down by the chair and put his arm round him.

'Don't cry now, love. It'll be all right.'

Mathew drew away so that he could see Phil's face.

'Is my mummy coming as well?'

'No, love. She's at university. She'll be waiting for you, though, when we get home.'

Phil gently lifted the pad from Mathew's eye.

'Are we going home now, daddy?'

'No, we're going for a ride to the hospital first, to let the doctor have a look at your cut.'

There was a deep nick under the eyebrow. Phil leaned over him and examined it intently like a boxer's second. The bleeding had been staunched and there was an oval stain on the lint like a lipstick blot.

'I don't want the doctor to look at it. I want to go home to my mummy.'

Phil replaced the lint on Mathew's wound as carefully as a stone over a sleeping toad.

'He'll not hurt you, love. You'll have to go and see him, though, to make it better.'

Mathew's lips began to tremble and tears came to his eyes again. Mrs Lockwood quickly stepped forward and stroked his hair.

'He's been ever so brave, Mr Downs. He's ever such a big boy now, you know.'

It worked, and instead of crying, Mathew managed a shy smile. If he had been a year or two older, he would have blushed. Phil, who was still kneeling by the chair, became aware of Mrs Lockwood's legs at the side of him. She was wearing open-toed shoes and he could see her painted toenails underneath her tights. He looked up at her.

'What happened to him?'

'He said he was playing at helicopters.' As she raised her arms to demonstrate, a gap appeared between the buttons of her blouse and he glimpsed pale flesh. 'He must have made himself dizzy spinning round, and fallen into the corner of the wall. I'm afraid he crashed, didn't you, Mathew?'

Phil wished that Mrs Lockwood would crash and fall on top of him. He stood up, making sure that he had his back to her.

'Come on then, Mathew, let's go and see that nice doctor at the hospital.' He tried to make it sound exciting, like a visit to the seaside, or a trip to the zoo. 'Where's your anorak?'

It was on Mrs Lockwood's desk. She helped him to put it on.

'There you are,' she said, straightening his collar. 'What about Tracey, Mr Downs? Will there be anyone in when she arrives home?'

'Well, Mrs Thorne, our next-door neighbour, usually collects them when Lucy's not in, and brings them home with her two. She'll have to stop there until one of us gets back, that's all. She'll not mind. I suppose she's used to it by now.'

Mrs Lockwood wasn't sure if he meant Mrs Thorne or Tracey, but judging by the bitterness in his voice, she guessed that he was referring to his daughter.

As they crossed the room towards the door, Mrs Lockwood said, 'How's your wife getting on at university, Mr Downs?'

'All right, as far as I know.'

'Is she enjoying it?'

'She must be. She spends enough time there anyway.'

'I think it's very brave of her taking on something like that. It must be terribly difficult doing a full-time course and running a home at the same time . . .'

'Running a home!' Mathew glanced up at him apprehensively. He recognised the tone. It usually signalled the start of an argument. 'The kids never see her these days. I'd to show them a photograph of her the other day; they'd forgotten what she looked like.'

Mrs Lockwood stood in the doorway and watched them walk away hand in hand. In his anger, Phil had forgotten about Mathew's injury and he was almost dragging him down the corridor. Mrs Lockwood was upset to see them leaving like that, but she was glad that she had found out about the problem. In her job, such information was vital.

*

99

Lucy could not understand it when she arrived home and there were no lights on in the house and no car on the drive. At first, she thought that Phil must have taken the children out somewhere, but she could not imagine where to. The only possibility seemed to be her parents' house, but it seemed highly unlikely Thursday teatime after work.

When she switched on the light in the kitchen, and saw that everything was as she had left it that morning, her immediate response was selfish and irrational: at least he could have washed the pots! Then she panicked. Something must have happened to him. He must have had an accident at work. They had probably been searching all over for her while she had been working in the library. And what about the children? Where were they?

Lucy ran out of the house to see if they were at Judith's, next door. She knocked on the kitchen door and went straight in. Judith and Tony were in the middle of a meal, but Lucy was so agitated by this time that she did not even apologise for interrupting them.

'Are the kids here, Judith?'

Lucy had to endure an unbearable pause while Judith swallowed a mouthful of food.

'Your Tracey is. Phil's taken Mathew to hospital.'

Hospital! Lucy pricked all over and started to sweat. Her head throbbed. She thought she was going to faint.

'Why, what's happened to him?'

She held onto the draining board for support, expecting Judith to say that Mathew had been knocked down. But before she could say anything, Tracey, who had been waiting impatiently for her mother for over an hour, yet had still delayed her entrance to watch the explosive last seconds of a cartoon on television, came running into the kitchen, her eyes bulging with pent-up excitement.

'Mummy! Mathew's cut his head open at school and my daddy's had to take him to hospital to have it sewn up!'

She made him sound like a rag doll. Lucy turned to Judith for a more measured assessment of the accident.

'I don't think it's serious. Mrs Lockwood said that he fell down in the playground and cut his eye. She thought it best to send him to hospital in case it needs stitching.'

'Poor little thing.' Lucy gave Tracey a hug big enough for two. 'Did they have to fetch Phil from work?'

'Mrs Lockwood said that she tried to contact you first. She said that she phoned you at home, and then at the university, but they couldn't find you anywhere.'

Phrased like that, it sounded as if Lucy had been trying to avoid discovery.

'I was in the library all afternoon, working.'

It was obvious from Judith's censorious silence where she thought that Lucy should have been. Tony finished his dinner and pushed his plate away.

'Put the kettle on, Jude.'

'Wait a minute. I haven't finished yet.'

Tony leaned back and reached for the newspaper off the worktop.

'Sit down, Lucy. We'll have a cup of coffee in a minute.'

'No, thanks, I'd better get back now, they'll be home soon. Where's your coat, Tracey?'

As Tracey walked into the hall to fetch it, Lucy noticed that she had taken off her shoes as well.

'That's all right. She's not a bit of trouble. She's just like one of the family now . . . In fact, they both are.'

Tracey returned carrying her coat, and treading down the heels of her shoes which she had taken off without unfastening.

As they were leaving, Judith said, 'Tracey's had a good tea, Lucy, so you've no need to worry about her.'

They had only been in the house a few minutes when Phil and Mathew arrived home. Lucy, who was listening for them as she washed up, had left the hall door open and resisted switching on the radio so that she would hear the car when it turned into the drive. Tracey heard it too in her bedroom, and they converged at the front door. Lucy fumbled with the latch in her anxiety to get out, and Tracey watched her impatiently like a dog eager for its walk.

'Hurry up, mummy.'

'What do you think I'm trying to do, you silly thing?'

Lucy opened the door, and Tracey almost pushed her down the steps as she surged past. Mathew was sitting in the back of the car waiting for someone to open the door for him. He had been treated like a prince for the past few hours and he was enjoying it. He emerged patched up and smiling like a wounded hero, but all his manly pretensions were immediately destroyed by his mother, who picked him up and transformed him back into her baby with fierce hugs and sloppy kisses. Mathew was suddenly relieved that the reception party was no bigger after all.

Lucy carried him into the house and sat him on the sofa in front of the fire. She sat down beside him and Tracey sat at his other side. Phil put the car away and closed the garage door; and while Lucy was waiting for him to come in with the full story, she fussed over Mathew and inspected the dressing over his eye.

'Poor little love. Does it hurt?'

'Only a bit now.'

Tracey leaned across him for a closer look.

'Did they put some stitches in it?'

'Two, my daddy says.'

'Is that all?'

It was obviously an anti-climax after such a long wait. Lucy angrily pushed her away from him.

'Isn't that enough?'

Undeterred, Tracey edged closer again.

'Did they sew it up with needle and cotton like my mummy with my teddy?'

'Tracey, just shut up about it now, will you? He's had enough for one day.'

Tracey did as she was told, but she continued to stare intently at the strip of elastoplast above his eye as if willing it to fall off. Lucy tried to cuddle Mathew, but he remained slightly resistant and did not give in to her in his usual way. At first, Lucy thought that he was protecting his wound, but when Phil came into the room and Mathew immediately went across and sat on his knee, she knew that it was more than that. She bumped up the cushion where he had been sitting, then turned to Phil.

'Is it bad then, his eye?'

'It's nothing to worry about. He's had a couple of stitches in it. The doctor says it should heal up all right, though.'

'Did you have to wait long? I can remember Judith saying she had to wait ages that time she took their Joanne when she dislocated her thumb. She said she was in agony.'

'It wasn't too bad. I bought him some comics to look at. He was as good as gold. And when the doctor put the stitches in he never made a murmur. He was ever so brave.'

Lucy felt the tears prickle her eyes. She wanted Mathew to be on her knee while they were discussing him. It was as if they were talking about someone else's child.

'I'm sorry they had to fetch you from work. I'd have taken him. You know that, don't you?'

Phil did not reply.

'I was in the library doing an essay. I couldn't do it at home because I had to use some reference books.'

She was lying. All the books that she needed were in her bag. But how could she tell Phil that she preferred to work in the library after what had just happened? It was easier to tell lies. She was becoming expert at it these days.

Phil reached down the side of the cushion and pulled out a model racing car. He ran it up and down the chair arm, then turned it over and started to flick one of the wheels as if it was a cigarette lighter.

'It can't be helped, can it?'

But his sullen tone contradicted his resignation. Mathew took the car off him.

'Daddy, you'll break it doing that.'

Lucy smiled and leaned towards him.

'I know, Mathew. We'll go into town on Saturday and buy you a new car for being such a brave boy.' She pulled Tracey to her to fill the gap that Mathew had left. 'And something for you as well, love. We'll all have a day out together. It'll be nice.'

When Mathew saw his mother making such a fuss of Tracey, he scrambled off Phil's knee and ran back to her for his share of affection. Lucy joyfully enfolded him with her other arm.

'Can I have a helicopter, mummy, like Stephen Ellis at school?'

'You can have anything you want, love.'

Mathew fixed her with a slow, wondering smile.

'Anything?'

'He can if he's fit to go.'

Lucy looked across at Phil from between the children's heads. They looked like a family group posing for a photograph.

'What do you mean?'

'Well, the doctor said he's to take it easy for a day or two in case there's any reaction. He said he's to stop off school tomorrow as well.'

Lucy nodded sympathetically and for a moment or two did not realise the implications of what Phil had said. Then it hit her. *Stop off school?* And who was going to look after him? Why, *she* was of course. Who else could? But she had work to do. She had to go in to university. She had a tutorial with Dave. Her heart bumped so hard that she was afraid that the children would feel it and say

103

something. Perhaps Judith would look after him . . . ? No, she couldn't possibly impose on her any more. What about her mother . . . ? No, she knew there was little chance of sympathy or assistance from her . . .

She had no choice; she would have to stay at home and look after him herself. Yes, like any normal mother would, she thought, suddenly ashamed that she had considered anything else. And she would start now. This very instant. She would prove to Phil that she was a proper wife and mother, and that her family came first in spite of what he, and her mother, and some of her friends thought about her.

And she did. She went into the kitchen and made Phil's dinner. She made a separate little tea for Mathew, then washed up, bathed the children, read to them and put them to bed. Even then she did not open her books. She dusted the lounge, then sat on the settee with Phil, and let down the hem of one of Tracey's dresses while he watched the television. He seemed pleased with her efforts to redeem herself and, later, he rewarded her in bed.

Things were almost like they used to be, before she went to university.

Mathew appeared to have fully recovered the following morning. He got up at the usual time, ate a good breakfast and wanted to go to school with Tracey. He was so persistent that Lucy was tempted to let him. As she was helping Tracey on with her coat, she caught him turning his head to admire his dressing in the hall mirror. Poor little thing. What was the point of being a hero in private? He wanted Miss Butler to make a fuss of him, and to tell all his friends about being stitched up at the hospital. But she could not risk it and, finally, she resigned herself to a day at home.

She would catch up with a few jobs in the house, go to the supermarket and enjoy being with Mathew for a change. She would read to him, play with him, take him for a walk if he felt like it. Down to the brook perhaps? Yes, he would enjoy that. She felt better already. They were going to have a good time together. She was determined to repair her neglect.

But first she must thank Mrs Lockwood and tell her how Mathew was, and then contact the university to tell them that she would not be in. It did not matter about the Politics lecture; no one would miss her, and she could copy up the notes later. But the tutorial was different. It was only courteous to let her tutor know she wasn't coming.

After she had spoken to Mrs Lockwood, she telephoned the Literature Department and asked for Dr Pybus's room. It seemed strange calling him by his academic title. It did not sound like the same man. Dr Pybus sounded older and more dignified than Dave. While she was waiting for the secretary to connect her, she watched Mathew feeding the goldfish in the kitchen. He was sprinkling enough food on the water to feed a whale. If she had been speaking to her mother, or a friend, she would have interrupted the conversation and shouted through to him from the hall. But she was so tense as she waited for Dave to answer that she felt powerless to intervene. She did not care what he did. Her attention was elsewhere.

'Hello.' It was the secretary again. 'I'm afraid Dr Pybus isn't in his room. Would you like to leave a message?'

Lucy hesitated. No, she wouldn't. She decided to ring back. But what if he wasn't in next time either, and she was forced to leave a message after all? The secretary would wonder what she was making such a fuss about. Why did she need to speak to Dr Pybus personally just to tell him that she could not come in? It was nothing unusual. She passed on similar messages all the time.

'Yes, all right then . . .'

After she had replaced the telephone, Lucy went into the kitchen, where Mathew was still feeding the goldfish on the windowsill. He was prodding the water to make the food sink and the fish were being showered by their own dinner. If she could have spoken to Dave, Lucy wouldn't have cared if Mathew had tipped a bucketful of food into the tank; she would have teased him and said that they would soon be too fat to swim around. But because Dave wasn't there, she scolded him, and warned him that he would kill them by overfeeding them like that.

Lucy made another cup of coffee and sat down at the table with the newspaper. On the front page, there were reports of continuing conflict in the Middle East, an American trade embargo against Russia, a further rise in unemployment and the resignation of two cabinet ministers. But the problems of the world did not interest Lucy just then, her concerns were more private. She felt listless, unable to concentrate. She turned the pages impatiently, then finished off her coffee and stood up.

'Have we to go for a walk, Mathew?'

Mathew scrambled out from under the table, his pop-up alphabet book immediately forgotten.

'Can I go on my bike, mummy?'

Lucy crouched down in front of him and held him by the arms.

'You can if you feel well enough. If not, we'll stop in and do something else.'

'I am, mummy! I'm better now. I want to go!'

He looked healthy enough. Yesterday's pallor had gone and she could feel the pent-up energy inside him. If she had released his arms, he would have sprung into the air like a jack-in-a-box.

'Come on then, I think you'll be all right if we don't stop out too long.'

Lucy made him a drink of hot chocolate first, then dressed him warmly in an extra jumper, duffel coat and scarf. Mathew endured all this cosseting with fortitude, but when Lucy produced his mittens, he became agitated and began to shake his hands about.

'No, mummy. I don't want them on.'

'Why not?' she said, trying to encase his recalcitrant fingers.

'Because they're too big. I can't ring my bell properly when I've got them on.'

'You'll have to wear them, love, it's frosty outside. Anyway, what about motorbike racers? They always wear gloves.'

'I know they do. But theirs have got fingers in, haven't they?'

Fingers or not, Lucy forced them on; but she could see what he meant when he emerged from the garage trying to ring the bell. His hand moved shapelessly inside its confines like a ferret in a bag.

Mathew rode beside her until they reached the end of the road, but he was soon bored by her steady pace, and he pedalled away into a world of fantasy, where his tricycle was transformed into every form of transport from a spaceship to a speedboat. Lucy was left on her own for much of the time, which suited her mood and gave her time to think.

She began with a fleeting kaleidoscope of topics: university, family, friends, but gradually her thoughts focused on the events of the previous day, and as she walked along the Crescents, Drives and Avenues of the estate, she became increasingly angry and entered into a furious argument with herself.

Why should I feel guilty about what happened? Why should Phil have been annoyed because he had to take Mathew to hospital? He's got as much right to go as me, hasn't he? After all, he is his dad! Yes, but he was at work. And where do you think I was? I know, but that's different. It would be, wouldn't it? But

Phil's the breadwinner. So what? He didn't lose any money, did he? Anyway, that's not the point. What you're really saying is my work's not as important as his, that really I'm just messing about. And another thing; even if I had been out at work earning a living like Phil, they'd still have phoned me up to take him to hospital, and it would still have been me who would have been expected to take today off and look after him. But you're his mother. Yes, and Phil's his dad. But you brought him up. I had no choice, had I? Do you mean you didn't want to? Of course I did! I enjoyed them when they were little. It seemed like the natural thing to do. Well, there you are then. What do you mean, there I am? It's not as easy as that. Decisions are not always made in a clear-cut and logical way. I did what was expected of me without considering anything else. I never felt that I'd made any decisions. They'd all been made for me somehow. I just went along with them, like everybody else I knew . . .

Lucy suddenly became aware that she was grimacing and muttering to herself at the conflict within her. She glanced round furtively to see if anyone was looking. If there had been, they would have thought she was demented. But the only people in sight were a young mother wheeling a pushchair on the opposite pavement and two little girls playing with their prams on a drive. And they were all too involved with their babies to take any notice of her. A man came out of a house and got into his car. As he drove away, his wife came to the door and shook a duster outside. It could have been a wave but, if it was, the snap of the cloth, and the disgruntled expression on her face, suggested good riddance rather than goodbye.

They reached Lapwing Rise, which was the last road on the estate. Some of the houses were still for sale and their gardens were as wild as the adjoining meadow. Mathew turned down a pathway between two houses. He knew the way. Lucy had brought him here regularly before he started school. As she followed him down the rough track, she realised that it was the first walk she had taken since the summer.

She felt calmer once she was out in the fields. It was a hazy morning of weak sunshine, with patches of mist lingering like gunsmoke near the hedgerows, and frost lining the plough furrows. Mathew toiled along the hard rutted path, his bell ringing involuntarily every time he hit a bump. Lucy could have overtaken him now, but she stayed behind so as not to hurt his pride. The walk across the estate had warmed her up. She felt snug in her winter coat and boots and the tingle in her cheeks was invigorating.

The path ran alongside a hawthorn hedge which separated two fields. Most of the leaves had fallen but the branches were still bright with berries. Lucy stopped and plucked a handful, polished one up on her sleeve like a miniature apple, then threw it at Mathew. It missed, so she threw another. This one hit him on the back of the head and he turned round feeling the spot. Lucy threw a third, and as the berry bounced off his duffel coat, Mathew laughed and tried to catch it.

'What are they, mummy?'

Lucy caught up with him and showed him the berries in her hand.

'They're berries. Like the ones there on the hedges. They call them haws.'

Mathew took one between his finger and thumb and examined it.

'They've got seeds inside them. Look . . .'

She crushed it and revealed the stone embedded in the green pulp.

'When they fall off the hedges, they go into the ground and make new little trees, like daddy's seeds in the garden.'

Mathew put his berry to his nose and sniffed it.

'Can you eat them?'

'I wouldn't risk it. They might be poisonous.'

'Would I die?'

'I don't know about that. But they'd probably make you poorly.'

She crouched down beside him and enclosed his hands on the handlebars.

'Have we to go back now? I don't want you to tire yourself out. The doctor said you'd to take it easy today. We don't want you in bed poorly all weekend, do we?'

Mathew released his hands and turned his front wheel.

'I'm better now, mummy. My head doesn't hurt at all now.'

'All right then. But we're only going as far as the bridge.'

'Can we play at boat races when we get there?'

Lucy kissed his cheek and stood up.

'We'll see.' She considered the haws in her hand. 'Do you want to take these berries home, Mathew, and plant them?'

Mathew scarcely looked at them. All he wanted was to get going again.

'I know. We'll leave a trail like in *Hansel and Gretel*. Then we'll be able to follow it to find our way back.'

'Have we, mummy?'

'What if the birds eat them all up though, and we get lost?'

Mathew looked worried. He was so taken up with the idea that he had conveniently forgotten that he could have found his way home on his own anyway.

'They won't, will they?'

'They might do. Birds like berries.'

'Don't they make them poorly, like people?'

Lucy dropped the first berry and gave Mathew a push to start him off again.

'Birds and animals can eat different things to people.'

'Why can they?'

'Well; they've got different kinds of tummies.'

Mathew seemed satisfied with this explanation and he turned round and pedalled away. Lucy was relieved to see him go. If he had persevered with the question, she would not have known how to answer him. She wasn't even sure if what she had already told him was true.

But even though she knew little about the metabolism of animals, she certainly knew more about natural history than when she had arrived from the city. She had grown up familiar with two types of bird: house sparrows and starlings; two types of animal: cats and dogs. How she had looked forward to leaving their back-street terraced house to come and live in the country. It would be nicer for children too, they always said. They used to drive out most Sunday afternoons to see how the house was progressing. Phil had already planned the garden before it was finished. Lucy had done the same with the furniture and fittings. How exciting it had been when they first moved in. Lucy remembered wakening and listening to skylarks singing above the adjoining fields. She bought books to identify the birds, wild flowers and trees, and now, as she followed Mathew along the path, she could recognise most of the things around her. She saw a dunnock flitting along the hedge bottom (it's like a robin without its bib, she had once described it to Tracey), and on a higher branch, a missel thrush was greedily stripping haws. But she wasn't sure about the large flock of birds cawing and wheeling overhead. She did not know if they were rooks or crows – there may even have been some jackdaws among them. But, whatever they were, there were too many of them for Lucy's liking and she felt threatened by their presence. They seemed to have gathered with intent, like vultures. Mathew noticed them too, but he wasn't frightened. He just pointed and laughed and said what a lot of noise they were making.

Then, as suddenly as they had arrived, they swirled away as if by a pre-determined signal. Lucy was glad to see them go, and as they departed, it looked as if the sky was being swept clean.

At the end of the path, Mathew dismounted and climbed over a stile. Lucy followed carrying his tricycle, and they continued down a narrow lane in the direction of a stone bridge a few hundred yards away. The unmade surface of the lane had been worn into two deep ruts divided by a mane of coarse grass, and as Mathew bumped along it trying to reach the bridge first, Lucy shouted after him to be careful or he was going to fall off and bang his head again.

By the time Lucy arrived at the bridge, Mathew had already gathered two small piles of twigs and leaves and placed them side by side on one of the parapets. Lucy knew what they were there for and she picked up a twig. Mathew was staring down into the brook.

'The water's running fast, mummy.'

'That's because there's been a lot of rain.'

'It's not raining now though, is it?'

Lucy was about to explain how it ran down from the hills, but Mathew lost interest and picked up a twig from his pile.

'Are you ready, mummy?'

They held out their twigs over the parapet, and when Mathew said, 'Go!' dropped them into the water and ran across the bridge to see which one emerged first. Mathew leaned so far out trying to look under the bridge that Lucy had to pull him back to stop him falling over. But he wrenched himself free as the twigs appeared and began to jump up and down in excitement.

'I've won! I've won, mummy! Mine's first!'

It was debatable, but Lucy gave him the benefit of the doubt. They walked back across the bridge and repeated the per-formance. The course was so short that it was a close race every time, especially when the contestants were twigs. They fell straight down and hit the water together, and there was never more than a length in it at the finish. It was usually more clear-cut with leaves. They drifted down haphazardly, and one of them often gained a start which it rarely relinquished: the race was decided before it had begun.

Lucy was more interested in what happened to her contenders

after the race had ended. She liked to stand at the parapet and see how far they could make it downstream. They had to negotiate fallen branches, protruding stones and trailing reeds. Sometimes they lost the current and became marooned in the shallows near the bank. When this happened, Lucy wanted to climb down and start them off again. She wanted to release the ones that got trapped. She urged them to break free, to keep going, and occasionally, when one of them avoided all the obstacles and mastered the course, she cheered silently and accompanied it in spirit as it sailed out of sight.

After the first series of races, Mathew began to assemble fresh craft, but Lucy said that she wanted to rest and told him to play on his own. Mathew did not object to this, and he varied the game by spitting into the water, then trying to spot it in the bubbling current at the other side of the bridge.

Lucy leaned against the parapet and looked out across the ploughed fields. The mist had evaporated now and the sun glinted on the long smooth flanks of the furrows. Trees stood in winter silhouette against a clear sky, and along the bank of the stream a cock pheasant was feeding under an oak tree. Every time it raised its head, its plumage shone like shot silk in the sunlight. Lucy did not show it to Mathew. She was afraid that he might start pointing and frighten it away. She wanted it to stay. It belonged to the peaceful landscape. It belonged to her peace, standing here on this ancient bridge, down this quiet lane. This was her secret place. The sloping fields concealed the estate in the distance, and the only sounds she could hear were running water and occasional birdsong.

Lucy enjoyed coming here. She had discovered it before the children were born, and had started bringing them while they were still toddlers and needed pushing most of the way in their buggy. Tracey had always insisted on having a picnic regardless of the season or weather. Lucy smiled as she remembered the number of times she had stood shivering underneath the umbrella, pretending to enjoy a jam sandwich and cold orange juice. Hectic, happy days. Her life was simple then. She looked after the children. She looked after her husband. She looked after the house. And now she was looking after herself for a change. She looked at her watch. If Mathew had been at school, she would have been in a Politics seminar now, considering the differences between positive and negative freedom. Closing her eyes, she concentrated and tried to remember what they were.

Negative freedom? That meant the absence of restraint. And positive freedom? That meant restraint for the greater good. Now then, which side were the political theorists on? Hobbes: he was authoritarian and believed that life was nasty, brutish and short. He believed in negative freedom. Who else? Mill and Locke. They did too. They were all individualistic political theorists, whereas Rousseau was less authoritarian. He believed in (a) (she used her fingers to make each point), rule by general will; (b) that community interests should come first; and (c) that constraints on individuals led to greater freedom for the whole . . . And what about Hegel and Marx, where did they fit in? It was all so confusing. Such hard work . . .

She opened her eyes. The sun was still shining, the birds were still singing and Mathew was still running backwards and forwards across the bridge. Why was she doing it? Why was she making life so difficult for herself? Wasn't it enough to be here, on a crisp autumn morning looking after her injured son? What's it all for in the end, Lucy? her mother often asked. She wasn't sure, but she was certain of one thing: like the leaf which Mathew had just dropped into the water, there was no turning back.

The following day, they all went into town together. Mathew had suffered no reaction from his accident, and during the journey, Lucy heard Tracey whispering to him in the back of the car, trying to persuade him to remove his dressing so that she could have a look at his wound. But Mathew refused. He told her that it had to stay on until the stitches were taken out. But Lucy knew that it was more than that. The strip of sticking plaster was like a badge of courage and he was revelling in the attention he was receiving because of it.

Before they reached the city centre, Phil turned off the main road and made for his usual parking place behind a disused warehouse. When he had come across this neglected backyard several years ago, he had been so excited by his discovery that he made Lucy promise not to tell anyone else about it. Lucy could not understand what all the fuss was about. She thought it was ridiculous parking half a mile away from the shopping centre. But Phil seemed to regard it as a great victory not having to use a parking meter or a multi-storey car park. It was a triumph of the individual rights of the motorist against the forces of bureaucracy. But these rights seemed only to apply to him. He resented anyone else using the space, and when occasionally it was full he

112

behaved as if it was his land and the other cars were trespassing. Lucy dreaded this happening, because somehow Phil always managed to shift the blame onto her, as if it was her fault that there was no room.

But there were no problems today. There were only two cars in the yard, and neither of them were in Phil's favourite place near the wall. Lucy felt relieved. She did not want the trip spoiled from the start by a bout of sulking. She wanted to enjoy herself. She wanted a pleasant day out with her family. Lucy tried to remember the last time they had been in town together . . . It was just before she had started university, when she had come in to buy her books.

They went to a café for a drink, all snug round a corner table deciding what to do and where to go first. To the toyshop, Mathew proposed. Tracey seconded it and the motion was passed unanimously. Phil and Lucy knew that, if the children were settled, there was a much better chance of the day passing harmoniously. They would have nothing to grumble about then. And Lucy wanted none of that today. There were going to be no threats and surreptitious smacking; they were going to have a good time together.

Lucy decided that the grown-ups should have a treat too. It was treats day all round, she announced. She was going to buy herself a new book, a novel. She might even go mad and buy herself a hardback! Phil laughed at her enthusiasm. He did not know what he was going to buy, he said. There was nothing he really wanted. It was enough for him to be sitting here, watching Lucy fuss over the children while they drank their orange juice. But Lucy insisted. Everybody had to have a present today, she said. It was a special day. The children agreed with her.

'All right then,' Phil said. 'I'll have a motor magazine.'

The children groaned and Lucy pulled a face. She nearly asked him why he didn't go the whole hog and buy a sparking plug, or a can of anti-freeze. But she resisted the temptation. There was to be no sarcasm today; not a hint of dissension between them.

'That's not a treat,' Tracey said. 'You buy a motor-car magazine every week.'

She was strongly supported by Lucy and Mathew, so Phil said that he would think of something later. Lucy would have liked another coffee. She was enjoying herself sitting here making plans. It was like Christmas, when the preparation was as pleasurable as the occasion itself.

But the children had sucked their glasses dry and were eager to go. Phil was ready to leave too, so Lucy put the wishes of the others first and they paid the bill and left.

In the toyshop, Lucy went with Tracey to look at dolls' outfits, while Phil took Mathew to look at the models. Lucy was aware of what was happening even as they separated, and she watched her husband and son running up the stairs to the first floor. But she did not know what to do about it. Perhaps she should have insisted that they walked round the shop together and looked at *all* the toys before allowing the children to make their choice. But she knew that it would not have made any difference: she had tried it before. They would still have finished up in the same departments. There was no point in trying it anyway with Phil there, he had no patience with such liberal agonising. 'What are you trying to do, turn him into a poofter?' he complained one day when he came home from work and saw Mathew dressed in one of her skirts, wheeling Tracey's pram around the house.

Lucy thought of Tanya arguing furiously with Chris and Robert in the pub after the last play rehearsal. The boys had been ridiculing the mixed football match which had been played during Rag Week. The girls had turned it into a farce, they said. They should have all been sent off for unladylike conduct and reported to the FA for bringing the game into disrepute. They then progressed to ribald speculation about the unfair advantage that women enjoyed by being able to carry the ball in their cleavage, and the impossibility of dispossessing them without being penalised for 'hands'. But they agreed that there were certain good points (much laughter) about the experiment, mainly the prospect of mixed showers afterwards. But Tanya took all this very seriously, and at one point Lucy thought she was going to hit them over the head with her pint pot. It was no good trying to disguise their sexist attitudes with badinage, she told them. People were often at their most serious when they were making jokes. But she did agree with Chris and Robert on one point, that the girls should not have been taking part in the first place . . . Not true! Not true! they objected. Fiona Holt was the best player on the field! And off it, Robert added. (More laughter.) But Tanya refused to be diverted. The girls had been included for sexist reasons, and if they did want to play football, they should set up their own organisation independent of men. That was the only way they would ever be taken seriously.

Lucy wondered what Tanya would have said to Tracey as she

chose a new outfit for her Cindy doll. She would have probably pointed out that they all conformed to the stereotype (one of Tanya's favourite words) of women. And that she couldn't see any train drivers' or firemen's outfits on the shelves. She might have even thrown Cindy away and made her share Mathew's Action Man. On the other hand, she might have thrown that away too on the grounds of macho indoctrination. There were so many ramifications to the question that it was difficult to know what to do; but she had to smile at the thought of Action Man dressed in the ballet dancer's costume which Tracey was considering.

She replaced it on the shelf and picked up a nurse's outfit.

'I think I'll have this one, mummy.'

Lucy took the package from her and glanced at the uniform, which consisted of a white apron and cap decorated with symbolic red crosses.

'Are you sure this is what you want?' She pretended to search through the other packages on the shelf. 'Why don't you choose a doctor's outfit for her?'

Tracey looked up at her, puzzled.

'Because they haven't got any doctors' outfits.'

'Haven't they?' Lucy tried to sound surprised. 'Why do you think that is?'

'Because doctors don't wear outfits. They just wear ordinary clothes.'

They wore them on the first floor though, where Action Man was sold. When he had finished his surgery, he could take off his overall, pack away his stethoscope in his little black bag, and employ his extraordinary talents in any number of adventurous occupations, ranging from deep-sea diver to astronaut. There were no prams and tea sets up here. This was a military, masculine world of model aeroplanes, motor cars and construction kits.

Lucy found Phil and Mathew watching the model railway. The track had been laid on a green baize board, and a convincing miniature landscape created with tiny fences and trees and cattle grazing in the fields. There was a signal box and a station with passengers waiting on the platform, and a porter wheeling a barrow containing suitcases no larger than ant eggs. Phil pointed to the lorry waiting at the level crossing.

'I hope his wife hasn't got his dinner ready for him, or he's going to be in trouble when he gets home.'

Mathew did not hear him. He was too engrossed in the two

115

trains running round the track. They were travelling in opposite directions and he was waiting for them to crash. But they never did, even though it looked inevitable at times. Their speeds had been coordinated and the lines cunningly laid to avoid collisions.

Mathew took no notice of Lucy and Tracey either when they approached and stood beside him. Lucy smiled at his expression of sheer wonder as he watched the trains go round. But she could understand his fascination: they produced a hypnotic effect, like watching tropical fish. It was a reassuring little world set out before them. Time stood still on the station clock. The fields were summer green, and passengers travelled endlessly through a cosy landscape in Pullman coaches.

Lucy said that she wanted to go to the bookshop next: it was time for her treat now. Phil said that he wouldn't mind treating himself to a couple of pints and meeting them later, but Lucy would not hear of it and they all went to the bookshop together.

They separated as soon as they got inside. Lucy went straight to the fiction shelves, Tracey and Mathew disappeared into the children's department, and Phil wandered from section to section glancing at titles indiscriminately, as if he was choosing bathroom tiles.

The recent hardback novels were displayed separately on a table in the middle of the shop. Lucy walked round them reading the titles and occasionally picking one up to read the synopsis. She liked the feel of the glossy dust jackets and the smell of the clean stiff pages when she looked inside. What a pleasure it was handling new books.

But she could not find anything to tempt her. Thrillers bored her, she wasn't interested in the colonies, and she had little sympathy with the minor emotional crises of the English middle classes. She turned away disappointed and considered buying a paperback. But that wouldn't be a real treat; she could buy a paperback any time. She would have to think of something else; something different. Why not forget about books for a change? She did. She thought of something straight away. She would buy some new knickers. She would go to Marks and Spencers and buy a whole new bunch. She looked at the price of one of the novels on display and calculated how many pairs she could get for the same money . . . Six. At least! And there was going to be no sexist behaviour either when she told the others what she was going for. She wasn't going to allow Phil to slope off with

Mathew to look at power tools or exhaust systems, while Tracey went in the shop with her. No, there was going to be none of that. Lucy looked round for Phil. He was standing at the shelves looking through a book. She was too far away to see what it was, but as he seemed to be interested (it was probably a book on gardening or do-it-yourself), she went downstairs to the children to give him a few more minutes on his own.

When they returned, Phil was waiting by the counter holding a paper bag. He looked quietly pleased with himself so Lucy, more out of courtesy than enthusiasm, asked him what he had bought. He grinned at her.

'You'll never guess.'

She did not try. She just took the bag from him and opened it. He was right. It was a cookery book: *Great Dishes of the World*.

Lucy tried to smile but she was furious. If this was his idea of a joke, she did not think much of it. It just seemed like an unnecessary taunt, especially as they were all having such a good time together. She glanced at the price, an expensive taunt too, then handed back the book.

'I'm afraid I'm not going to be able to do much justice to that.'

Phil continued to smile.

'You? It's not for you. It's for me.'

Lucy stared at him in disbelief.

'Well, if I'm going to cook, I might as well do the job properly, hadn't I?'

He replaced the book in the bag and tried to seal it again with the used sellotape. Lucy, who should have been delighted by his initiative, was unexpectedly touched instead, and suddenly close to tears. She linked Phil's arm and gave it a hard squeeze for reasons she could not clearly identify.

As they were leaving the shop, Dave came in with a woman. Lucy was so put out that for a moment she did not know what to do: it was like seeing a teacher out of school. She blushed and tried to avoid him; but it was too late, and they came face to face just inside the door. There was nothing equivocal about Dave's response, however; he was obviously pleased to see her and he stepped forward and touched her arm as if there was no one else there.

'Hello! Fancy seeing you here.' He did not seem to have noticed Phil and the children. 'You've obviously recovered then?' He could see that Lucy was puzzled by this question, so he had to carry on. 'I had a note from Denise in the office Yesterday, was it

117

. . . ? That's right. She said you were ill or something and wouldn't be able to attend the tutorial.'

Lucy shook her head.

'It wasn't me that was ill, it was Mathew.' She took Mathew's arm and stood him in front of her. 'He banged his head at school and had to have a couple of stitches in it. I had to stay at home and look after him.' Dave barely glanced at the boy. 'By the way, this is my husband Phil, and my daughter Tracey.'

Dave raised his hand briefly.

'Hi. This is Melissa.'

Melissa was smiling. She appeared to be quietly amused by the scene, as if intuitively she understood what was happening.

'That's right!' Dave clicked his fingers in an exaggerated gesture of remembrance, 'Denise did say something about a head injury. I thought she meant you, though. She must have got it wrong.'

But Lucy knew that she hadn't. Dave was bluffing; he had obviously forgotten. He probably hadn't given the message a second thought. She could see him now, picking up his telephone in his room, nodding impatiently as he listened, then immediately resuming work . . . All that fuss for nothing. She had made a fool of herself. She felt humiliated. She looked at Melissa in her pert hat and trailing woollen scarf. Lucy could have strangled her with it. She wanted to knock that smile right off her face! And as for Dave! She could have murdered him too . . . She became aware of Mathew rubbing up against her and heard Melissa talking to him about his accident . . .

'. . . and it won't hurt one little bit having the stitches out. It only takes a minute.'

She produced a bag from her coat pocket and held it towards Mathew.

'Would you like a coffee cream? They're ruinous for the figure, I'm afraid' – Lucy gave her a quick look over, but they seemed to have done her no harm – 'but wonderful for cut heads.'

Mathew hesitated and looked up at his mother for approval. Lucy nodded and Mathew reached into the bag. Tracey watched intently to see what he brought out, and when her turn came, she looked inside the bag first to see if there was any choice. Lucy and Phil declined her offer, but Lucy would have loved one. Coffee creams were her favourite chocolates. But they were so expensive, such a luxury, especially when the children were there. Two each and they were all gone. Coffee creams in a pretty bag were

118

best enjoyed leisurely by two people, not shared out strictly between a family and squabbled over if there were any left.

As Melissa held out the bag to Dave, Lucy noticed how the colour of her nail varnish matched the maroon stripe in her scarf. Like carpet and curtains, she thought, as she clenched her hands to conceal her own chipped nails. Who was this woman anyway? She was too smart, too expensively dressed, to be a student. She was more like a model. Perhaps it was some empty-headed glamour puss who he had picked up at a party somewhere! Or his wife? Yes, it could be his wife come up from London to visit him for the weekend. (Better her than someone new.) But Lucy could not convince herself. Melissa was too relaxed and attentive to be an estranged wife. Whoever she was, Lucy wished they had never met. She hated her! She had ruined her day.

Dave slowly bit through his chocolate. 'I suppose we'd better be going.' Then, popping the remaining half into Melissa's mouth, 'Melissa's looking for a book on Sanskrit.'

Outside the shop, Phil said, 'Who was that?'

'Dave Pybus. He's my Literature tutor. I've told you about him.'

'He's young, isn't he?'

'I suppose so.'

'I didn't expect him to look like that.'

Lucy was irritated by this remark. She felt like saying something sarcastic to humiliate him. Then she realised that it was possibly the first time that he had seen a university lecturer, never mind spoken to one.

'Who was that bird he was with, his wife?'

'I've no idea.'

'She was a bit of all right, wasn't she?'

Lucy did not reply.

'Where do you want to go next then?'

Marks and Spencer was just across the road, but Lucy had lost all interest in new knickers. She had lost interest in everything. She just wanted to go home.

As they stood on the pavement deciding what to do, Lucy noticed Mathew trying to click his fingers just like Dave.

The props for the play included an armchair. Tanya said there was one at their house they could borrow, so one evening she picked up Lucy at the university and they went to fetch it. As they drove along in the transit van, Lucy asked her who it belonged to.

'All of us,' she replied.

They passed the railway station, then stopped at a set of traffic lights opposite a hoarding advertising women's tights. The poster showed a pair of slim glossy legs wearing high-heeled shoes and a short black underskirt. Lucy looked to see what brand they were. When Tanya noticed the advertisement, she slid open the van door, strode across the pavement, and with a black marker printed SEXIST diagonally across the legs.

The drivers in the vehicles behind the van sounded their horns at her, especially when the lights changed and they could not move. Tanya gave them the two-fingered victory salute and walked unhurriedly back to the van.

'Bastards,' she said as she climbed in and released the hand-brake. Lucy was sweating with embarrassment. She wanted to jump out and run away. She did not want to be sitting there when they were overtaken, and everyone looked round to see who the two lunatics were. But she need not have worried. As they drove off, the lights changed back to red and they left all the others behind.

'Serves the fuckers right,' Tanya said, watching the diminishing line of traffic in her driving mirror.

Lucy was surprised at the direction they had taken. She had expected Tanya to live in the leafy Victorian suburb near the university, where many of the students rented rooms and flats. But they had driven across the city to a district not far from where Lucy had been brought up, and where she and Phil had bought their first house. It was a shabby neglected area, inhabited mainly by blacks and poor whites. The first West Indian immigrants had settled here during the 1950s, and when Lucy was young, her mother used to tell her to keep away from them. She had nothing against coloured boys, she said, but everybody knew what they were like. There had been enough of that sort of thing during the war with the American servicemen . . .

They turned into a street of three-storey terraced houses, some of which were boarded up, and the rest in urgent need of repair and decoration. Fancy living here, Lucy thought, as she compared them with her own cosy home. Judging by the dingy curtains, she guessed that most of the houses must be divided into flats and bedsitters. She had never asked Tanya where she lived, or anything at all about her private life, for fear of sounding naive and old-fashioned. But she was curious to find out.

They stopped outside a house which looked in no better repair than the rest except for the front garden. The tiny plot had been planted with herbs and flowering shrubs, and a clematis had been trained up the wall by the door. A light was on in the front room, and between partially closed curtains Lucy could see a white paper lantern and an Indian bedspread hanging on a wall.

As they climbed out of the van, she said, 'Have you got a flat here?'

'Well, sort of. Four of us rent the house. We have our own rooms and share a communal kitchen.'

Lucy followed her up the steps to the front door. There were plant pots on every step, and at the top, a tub containing a frost-bitten geranium. Lucy pulled off a withered leaf and recalled that Phil had taken his geraniums into the greenhouse weeks ago. Tanya unlocked the door and they stepped inside to the smell of cooking, a savoury, spicy smell which Lucy did not recognise, and the sound of laughter from somewhere at the back of the house. The narrow hall was made even narrower by piles of books on either side and a bicycle leaning against one wall. A worn Turkish runner covered the bare boards, and as Lucy followed Tanya along the passage, she wondered if the books were moved when the hall was cleaned, or if they just left them there and cleaned around them. At the far end, the wall was decorated with a framed poster depicting a group of peasant women. The slogan was in a language that Lucy did not understand, but she could tell by their defiant attitudes that they were not advertising cosmetics.

Tanya led Lucy into the kitchen, where three women were eating at a long table in the middle of the room. A toddler, playing under the table with a cardboard box, paused and stared up at them. After the introductions – Liz Helen Carol, and the crouching baby, Darren – Liz half stood to look into the casserole in the middle of the table.

'Have some food. There's plenty left.'

Tanya shook her head.

'No, thanks, I've already eaten.'

'Lucy?'

'No, thanks. I had something before I came out.'

She could have eaten some more though. It looked delicious: a kind of thick vegetable stew with chunks of French bread in a basket.

'Have some wine then. If there's any left, that is.'

She peered at the dark bottle to see if she could fulfil her offer, then Helen stood up and fetched two glasses from the cupboard.

'It's only plonk, I'm afraid,' she said, emptying the bottle. 'But it's drinkable.'

She need not have apologised to Lucy, who knew very little about wine. They rarely drank it at home, and on the few occasions when they ate out with friends she just followed the lead of the others. She had a sip and tried not to pull a face. But, even though she was not keen on the wine, she approved of the good simple food, the plain sturdy crockery and the wooden bowl of fresh fruit.

Tanya bent down and said a few words to Darren, then walked across to the noticeboard. As she was reading the telephone messages, Liz said, 'Harriet told me to mention that Rosie Dunlin phoned from the printing co-op. She says she'll ring back later.'

'Is Harriet not in?'

'No, she's gone to the Housing Association meeting.'

There was a commotion then, because Darren stood up under the table and banged his head. Lucy had been wondering who his mother was, and now she found out as Carol reached down for him and lifted him onto her knee. Lucy was as concerned as the others about Darren's condition, especially after Mathew's recent accident, but, being a stranger in the house, she did not want to appear officious, and she remained at the back of the ministering throng.

It was soon obvious that Darren was not seriously injured; there was no cut, not even a discernible bump. (Rub some butter on it, her mother would have said.) As Lucy stood back and watched the others trying to soothe the crying child, she realised that Carol was the odd woman out. She was dressed more conventionally, in sweater, skirt and high-heeled shoes. Her hair was longer and she was wearing make-up. But there was something else . . . Then Lucy noticed her wedding ring. That was it! Carol looked married, whereas the others looked complete in themselves and determinedly independent. Lucy wondered what *she* looked like, and if she looked married too. She was wearing jeans (she had not graduated to dungarees yet), but her sweater was more like Carol's than those of the other three. Lucy wondered where they got them from. Jumble sales or the Oxfam shop, by the look of them: but certainly not from the places she shopped at. Liz's jumper looked as if it had been cast off by a heavyweight wrestler, while Helen's was so skimpy that it flattened her breasts. Lucy decided that they probably had a common stock of woollies which they dipped into at random, then put on whatever they fished out.

After the baby had been mollified with an oatmeal biscuit, Tanya turned to Lucy.

'We'd better go and fetch that chair.'

Liz rinsed out the coffeepot and set out the cups on the table.

'How's the play going?'

'Reasonably well, I think!' Lucy nodded in agreement. 'We managed to get a super mangle. One of those clanking monsters with wooden rollers and an iron handle. It should dominate the stage. The play should revolve around it, as far as I'm concerned . . .'

She paused and looked across the table at Lucy as if expecting a challenge. She might have got one too if they had been on their own, but Lucy felt inhibited with the others there; she sensed that she would have been heavily outnumbered.

'What's it about?'

It was the first time that Carol had spoken, except to quieten the child.

'Perhaps you'd better ask Lucy. Her interpretation tends to be more balanced than mine.'

Lucy felt her colour rising as they all looked at her. Even baby Darren seemed to be waiting for her to speak.

'It's about a young woman who's just got married. Her husband's a brilliant local footballer and two scouts come from Tottenham Hotspur to sign him on. Alice – that's the woman in the play – is really keen to go. She sees it as an escape from the dreariness of her own life . . .'

'What happens?'

'Nothing much. Her husband never arrives home from work. The scouts leave, and Alice is back where she started.'

'Typical.'

There was a bitterness in Carol's response which suggested that she knew the story well. As Carol sat there hugging the baby to her and staring moodily towards the fireplace, Lucy realised what an excellent Alice she would have made. She would have been much more convincing than Julie, who continued to portray Alice in the traditional manner of the cheeky charlady. Dave had been annoyed with Lucy after one rehearsal, when she said that all Julie needed was a set of rollers underneath her headscarf to complete the caricature.

Tanya and Lucy finished their wine and went upstairs to fetch the armchair. When they were out of earshot, Tanya said, 'Carol's staying at the battered wives' refuge down the road. Liz helps out there. She often brings someone back for a meal. It does them good to get out for a while.'

'Why is she staying there?'

'Because her husband gets violently drunk occasionally, then goes home and beats her up.'

'What'll happen to her, do you think?'

'She'll probably go back to him. They often do. We've told her that she can stay here if she likes, but she doesn't seem terribly keen.'

They reached the first-floor landing and Tanya opened a door. 'This is my room. Harriet lives there.' She nodded towards a door across the landing. 'And Liz and Helen share the two rooms downstairs.'

She switched on the light and they went inside. Lucy had expected the room to be cluttered and untidy. She was wrong: it was sparse and neat. There was a mattress in the corner, a wardrobe, and a table and chair in front of the window. The furniture looked as if it had been bought as a job lot, and the only personal effects in the room were the books on the table and the suitcase on top of the wardrobe. As Tanya took off her coat and scarf, Lucy said, 'What do the others do?'

She felt free to ask now that she had been introduced to them.

'Liz teaches at Highcliff FE College. Helen's an architect, and Harriet's just opened a health-food shop with two other women.'

There was a movement in the bed, and a cat crawled out from underneath the covers yawning and blinking against the light. It stretched by walking away from its back legs, and when it arched its back, its paws came so close together that it could have been picked up like a bunch of flowers.

Tanya wagged her finger and spoke to it with mock severity.

'You naughty boy. You know you shouldn't be under there. I don't want your fleas infesting my bed.'

Lucy walked across the room to stroke it. She liked cats, but Phil would not have one. It would scratch up the garden, he said.

'What do you call it?'

'Walter.'

Lucy laughed, and Walter pushed his head forcefully against her hand when she stopped stroking him to look round at Tanya.

'I suppose that's what you call emasculation by nomenclature, isn't it?'

124

Tanya gave her a slow smile. She was surprised by Lucy's remark. Up to now, she had thought her incapable of such trenchancy.

'Well, it wasn't quite as deliberate as that. He's just such a big softy, that's all.'

Lucy presumed that she was referring to Dennis the Menace's chief victim in the *Beano*. She tickled Walter's outstretched chin. He was purring so loudly that he was beginning to slaver.

'I'm surprised at you having a tom cat. I thought you would have objected on principle.'

She was also surprised at her own audacity. She blamed it on the wine. She might not have enjoyed it much, but it had certainly taken effect.

'He was a stray. We had him neutered of course . . .' She smiled in a sly, self-mocking kind of way. 'I'm all in favour of neutered toms of course.'

Lucy was not sure if she was or not, but she did not have time to consider the matter further because Tanya crossed the room towards the door.

'We'd better fetch the chair. It's up in the attic.'

When Lucy saw the size of it, she wondered how they were going to get it downstairs. She thought it was too big anyway: they would never have had a bulky thing like that in the kitchen of a terrace house; it would have taken up too much room. But it might have sounded presumptuous of her to object; after all, she was only assistant props on the production.

'It must have been a big job getting this all the way up here,' Lucy said, as they pushed it, squealing on its castors across the floor.

'It was already up here when we moved in. We've never had reason to move it.'

Lucy looked back when they reached the door. She had always liked the idea of an attic bedroom with a sloping roof and a window in the slates. She remembered that the heroes in children's stories often slept in attics. Their adventures began there at night.

The room looked bare now that the chair had been moved. The only items of furniture left were a chest of drawers and a single bed containing a pile of folded blankets.

'We shall have to turn it on its side, Lucy, to get it out.'

They tipped the chair over, then dragged and pushed it through the doorway onto the landing. It was like forcing an unwilling racehorse into a starting stall. Lucy was sweating already and they had only just started.

'Right, we'll get it back onto its feet now. Would you prefer to be at the front or the back?'

Glancing down the precipitous staircase, Lucy decided that both positions were equally suicidal. They would never manage it on their own; two men perhaps, but not two women. At home, Phil would have fetched Tony from next door to help him, while Lucy made a cup of tea for them when they had finished. It seemed like an increasingly sensible arrangement: handling teabags was a much safer proposition.

'I don't mind really. Whatever suits you.'

On second thoughts, Lucy hoped that the front suited Tanya. The prospect of being at the front, with the chair looming over her as they descended the stairs, terrified her. It would be like being threatened by an avalanche. What if she slipped? Or Tanya let go? She imagined the headline in the newspaper:

MOTHER OF TWO CRUSHED BY RUNAWAY ARMCHAIR!

Perhaps the women downstairs would help? Five of them should be able to manage it all right. But how could she suggest it to Tanya without appearing weak or cowardly? Or possibly both?

She did not have to bother, because just then Helen shouted up the stairs to see if they needed any help.

Without hesitation, Tanya called back, 'No, thanks! We should be able to manage! Anyway, I think the stairs are too narrow. We'd get in each other's way!'

Get in each other's way! Lucy was dumbfounded. That was what she wanted. Safety in numbers! A gang! And, even if Tanya was right, it would still have been reassuring to have the others there. They could have offered encouragement and advice, and acted as a kind of buffer or long-stop if anything went disastrously wrong. Tanya said, 'All right then. I'll take the front.'

Lucy immediately felt guilty. By evading the question of which position she preferred, she had thrown the onus back onto Tanya in the hope that the matter would be settled to her advantage. It had been; but she wasn't happy about it. And, knowing Tanya, she had probably guessed her thoughts and chosen the most dangerous position on purpose to protect her. She tried to justify her conduct: she was a married woman with a husband and two children to think of. It was her duty to be careful. She had responsibilities. Tanya on the other hand could afford to be

reckless. She was single. Her responsibilities were only to herself
. . . But it was a cowardly argument and she knew it. Even so, she
did not offer to change places and go to the front.

They pushed the chair to the brink of the stairs, then Tanya
walked down a few steps and turned round.

'Tilt it, Lucy, and we'll take it down one step at a time on its
back legs.'

And they did. Very slowly. Bump. Bump. Bump. With Tanya
descending backwards supporting the bottom, and Lucy hunched and off balance above her, threatening to pitch forward into
the chair at any moment. That really would have been a spectacu-
lar end; first running over Tanya then careering headlong to her
own doom.

It might have been a giant step for mankind when the first
astronauts stepped onto the moon, but it was an even bigger step
for Lucy when they reached the first-floor landing. She was
exhausted but elated; and she was still alive! The rest of the way
down should be easy now. The main staircase was wider and not
as steep. It would have been possible for the others to have
helped them now, but Lucy did not want them to. She wanted to
finish the job with Tanya; just the two of them.

'Do you want a rest, Lucy?'

Of course she did, but she wasn't going to admit it.

'No, let's carry on and get it over with. Do you want to change
places?'

Tanya's answer was unimportant. She had expiated her guilt.

'No, I'll stay where I am if it's all right with you. I've got the
hang of it now.'

Walter the cat peeped round Tanya's door to see what all the
noise was about. When he saw the armchair, he jumped up onto
the seat and proceeded to sniff the material.

'Are you coming for a ride then, Walter?' Tanya said, as they
dragged the chair into position at the top of the stairs. 'Hold tight
then.'

But Walter did not like it when the chair was tilted. He liked it
even less when they jolted down the first step, and with a
desperate, soaring leap he cleared Lucy's shoulder and regained
the safety of the landing. Lucy was so startled that she nearly let
go of the chair. Tanya nearly fell backwards down the stairs with
laughing. There was a brief crisis as they fought for balance and
control, while Walter gazed down at them in silent wonder from
the safety of the attic steps.

They steadied themselves and managed to check the threatened plunge. Then, chastened by their narrow escape, they continued downstairs carefully and in silence. Three steps from the bottom, Tanya started to giggle at the memory of Lucy's expression when the cat had flown past her face, and by the time they bumped down into the hall she was laughing uncontrollably. Lucy joined in, but more in triumph and relief than at the incident on the stairs. They had done it! The two of them. Thirty-five treacherous steps from attic to hallway all on their own. She flopped down in the chair, still smiling. Tanya stood behind her with her hands on the back as if she was going to wheel her round in celebration.

'I think we deserve another drink after that, don't you?'

Lucy looked up over her shoulder.

'You haven't got a cigarette, have you?'

'I didn't know you smoked.'

'I don't, except on special occasions.'

Tanya squeezed her shoulder and smiled.

'Come into the kitchen. Someone might have one in there.'

Phil was sitting on the settee reading his cookery book. He occasionally glanced up at the television, but he wasn't following the programme. He had switched it on out of habit, for company. He was looking for a recipe for tomorrow's dinner. It had to be something that the children liked. It was too much trouble preparing two separate dishes. Tracey was no problem, she would eat most things, but Mathew could be finicky at times. *Trout with almonds?* No chance. Fish fingers, yes. But not with the head and tail still on! He might as well have asked him to eat his goldfish. That was going to be the next big problem, when Mathew realised what meat and fried fish *really* were. *Chicken casserole?* That sounded more like it. He could call in at the butcher's on his way home from work. How long did it take to cook . . . ?

While he was studying the recipe, Tracey entered the room. She came in so quietly that she was halfway across the carpet before Phil noticed she was there. She was wearing her nightdress and her feet were bare.

'Hello, love, what are you doing here? You should be fast asleep by now.'

He looked at the clock on the mantelpiece. He had put her to bed over an hour ago. Tracey sat down beside him on the settee.

'I can't go to sleep, daddy.'

She was already watching television.

'Do you feel poorly?'

'No, I just keep lying there awake.'

'You'll be tired out for school in the morning, you know.'

But, instead of sending her back upstairs, he put his arm around her and pulled her close. One cheek was flushed where it had been pressed to the pillow, and her nightdress was still warm as if it had just been ironed.

'Just five minutes then. Then I'll take you back to bed.'

Tracey stuck out her legs and twiddled her toes with satisfaction. If she had been a cat, she would have purred.

'What are you reading, daddy?'

'I'm trying to find something for tomorrow's tea.'

'What time is my mum coming home?'

'I don't know. She shouldn't be long now, though.'

He tried to sound optimistic, as if she was due home any minute, but he was pretending for Tracey's sake. There was no knowing what time she would be home these days. Rehearsals seemed to start earlier and end later every time she went out. There were more of them now, too.

'Will you read me a story, daddy?'

'It's a bit late to be reading now, Tracey. You should be fast asleep in bed.'

Phil looked at the television while he made up his mind. On the screen, a woman was attending to her husband, who lay dying in bed.

'Go on then, fetch a book.'

It was a good job that the scene had not registered, or he might have been overcome with bitterness and self-pity and refused. Tracey went to the shelves for a book: Lucy's shelves with the brick supports which Phil had since glossed up with polyurethane. She quickly found what she was looking for, then turned off the television and ran back to the settee.

'Hey! What have you done that for?'

'My mummy always turns the television off when she reads to us. She says she can't concentrate properly when it's on.'

'Well, your mummy's not reading to you tonight, is she?'

He was angry with Tracey, but he did not make her switch it back on.

Tracey had selected *The Water Babies* by Charles Kingsley. It was a new paperback edition with a glossy cover and coloured illustrations. Phil opened it and looked at a picture of Tom being shoved up a chimney by his cruel master.

'I thought you'd read this.'

'I have, but my mummy's reading it to me again.'

'It'll take her a long time, the way she's carrying on. They'll have turned into water pensioners by the time you reach the end.'

Tracey ignored him and turned the pages purposefully, looking for a particular place . . .

'There.'

Phil opened the book so wide that the spine cracked.

'My mum says that it spoils books doing that to them.'

Phil resisted further sarcasm and Tracey settled down beside him to listen to the story.

It was the part where Tom, still sooty and dressed in rags, falls asleep in the cool clear stream after escaping from the wicked chimney sweep. Tracey concentrated on the full-page illustration while Phil read the accompanying text. It showed Tom being washed by the fairies, and she liked to imagine how fresh and clean he would feel when he woke up. But Phil's reading was not feeding her fantasies. He kept faltering, and he was so concerned with pronunciation that he ignored the punctuation and lost the rhythm of the prose.

After a few paragraphs, Tracey lost interest and looked up at him, which made Phil even more self-conscious. He began to sweat. It was like reading round the class at school. He suddenly stopped in mid-sentence after mutilating *amphibious*.

'What are you looking at, Tracey?'

'You're not reading it properly, daddy.'

'I'm doing my best, love.'

'You're reading it all jerky. Not like my mummy reads it. She makes it exciting.'

Phil slammed the book shut and threw it onto the settee.

'Well, you'd better ask your mum to carry on then when she comes in!'

Tracey's lips quivered and she started to cry. Phil felt like crying too. He lifted Tracey onto his knee and tried to comfort her.

'I'm sorry, love. I didn't mean to shout at you.'

He patted her rhythmically on the back to ease her sobbing.

'Come on now, stop crying.'

'I want my mummy.'

'I know you do, love. She'll not be long now. Do you want to go to bed, and I'll tell her to come up to you as soon as she gets in?'

Tracey shook her head against his chest.

'Have I to read you a bit more of your book then?'

Tracey nodded and Phil picked up the book and started again where he had left off. His reading did not improve much, but he persevered, and after a few pages he became interested in the story himself.

When he reached the end of the chapter, he looked down to ask Tracey if she wanted him to continue, but she was asleep. He smiled with relief, took her thumb out of her mouth, then carried her gently up to bed.

Lucy was sitting at the table in Tanya's kitchen. Darren had fallen asleep on Carol's knee and Helen had opened another bottle of wine. She filled up the glasses. Lucy accepted another cigarette.

'Me and Phil gave up smoking together when we were saving up to buy the house. We made a pact. He'd kill me if he saw me now.'

She lit Carol's cigarette, then her own, from a box of matches on the table.

'He sounds as bad as my husband.'

Lucy shook her head and the burning match in emphatic, double denial.

'I didn't mean it literally. I meant that he'd be mad if he thought that I'd started again, that's all.'

She wondered if her eagerness to dissociate Phil from Carol's husband sounded callous. But it was important to her, even at the risk of appearing subservient, that the others knew that she was not married to a brutal man. Phil might have his faults (who hasn't?) but, in ten years of marriage, he had never once threatened her with violence. At least that was something to be grateful for, especially after listening to Carol's experiences.

'Do you know what he did the other night?' she said, sipping her wine as if it was whisky. 'He came in from the pub and threw the teapot straight through the television screen.'

Lucy knew the feeling. She had often wanted to do the same thing herself.

'What did he do that for?'

'He's always the same when he gets drunk. It's a wonder he didn't throw it at me.' She blew a fleck of ash off the baby's head, then tapped her cigarette into the ashtray. 'At least it was rented,

131

that's one good thing. I just told the man from the shop that it had fallen off the sideboard. Just imagine if we'd bought it, all that money down the drain.'

Darren stirred and moaned in his sleep and Carol adjusted her hold to make him more comfortable.

'I suppose I ought to be going. He should be in bed by now.'

Lucy wanted to go with her to see what the refuge was like. Did Carol have a room of her own? Or was it like a hostel with dormitories? Who ran it? How long could she stay? She tried to put herself in Carol's place: picking Mathew up and taking him out into the cold night, back to a strange bed. The notion was unbearable. She thought of her own children, safe at home in their own beds in their cosy bedrooms. They were lucky. She was lucky. She had two healthy children, a good husband and a lovely home. What more could anyone want . . . ? The wine was making her maudlin. All she needed now was a rendition of 'Hearts and Flowers' and she would have started to cry. Surely Carol would be better off at home, however bad things were there. Anything was better than a refuge. It sounded like a Salvation Army hostel for down-and-outs.

Liz disagreed. Her advice was brutally direct.

'You mustn't go back to him, you know.'

Carol did not reply. An unfastened button on Darren's jumper suddenly seemed to be in urgent need of attention.

'It'll happen all over again if you do.'

Carol looked across the table at her.

'He's not like that all the time, you know, Liz. He can be ever so kind when he wants. And he thinks the world of Darren.'

'But how can you say that, Carol, after you told us what he did to him last week?'

Carol began to rock Darren even though he was sound asleep.

'I know, but he didn't really mean it. He just lost his temper, that's all. Kids can be trying, you know; especially at two o'clock in the morning when you're trying to get some sleep.'

Lucy nodded sympathetically. You did not have to be a battered wife to appreciate that. But she was the only one who did show any understanding. Liz, Helen and Tanya all looked exasperated with her.

'He was a different man when he was working. He's been out of work for over two years now, you know. It's bound to make a difference, isn't it?'

It sounded more like an appeal than a question, and she looked

132

at each one of them in turn. Lucy nodded again. She could not refute it. Helen could.

'But that's no excuse, Carol. There are millions of men out of work, but they don't go round beating up their wives.'

'How do you know? How do you know what men do to their wives?'

Lucy wondered if Carol realised the full implication of this question. Was it rhetorical? Or did she already know what Lucy was beginning to suspect; that Liz and Helen were probably lesbians?

'Anyway, there's not only physical cruelty, you know. There's a lot of mental cruelty goes on as well. Only that doesn't show up as easily as a black eye. I'm not sure which is the worst myself. At least with Ted it's soon over and done with. And he's always sorry afterwards.'

Lucy thought of Phil and wondered how he would cope with redundancy. Not very well, she imagined. He couldn't dig the garden and tinker with the car for ever. He would sulk. He would resent her going out. He was bad enough already, so God knows what he would be like if he was out of work and left on his own every day. The rows would start up again. Would he get violent like Carol's husband . . . ? No, she did not think so. He would get depressed and sullen. He wouldn't give her black eyes, just black looks. And Carol was right: such treatment could be just as damaging.

'Look Carol, it's no good making excuses for him, you know. It's nothing to do with unemployment. He's got a history of violence. You've said so yourself. You're going to have to leave him and make a fresh life for yourself.'

It was Tanya's turn to try and convince Carol now, and her approach was equally pugnacious and uncompromising.

'He'll come for me again you know, Tanya, when he knows where I am.'

'But you don't have to go with him. He doesn't own you, you know.'

'I know that, but he's lost when I'm not there. He's like a big baby really.'

Tanya had a drink of wine to help her to restrain herself. It did not work.

'Fuck him, Carol! You've got to start thinking about yourself for a change.'

Lucy was shocked at Tanya's language. She still wasn't used to

133

hearing women swear like men. She turned away in embarrassment and began to read the titles of the books on the dresser: *Combat in the Erogenous Zone, Sex and Subterfuge, The Girl's Own Annual . . . The Girl's Own Annual?* What was that doing there? Under scrutiny, no doubt, for examples of sexual stereotyping in children's literature. Perhaps one of them was writing a book about it.

But Carol did not seem perturbed by Tanya's rude outburst. She was probably used to it. Especially when her husband was beating her up.

'I know, Tanya. But where can I go? I can't stop at the refuge for ever.'

'You can stay here until you find another place.' Helen and Liz nodded their agreement. 'We'll help you. We'll get in touch with the social services and the council. We'll ask Harriet about the new flats that the Housing Association have built at Ashbrook . . .'

But Carol did not seem enthusiastic about any of these proposals. She just sat there, staring in the direction of the sink and allowing the ash to lengthen on her cigarette. Poor pathetic Carol. Lucy felt sorry for her. She understood her dilemma. Yes, she might have a brute of a husband, but he was still her husband nevertheless. (Lucy remembered her own mother's lack of sympathy when she had run home after an argument with Phil soon after they were married. 'You've made your own bed, now you can lie on it,' she had curtly advised her.) And Carol had a home and her own furniture, and she would have friends and neighbours. It was so much easier to go back than to start again on her own, in spite of everything. It wasn't as simple as the others were trying to make out. Lucy felt that she understood Carol better than they did. Not merely because she was married and had children too, but because they both came from the same social background. And, although Lucy now lived in a respectable suburb, and was studying for an Honours degree at university, she still felt closer in spirit to Carol than she did to Tanya, Helen or Liz. She had never known women like these before. They were independent, articulate and assured. They were friendly enough, but formidable, and Lucy was a little overawed by them.

She glanced round the kitchen at the collection of old plates on the dresser, the casseroles and earthenware dishes on the shelves, the wine rack in the corner and the noticeboard on the wall by the cupboard. She tried to read the items on it. There were telephone messages and reminders, a shopping list (muesli, lentils, brown rice), postcards from foreign countries, leaflets from anti-vivisectionists, Friends of the Earth, Greenpeace and CND. There were two tickets for the Halle Orchestra, an invitation to a series of lectures on Marxism organised by the WEA, and the season's programmes for the City Art Galleries, Theatre and Film Society. There it was, the cultural difference neatly summarised on four cork tiles.

What would Carol do? Lucy had a good idea, in spite of the convincing arguments being put forward by the other three. What if Carol turned to her for advice as a fellow wife and mother? What would she tell her . . . ? She wasn't sure. She hoped she wouldn't ask. Her uncertainty might be regarded with hostility in this household. Lucy had never known anything like it. Here she was, sitting with a group of women who were unequivocally advising another woman to leave her husband, give up her home, and start again on her own. They hadn't even mentioned the baby, and what might be best for him! With them, Carol came first, not as a wife or a mother, but in her own right, as a woman. It was usually the other way round.

Lucy recalled past conversations with tearful friends whose marriages were in trouble . . . They never seemed to talk any more, except to argue. He was never in. She wondered if he had met somebody else. She felt drab. He said he was fed up of her being tired all the time. She did not know what to do. (It always seemed to be the wife who carried the blame.) Perhaps they ought to split up? Yes, she would definitely leave him, if it wasn't for the children. But they had to come first, didn't they? If only they were older, it would be easier then, they would understand what it was all about . . . If, if, if . . .

There were no 'ifs' in Tanya's kitchen, just cast-iron certainties. But Carol had had enough for one night and said she ought to go; it was time Darren was in bed. The frustration in the room was palpable, but no one tried to persuade her further and Liz asked her if she would like another coffee before she went. Carol refused, and Lucy thought that she seemed eager to get out of the house before they started on her again. As Carol stood up, Tanya said they would give her a lift back in the van.

Lucy had forgotten all about the original purpose of the visit, and that the armchair was still standing in the hall, waiting to be taken back to the drama studio. Helen and Liz helped them to load it into the van, and Carol said that she might as well travel in style and climbed in after it.

Liz slammed the doors behind her and turned to Lucy.

'It's been nice meeting you. You'll have to come round again. Perhaps for a meal some time?'

Lucy was flattered, even though she realised that nothing might come of it. Perhaps Liz thought that she had marital problems too and needed some advice. But, whatever the reason, Lucy was grateful for the invitation. It reassured her, especially as she had contributed so little to the discussion and might have appeared uninteresting.

'Thank you. I would like to.'

And she meant it. She did want to come and see them again. To eat at the big kitchen table, and talk and drink wine. Their first meeting had disturbed her, but it had excited her too. Lucy had never known women like these before. Their priorities were so different from her own, and those of all the other women she had known. She was grateful to Tanya for bringing her.

Phil plugged in the iron and reached down into the clothes basket for a shirt. He had never seen the basket so full. (He had never seen his shirt rail in the wardrobe empty either!) Even when the children were at home all day, Lucy had always managed to keep up with the ironing. Perhaps they ought to have another one and get her back into the old routine. Phil read the dial on the iron, then looked inside the collar of his shirt to see what material it was made of. His mother had bought him this shirt the Christmas before she died. He had never really liked it, but it seemed disrespectful not to wear it, and, typically, it would not wear out. Other shirts came and went, but this one went on for ever. Sometimes (but not recently) Lucy used to tease him about it. 'You're only scared of what your mother'll say to you if you meet her in heaven,' she would say to him. 'She'll buttonhole you as soon as you get through them gates.' Then, in a cruel but accurate impersonation of her former mother-in-law, 'Now then, Philip, what about that shirt? I'd never have bought it if I'd known that you weren't going to wear it. Sheer waste of money. Hard-earned money as well . . .' Phil always felt uneasy when Lucy mocked his mother like this. He wasn't religious, but he still considered such irreverence dangerous. It might rebound later. It was wiser to play safe.

Phil had never ironed a shirt before. He tried to think how Lucy did it, but he had never watched her properly. His main impressions of her ironing were the sounds: soft bumps and slithering, punctuated by the clatter of the iron on the asbestos square.

He decided to start on the back, then, if anything did go drastically wrong, he would still be able to wear the shirt with a sweater. He spread out the material with the arms hanging down the sides, then started at the bottom, rubbing quickly and jerkily for fear of scorching it. He had to keep pulling at the material to keep it smooth, or the folds fled before him like ripples on a pond. He overtook them once and ironed creases *into* the material.

It wasn't as easy as he thought. The shirt always seemed to be slipping away from him, and there was always more material off the board than on it. And what about the sleeves? There seemed to be no other way but to lay them flat and press them like trousers. But, after he had finished both sides, the first side looked just as crumpled again. There ought to be an attachment, something arm-shaped, like a short length of fall pipe to pull the sleeves onto. Perhaps he could design and patent one? He might make a fortune out of it like the man who invented cats' eyes.

There was only the front and collar to do now, and he quite enjoyed nosing and gliding between the buttons. It was like riding on the dodgem cars at the fair. But he could not get the collar right: there was one crease which would not disappear. Normal pressure would not erase it, but he was afraid of pressing harder or leaving the iron standing for a few seconds, in case he scorched the material. He would have been furious with himself if he had done that now, when he had almost finished. It would have been like tripping over the doorstep and breaking a precious holiday souvenir.

So he approached the recalcitrant crease stealthily, and tried to nudge it off the edge of the collar. But it would not go where he wanted it to; it kept changing course and evading the bow of the iron. He felt at the collar. It was dangerously hot. If he wasn't careful, he was going to ruin it. He felt like pressing the iron down on the crease and holding it there until the shirt went up in flames. But he resisted the temptation, and after a good curse and threatening it with violence (it was a good job that no one was listening at the door or they would have called the police), he tried again. But he was outmanoeuvred a second time, and after several more unsuccessful attempts, when the ironing board was in constant danger of being kicked over, and the iron flung through the window, he conceded defeat and left the crease trapped, but defiantly obvious in the point of the collar.

Phil fetched a coat hanger from upstairs, and hung the shirt on the door handle to inspect it. It wasn't as good as Lucy's work; there was no comparison. But it wasn't a disgrace either, and it was definitely wearable. He would get better with practice. His first attempts at cooking had been nothing special either, but look at the dishes he was attempting now! Perhaps there were books on ironing too.

The posters advertising the play were on display all round the university, but with only a week to go before opening night, Lucy could not possibly imagine how it was going to be ready in time. She also had a long essay to hand in before the end of term, but, when she began to worry about it, she consoled herself with the knowledge that the other students involved in the production could not be doing much academic work either. Working on the play was a full-time job. It became an obsession. Every spare minute was spent at the drama studio in increasingly feverish activity . . . Some of the scenery still needed painting. They were still undecided whether to have pictures on the walls or not. They still hadn't found a period lampshade, and they still needed two old caps, having discovered that the ones in the wardrobe were all too modern.

But, much more worrying, with such a short time to go, were the performances of the actors. Robert and Chris were still unsure of their lines and Julie was still having trouble with the accent.

'I wonder if all steelworkers' wives speak like debutantes?' Tanya said in the pub, after one particularly exhausting rehearsal. 'It's not her fault, though; she's been wrongly cast, that's all.'

Lucy looked across at Dave, who had left the others at the bar and gone to sit on his own by the fire. She had become increasingly fond of him during the past few weeks. Not because he encouraged her affection, or favoured her in any way (even though she was always on the lookout for signs of it), but because of the considerate way that he treated everyone in the group, and particularly his patience with the cast. He was firm with them, but never sarcastic or irritable when they made mistakes. Conflicting interpretations of the text were always settled by discussion and, although Dave usually got his own way in the end, he had the knack of making the actors feel that they were the ones who had initiated the changes.

Lucy walked across to his table and sat down, but Dave continued to stare into the fire as if the answer to his problems was hidden in the flames. When he eventually looked up, his greeting was more polite than enthusiastic, and Lucy felt that she had intruded on his privacy.

'Do you mind if I sit down?'

'Of course not. I'm not being anti-social. I was a little chilly, that's all.'

He leaned towards the fire and toasted his hands as if he had crossed the moors, rather than the road from the drama studio. But his performance was too obvious to be convincing.

'Do you mind if I have a word with you about something?'

Dave sat up and looked round at her.

'Don't tell me that you're not going to have your long essay finished on time?'

'I was saving that for another day. No, it's about the play.'

'What about it?'

Lucy hesitated. Who was she, assistant props and theatrical novice, to be giving the director advice? Someone laughed at the bar. Lucy glanced round instinctively, convinced that they were laughing at her.

'I was thinking about Julie . . .'

'Join the club.'

'Well, I think the main trouble is that she's concentrating on the accent too much. She's never going to get it right, so why bother? She'd be much more convincing speaking naturally.'

'What, in the voice of a solicitor's daughter from the Home Counties? It would turn the play into a farce.'

Lucy was furious at Dave's contemptuous dismissal, and when he picked up his glass to have a drink, she glared at it as if she was going to knock it out of his hand.

'Well, she couldn't be any worse than she is now, whatever she sounded like. One minute it's "grass" then it's "grarse". She goes "upstairs" then "apstairs". There's no consistency at all. You're on tenterhooks listening to her, just waiting for her to make mistakes.'

Dave stared at her, glass poised.

'I am trying my best, you know. Anyway, if Julie has any pretensions to being an actress, which she appears to have, then she's going to have to learn to master different accents.'

Lucy shook her head slowly. It was her turn to be contemptuous now.

'It's more than accents. She hasn't got a clue . . .'

'There's still time. When we did *What the Butler Saw*, last year . . .'

But Lucy refused to be diverted. She did not know anything about *What the Butler Saw*, but she knew something about this play.

'I think that what Alice does is more important than what she says, anyway. What really matters is all the work she has to do; all that washing and emptying tubs and getting her husband's dinner ready. The sheer rotten drudgery of it all. If she can get that right, the audience won't be bothered about her accent, they'll be too interested in what she's doing.'

Dave slowly lowered his glass and looked at Lucy for such a long time that she blushed.

'I think you should have directed the play, not me.'

'No, I should have been in it. I could have played Alice with my eyes shut.'

'You identify very strongly with Alice, don't you?'

'There's no wonder, is there? I know what it's like to be stuck at home all day like that. It's like being in prison.'

'Perhaps you should write a play about it: *The Prisoner of . . .* Where is it you live, Blackbird Avenue?'

Lucy laughed, but she did not correct him, Linnet Close sounded just as absurd.

'No, ex-prisoner,' Lucy said, accepting a cigarette from Dave.

'I'm glad to hear it,' Dave said, lighting it for her.

After she had smoked the cigarette and finished her drink, Lucy said that she was going home. Dave offered to buy her another one, but she refused and buttoned up her coat.

'Would you like a lift home?'

Again Lucy shook her head.

'No, thank you. I've got the car.'

Dave squeezed her hand across the table.

'In that case, why don't you come back and have coffee. It's on your way . . .' He met Lucy's quizzical look and conceded. 'Well, almost.'

Lucy dispensed with all pretence of refusing his invitation. She just took the car keys out of her bag and stood up.

'All right then, but I can't stay long. I've some work to do when I get in.'

*

As Lucy followed Dave's car, she found herself wondering about the state of her underwear. Which pair of knickers was she wearing? Was her bra clean? She was ashamed of herself. How could she, a married woman with two children and a good and faithful husband? Even so, she still wished that she wasn't wearing the tights with the hole at the top.

They turned off the main road and drove along an avenue lined with trees. The topmost branches almost met over the road, and when the wind blew, they appeared to be straining to touch each other. Lucy tried to forget about her tights by composing a poem about the moon. She began with the image of it being snared in the branches. Snared? Was that the right verb? Perhaps tangled might be better. Or even trapped. What about caught? *Caught in the latticework of branches, the moon* . . .

She was still working on it when Dave turned into a gateway and stopped in front of a large stone house. Lucy presumed that it was divided into flats like many of the houses near the university, but when she stepped into the warm comfortable hall she realised that it was privately owned. Surely Dave did not live in a house this size on his own. As she wiped her feet, she noticed the Turkish carpet, the polished balustrade, the vase of chrysanthemums on the hall table. Perhaps Dave lived with someone. She had never asked him directly. Perhaps he lived with the woman she had met in the bookshop: the one with the posh name. Lucy had often wanted to ask Dave who she was, but she was afraid of the answer. She preferred hopeful ignorance to the killing truth.

Would Dave turn and call her name? Or someone else's name perhaps! As she waited, she heard a persistent, scuffing sound and realised that she was still wiping her feet. She stopped abruptly, hoping that Dave had not noticed her humbling herself on the doormat. She was furious with herself. Anybody would think she had crossed a ploughed field rather than a few feet of dry asphalt. It was her mother's fault! Her rectitude, her obsession with propriety. Yes, she was the one to blame. Lucy could hear her now, as she fussed over her before setting out to visit someone's house . . . 'Don't forget your manners,' she always told her. 'And don't forget to wipe your feet before you go in.'

She hadn't forgotten. And here she was, still wiping them all these years later.

As Lucy hung up her coat on the hall stand, she noticed that there were no other women's coats on the pegs. There was a checked woollen scarf which she had never seen Dave wearing, but this one article hardly constituted evidence of female occupation.

Lucy was aware of Dave standing behind her, and when she turned round, thinking that he wanted to get to the hall stand, he pulled her to him and kissed her. Lucy was surprised by the speed of his advance: she had been expecting it later, after coffee and a chat. But his urgency, here in the corner of the hall with her back against the wall, excited her, and she opened her lips to receive his tongue. That started it, and she felt the heat between her legs as his hands went over her body. She watched him unfastening her blouse, saw his fingers trembling, felt him tugging at the buttons and revealing her bra, the white one with the missing hook. Dave did not bother with the hooks; he reached deep into the cups and lifted out her breasts. Lucy gasped, embarrassed, thrilled; they looked so big and vulgar held up like that. Dave lowered his head and kissed her nipples. She shuddered, her knees buckled, she wanted to lie down, she wanted to slide down the wall and sit on the floor with her legs open. She wanted it all, everything, everywhere. She wanted to do things that she had not done for years. She wanted to do things that she had never done before. Dave was trying to pull down her tights. His hands felt cold on her legs.

'Let's go somewhere else, Dave.'

He went down on his knees.

'I want to lie down. I want to get undressed.'

'Come on then, let's go in here.'

They were speaking breathlessly in hoarse whispers, as if afraid of being overheard. Dave led her into a sitting room at the front of the house. It was dark, the curtains were open and Lucy could see the moon through the window. It had broken clear of the trees, *cut itself free like a scythe*, Lucy thought as she took off her clothes. Dave lit the gas fire, and Lucy pulled him down onto the carpet, where she undressed him roughly, then hugged him and kissed his face and body.

'Now, Dave, now,' she said, rolling away from him and raising her knees. 'Yes. Yes. Oh, yes.' Her cries punctuated the hiss of the fire, and she could feel the heat on her body, a shifting heat as she thrashed around. She heard a voice. Someone was shouting obscenities, dirty disgusting things . . . It was her! It was her own voice she could hear. No. She began to shake her head. No. No! But the voice continued, and she could still hear it as the tears drenched her cheeks at each flaming stab.

She woke up still gripping Dave's hair. He felt surprisingly heavy now, and she wondered how she had managed to roll him over and pull him around so easily only a few minutes before . . . It wasn't her. It was that other woman. The vicious one with the wicked tongue.

Lucy told Dave that she wanted to get up, and as she raised his body, their damp skin peeled apart like a steamed envelope. Lucy stood up and began to get dressed, while Dave stretched out on the carpet and watched her. He kissed her feet, then her legs, moving slowly upward.

'That was marvellous, Lucy.'

Lucy stepped away from him and put on her shoes. Dave inserted his hand beneath one of the arches and held her foot. She seemed more distant now, as if she had swung up on horseback.

'Would you like a cup of coffee before you go?'

He presumed that she was going, by the brisk, silent way she had dressed. He wondered if she felt ashamed of herself, and was already regretting what she had done.

'No, thanks, I have to go now. I daren't look at the time.'

This was the answer he had expected; but she wasn't leaving because she was abashed, or afraid of arriving home late (that particular battle had been won); she needed to be on her own now, to reflect on what had happened.

Dave did not ask her again. There was no point. He could tell she had made up her mind. He followed her into the hall and stood at the door while she put on her coat. When she was ready to leave, he put his arms round her and hugged her. It was a bizarre embrace, with Lucy in her overcoat and scarf and Dave still naked.

'How do you feel?'

Lucy looked over his shoulder at a set of bird prints on the wall. She recognised the songthrush and the chaffinch, but she could not identify the other two. They looked like waders of some kind.

'Did you enjoy it?'

'Yes. I feel a bit overwhelmed, that's all.'

'I bet you wish you hadn't come now, don't you?'

'No. I wanted to come. I knew what I was doing.'

'I'm glad. It's all unethical though, you know. Lecturer and student. That kind of thing.'

'You don't have to worry about that. I'm hardly straight from school, am I?'

'No. Thank goodness you're not.'

143

He said it with such feeling that Lucy wondered if he was speaking from experience . . . ? Of course he was! He had probably been out with the lot, from worldly schoolgirls to innocent mothers of two like her. It was best not to think about it or it could spoil the evening.

Lucy noticed the goose pimples on his arms and felt him shiver.

'You'd better get dressed before you catch cold.'

'It's a bit late for that, isn't it?'

Lucy looked at her watch and winced.

'Yes, I suppose it is. You'd better go to bed then and take a hot-water bottle with you.'

Dave slid his hand inside her coat and squeezed her breasts.

'I should be taking you, never mind a hot-water bottle.'

'Yes, it would be nice, wouldn't it?'

'Perhaps some other time?'

'Perhaps.' Then, crushing his hand to her, 'I can't imagine how, though.'

'Listen, Lucy. If we really want it to happen, we'll make it happen.'

She was impressed by his confidence. It sounded like a maxim from the book on Positive Thinking which Phil had borrowed from Tony next door. But, however positively she thought, she could not imagine how she would ever be able to spend the night away from home with Dave. Did she want to anyway? If she was so keen on him, why was she dashing away now? Perhaps now that she had proved to herself that she was still desirable, she could relax and revert to being a loyal wife and mother again.

As she opened the door, Dave said, 'I'm pushing in an extra rehearsal tomorrow afternoon if you can make it.'

'I'll try. I usually fetch the children from school on Wednesdays though. I can't impose on the neighbours too much.'

But she was scheming already: goodbye family loyalties. Dave leaned across from behind the door and kissed her cheek.

'Don't worry about it, I understand. By the way, I thought it made a lot of sense what you said about Julie. Perhaps I should concentrate more on the business and let her accent take care of itself.'

Lucy looked out into the quiet shadowy night and turned up her collar.

'If she needs any advice on domesticity, just send her to me. I'm an expert.'

She walked down the steps and unlocked the car door. As she

swung out of the drive, she looked back, but Dave had already gone inside, and there was a light on in the sitting room. Lucy turned up the heat, switched on the radio and lit a cigarette. What if Phil smelled the smoke when he went to work in the morning? He was so particular about smells in the car, that if they bought fish and chips when they were out anywhere, they had to eat them outside – even when it was raining and the children complained that their chips were getting wet. Would she admit that she had been smoking, or say that she had given a friend a lift home . . . ? She twiddled the tuner on the radio to find some music and stopped worrying about it. She could always spray the interior with perfume when she arrived home.

It was snug in the car: snug and safe with rock and roll blasting out of the radio, and a tingle in her belly. Lucy wasn't especially interested in driving; she was usually glad to let Phil do it. But tonight she felt different. She was enjoying herself. She felt confident and powerful. She could have tackled anything as she sat there grasping the wheel, cut off from the world and singing along with the music at the top of her voice. She did not want to go home. She wanted to drive on, to keep moving, anywhere, it did not matter where to. She remembered Tanya's story about a friend who, after a row with her boyfriend, had driven furiously to London, then, when she arrived there, turned straight round and drove back.

That was what Lucy wanted to do: to drive along a motorway hour after hour, mile after relentless mile in the darkness, isolated, oblivious, mesmerised by the road ahead. And then, distanced by several cities, she would stop at a service station, buy a cup of coffee, ask a long-distance driver for a cigarette, then sit at a table on her own and listen to a love song on the jukebox. Yes! She would do it! Take off, point the car and drive through the night . . .

She looked at the petrol gauge. There was just enough left in the tank to get her home. But she did not want to go home! She wanted to go on a journey! She fiddled frantically with the radio as the music was replaced by a jingle for pork pies . . . But she was too late, the vision faded, her excitement ebbed.

As Lucy approached Hartford village, she looked out across the open fields. It was a still, silvery landscape in the moonlight, with dense shadows and trees and hedgerows etched clearly against a lighter sky. A peewit called repeatedly overhead and, although Lucy could not see it, the thought of it wheeling and tumbling in the darkness matched her own restless mood and made her cry. She cried shamelessly, and when she sobbed the tears fell from her face in clusters like raindrops from a shaken bough.

She could hardly see as she drove through the village, but she neither slowed down nor wiped her eyes. She no longer cared what happened to her, and she continued recklessly, looking for trouble, willing something to happen to her before she arrived home. But it was late, and there were no cars on the road or people crossing to give her an excuse to swerve and crash. There wasn't even a dog or cat to avoid (would she have really done it?), and she turned reluctantly into Linnet Close cheated and still unscathed. The sight of the house restored her senses, and by the time she drove into the garage she was calm enough to make sure that she did not scrape the front wings. The headlamps illuminated garden tools, Phil's workbench and a shelf containing paint tins and a bundle of cleaning rags. Lucy switched off the lights and sat in the darkness to compose herself before going in. After a few minutes, she could make out the shapes of most of the objects before her, but the rags left only a space between the tins.

Phil had left on the outside light for her, and as Lucy approached the kitchen door, she noticed that the wire birdfeeder hanging from a branch of the birch tree was empty. Poor birds. She never even thought about them now. And after all those years of feeding, and the hours of pleasure they had given her while she stood at the sink. They had been like friends, cheering her up with their antics during the long dreary days when the children were little, and she had been confined to the house. And now she couldn't even be bothered to buy them an occasional bag of peanuts. She had betrayed them. She felt like crying again.

Instead of going straight in, Lucy walked across to the birch tree and touched the trunk. How tall and sturdy it had grown. They had planted it to commemorate moving into the house. They had performed a ceremony, with Lucy removing the first spadeful of soil, then Phil taking over and digging a proper hole. How they had laughed, as Lucy stood on the doorstep and solemnly declared 'this tree well and truly planted'. It had only been a sapling then, a few feet high and strapped to a stake for support. But it had burst its bonds years ago. The top branches were level with Mathew's bedroom window, and Phil was wondering if they had planted it too near the house, and whether the roots would undermine the foundations. Lucy patted it affectionately like an old horse and went inside.

But she could not settle down. It was past midnight and she knew that she ought to go to bed, but she felt too restless to sleep. She decided to make a cup of coffee, then continue with her essay, but first she went upstairs to see the children.

Mathew was lying on his back with his mouth open, and as Lucy bent over him and smiled, she half expected him to open his eyes and smile back. She wanted to kiss his cheek, but she was afraid of disturbing him, so she tucked up his teddy beside him and quietly left the room.

Tracey was lying on her side with her teddy in her arms. Even by the faint light shining in from the landing, Lucy could see that she looked strained and pale. Lucy knew what was wrong with her, and she sat down on the bed and stroked the hair back from her eyes. She was almost inviting Tracey to wake up, so that she could hug her and reassure her that everything was all right, and tell her that once the play was over, she would be able to spend more time with her again. Just a few more days, that was all. She continued to stroke Tracey's hair, but gradually the implications of what this would mean stilled her hand. There would be no more rehearsals. No more visits to the Cross Keys. No more expeditions with Tanya looking for props . . . What would she do with herself? Tracey whimpered and turned over. Lucy was ashamed of herself. She would get on with her work and look after her family a bit better, that's what she would do! She would consider them for a change, and stop thinking about herself all the time . . . But her resolve did not last long, and as she left the room, avoiding the reproachful stares of the panda and badger on top of the chest of drawers, she was already wondering if there would be a new production next term.

She crossed the landing as quietly as she could in case Phil heard her and woke up. What if he switched on the light and looked at the clock? Where would she say she had been? What if he waited for her to go to bed and wanted to make love? How could she refuse him without causing an argument? Would he be able to tell? Perhaps she ought to go to the bathroom just in case. She paused at the top of the stairs. No, it was too risky, he might hear her through the adjoining wall. The thought of Phil listening to her getting washed after what had happened embarrassed her, and she started downstairs. A step creaked (she had never heard it before) and, in an illogical attempt to reduce her weight, she gripped the bannister and stood on her toes. As she proceeded, step by cautious step, she recalled the staircase at Dave's house with its wide steps and polished balustrade. She had wanted to straddle it and slide down. She suddenly felt randy again, and as she reached the bottom of the stairs, Dave's spunk oozed out of her, and she stood there shocked and excited at the sensation.

Lucy made herself a cup of coffee, carried it through to the lounge, and lit the gas fire. The central heating had gone off hours ago, but she did not want to switch it back on, in case the knocking in the radiators disturbed Phil. That really would have upset him, the thought of all that heat being pumped out in the middle of the night. She pulled up the armchair, and as she sipped her coffee, and stared at the glowing imitation coals, it was so quiet that she felt like the only person awake in the world. She felt privileged, as if she had been allocated secret time. It was too precious to waste. She felt alert and calm now, so she fetched her books from the shelves and sat down at the table to continue her English essay. She was looking forward to it, and after a quick read of her last paragraph, she settled down to work.

Phil could not understand it when he switched off the alarm and discovered that Lucy was not in bed with him. At first, he thought she must be in the bathroom, but when he couldn't hear anything, and he switched on the bedside lamp and saw that her place had not been slept in, he panicked and jumped out of bed. Where was she? Had she had an accident? (Was the car smashed up?) He glanced into the bathroom and the children's rooms, then hurried downstairs. What if she was still lying in a ditch somewhere. What would happen to the children? Would he have to give up work? She wasn't in the kitchen . . . Then he noticed the crack of light under the lounge door and went in. At first glance, he thought she wasn't in there either, then he saw her, asleep at the table at the other end of the room.

He stood in the doorway for a few moments to recover, but now that he had found her his relief rapidly gave way to anger.

'Lucy.'

She did not stir, so he walked across the room and touched her shoulder.

'Lucy, wake up.'

She immediately opened her eyes, but remained in the same position with her head on her arms, trying to work out where she was.

'What time is it?'

'It's six o'clock.'

She did not know whether he meant morning or evening. With the light on and the curtains drawn, it could have been either. She just sat there feeling hopelessly disoriented until it all came back.

'I must have dropped off when I'd finished working.'

She sat up grimacing as she tried to straighten her neck. Phil could have wrung it for her.

'What the hell do you think you're doing, stopping up all night? I wondered what had happened to you when I woke up and you weren't there.'

'I didn't mean to stop up all night. I wasn't tired when I came in so I thought I might as well do some work.'

As soon as she had said it, she realised her mistake.

'And what time did you come in?'

Lucy stretched luxuriously to give herself time to think. It was a tricky calculation. Her future actions could depend on the answer.

'Oh, not late. About quarter past eleven, I suppose. When the porter threw us out of the studio, we went round to Julie's flat and carried on there. She lives just round the corner from the university.'

Anyone peeping through the curtains would have witnessed a bizarre tableau, with Lucy sitting nervously at the table and Phil, wearing only his vest, standing menacingly behind her.

'Anyway, don't go on about it, Phil, I'm tired. I wanted to get that essay finished so that I could get home at a decent time today.'

She stood up and walked towards the door.

'Where are you going?'

'To bed, where do you think?'

'And what about the kids? Who's going to get them off to school?'

'I am. You don't think they'll let me stop asleep, do you, once they're awake?'

She left the room and, as Phil followed her receding footsteps up the stairs, he looked as if he was studying a successful sales graph on the lounge wall. When she reached the landing, he began to tidy up her books and papers. He was in awe at the amount she had written. He knocked the pages together like a pack of cards and read the title: *"The Alchemist" presents us with the acceptable face of capitalism. Discuss.* He read the first paragraph, then glanced up as the ceiling creaked overhead. It was difficult to associate his wife, up there, with the woman who had written

149

this essay. She had nothing to do with him, and as he stared at her name at the top of the page, it became increasingly unfamiliar.

Lucy knew that she would have to invite Phil to the play, but she kept putting it off, and she only mentioned it to him as she was getting ready to go to the dress rehearsal.

'Is it any good?' he asked, applying a spot of glue to one of the chairs from Tracey's doll's house.

'I think so.'

Phil held the tiny leg in position until it set.

'It ought to be, the time you've spent on it.'

He knelt down beside the doll's house and replaced the chair in the dining room. As he slid it under the table, he managed not to disturb any of the other chairs, even though he was working in such a restricted space. At the other side of the house, Mathew was trying to put the family to bed, but the covers kept slipping off their stiff little figures. He was beginning to grumble at them and whine, and it was only a matter of time before dolls, beds and bedroom suite were swept onto the carpet. That was what had happened to the dining chair when the family would not sit down properly for their dinners.

Lucy could see it coming. There would be another scene, with Tracey crying, Phil shouting and Mathew running away before he got smacked. Lucy crouched down to help him before anything happened. The dolls were made of plastic, and because their clothes were painted on, they had to sleep fully dressed. Mr Doll lay down in his suit, Mrs Doll in her dress and the two children, incongruously, in lederhosen. It was the first time she had noticed that it was a German family. She picked up the boy and turned him upside down. On the soles of his shoes it said: MADE IN TAIWAN.

'I don't think you'll like it very much though, Phil.'

'Why not?'

'Well, I don't think it's your kind of play, that's all.'

'What do you mean, my kind of play? I haven't got a kind of play. How can I have, when I've never been to see one?'

Tracey, who was drawing at the table, noticed the aggression in his voice and looked up.

'I'm going on the things you watch on television, that's all. I think it'll be too domestic for you.'

'Well, in that case, it'll be right up my street, won't it?'

He began to peel flakes of dry glue from his fingers and hurl them towards the fire. Lucy decided to leave her lipstick until she was in the car: it was time to go. She left the room and returned immediately, putting on her coat.

'Have I to get you a ticket then?'

She avoided Phil's eyes by fussing with the lapels and buckling her belt.

'You'd be disappointed if I said yes, wouldn't you?'

That made her look up.

'What do you mean? Why should I be?'

'Because you think I'll embarrass you in front of all your clever new friends. You think I'll sit there farting and belching, and laughing in all the wrong places.'

Tracey giggled at the rude word and Mathew, with an unerring instinct for vulgarity, shouted gleefully at the sleeping dolls, 'Farting and belching! Daddy's farting and belching!' He laughed into the bedroom, then looked round slyly, waiting for the reprimand. Lucy ignored him.

'Don't be ridiculous, Phil. Why would I ask you if I felt like that?'

'Because you'd no choice, that's why. It's a wonder you didn't wait until there were no tickets left and then ask me.'

Lucy blushed. It had crossed her mind. She sat on the arm of the settee and placed her hand on his shoulder.

'It's not true, Phil. Of course I want you to come.' She had to go all the way now to prove that she meant it. 'If you come on Saturday night, we'll be able to go to the party afterwards. We'll get a babysitter. It'll be really nice.'

She tried to sound enthusiastic, but it was a good job that she was sitting above Phil and he could not see the troubled expression on her face.

'What party? You never mentioned it before.'

'I didn't think there was any need. There's always a party after a show. It's a tradition.'

'Who'll be there?'

'The cast, and everybody else involved with the play. Friends. A few lecturers from the English Department, I suppose . . .'

'I don't suppose there'll be any welders there.'

Lucy laughed, her hopes rising.

'I wouldn't think so. They'll all be people from the university, I expect.'

She hoped this would be the ultimate deterrent. She was disappointed.

'I'll come if you like then. It'll be a change from the Malt Shovel on a Saturday night.'

'Good.' She could have knifed him. 'I'll reserve you a seat then.'

She went into the kitchen to fetch the car keys. Tracey picked up her drawing pad from the table and followed her.

'Mummy?'

'What?'

'I can't get this horse right. Will you draw it for me?'

Lucy barely glanced at it.

'It's all right, love. It's good.'

'It's not. Its legs are funny, look.'

Lucy ignored her and went back into the lounge for her bag. Phil had switched on the television and Mathew was sitting on his knee watching it with him.

'See that they're in bed at a decent time, won't you, Phil?'

Tracey tugged at her coat.

'Go on, mum, draw it for me.'

'I can't now, Tracey, I haven't got time.'

'It won't take you long. It's only its legs. It looks as if it's falling down.'

The horse was being chased across a field by a group of people. One of the pursuers had a gun. Tracey tried to force Lucy to look at it again, but she was too busy checking the contents of her bag.

'Ask your daddy to draw it for you, Tracey. I've got to go now.'

'I want you to draw it for me, mummy. You can draw best.'

'I can't, Tracey!' She twitched her coat free and closed her bag. 'I haven't got time.'

Her voice was sharp enough to make Tracey's lips quiver, and Lucy immediately regretted her impatience. She reached out to reassure her, but it was too late, the damage had been done and Tracey avoided her arms.

'I'll do it tomorrow for you, love, when you come home from school.'

Tracey ignored her and sat down at the table again.

'Right then, I'm going now.'

Phil and Mathew ignored her too. They were watching a wildlife programme. Two baboons were mating and Mathew was asking Phil what they were doing. Lucy bent down to kiss him, but he was more interested in the activities of the animals, and the whites of his eyes showed as he strained to see round her face.

As she left the room, Lucy realised how much he had changed

towards her recently. A few months ago, he would have accompanied her to the door and waved until she went out of sight at the top of the road. Now, he had not even noticed she was going.

Tracey listened to the door close and the car start up on the drive. She decided to put a rider on the horse's back, drew a head, then changed her mind and rubbed it out. But the ghost of the head remained. She hated it. It spoiled her picture and she rubbed and rubbed until the paper wrinkled and finally tore.

It took the actors two nights to play themselves in, and on the last night, when Phil went to see the play, they were confident and relaxed. All that work for three performances, Lucy thought, as she watched from the side of the stage. She wished that it would run for ever. She wondered if Phil was enjoying it. She could not see him from where she was standing as he was sitting near the back. She had not heard him laughing in the wrong places yet, but whether he was farting and belching she couldn't tell because he was sitting too far away. She hoped not, because he was sitting next to Professor Jupp, the head of the English Literature Department.

Poor Phil, she wondered how he was getting on out there surrounded by all those university people. He nearly had not come in the end. It would be boring, he said, a waste of a good Saturday night. Lucy wanted to agree with him, but when she feigned disappointment he changed his mind. There was worse to come. He put on his best suit. The charcoal grey one with the baggy trousers. Lucy could have wept. She hated him in it. It was too old-fashioned, too formal. The last time he had worn it was at his mother's funeral three years ago. But what could she say without insulting him? Especially as she knew that he was wearing it for her sake. It was an important occasion, and he wanted to look his best so that she would not be ashamed of him if he was introduced to any of her new friends. How was he to know that he would be overdressed, and that most of the men there would be dressed casually in denim or corduroy?

Perhaps she should have sat with him, instead of leaving him out there on his own? She could have done; there was only one set and no scenery to change. But she did not want to be in the audience; she wanted to be backstage where she could feel part of the show. She revelled in the atmosphere, and as she stood in the wings sipping a glass of wine, she was so moved by the intensity of her feelings that tears came to her eyes.

Dave came up behind her with a bottle and refilled her glass. She could smell the wine on his breath as he pressed up to her and rubbed his chin on her shoulder. He kept smiling to himself, and it wasn't just the wine. He was high on the success of the play. It had been fully booked for all three nights. The applause had been generous, comments from students and colleagues favourable, and the theatre critic of the local daily newspaper had said that it was the best thing that the Drama Club had ever done. He especially praised the authenticity of the set and the realistic production. Lucy had been pleased by his reference to the set, but Tanya was derisive. 'What does he know about it?' she said. 'As a man, he's not qualified to pass an opinion on such matters.'

The matters she was referring to were the strenuous household chores which Julie was performing on stage. She really was working out there. Lucy could see the damp patches under her arms as she lifted a dripping sheet from the washtub and placed it between the rollers of the mangle. ('No make-up,' Dave had said. 'We don't want mascara running down your face when you start sweating.') As Julie turned the handle, and the flattened sheet squeezed through, it looked as if the mangle was pulling its tongue out at the audience.

Lucy was impressed by her performance. She believed in her at last. She had no time for the histrionics she had shown at rehearsal. She was too busy trying to keep up with her work. In the first act, when Julie had been filling a tub with buckets of hot water from the boiler, Lucy had turned to Tanya and thanked God for the invention of washing machines. Yes, Tanya conceded, physical conditions in the home might be better now, but have the improvements led to greater freedom and independence for women? That was the important question. Maybe it was, Lucy thought, but, as she watched Julie open the oven door, she was glad that she did not have to light a fire every time she had to do some cooking. These were the 'good old days' which her parents and elderly relatives were always reminiscing about when they gathered at Christmas. Perhaps that was why she was feeling so emotional now. She was thinking of them, those poor, worn-out old people, and all the hardships they had endured in their lives.

Dave gave Lucy a parting squeeze and whispered that he would see her later; but she scarcely heard him or noticed when he went away. Her thoughts were on more important matters than Dave just then . . . . Had things *really* improved since those days? Or had they just been bought off with gadgets, as Tanya had suggested? She watched Alice trying desperately to persuade the two football scouts to stay a bit longer. If they left before her husband came home, then her hopes of a better life would disappear with them . . .

Alice: He could be at his mother's. He often calls in there on his way home from work.

Arthur: It sounds as if you're married to the Scarlet Pimpernel to me, missus. He could be here. He could be there. He could be anywhere by the sounds of it. I think it's time we were off.
         (He stands up. Then Sam Kirk stands up.)

Alice: You're not going, are you? I'll run round, if you like. She only lives in the next street.

Arthur: We haven't got time. We'll miss the train if we stop any longer.

Alice: It'll not take a minute.

Arthur: No. After all, he did know we were coming.

Alice: He's probably got the wrong day. Perhaps he thinks you're coming another day.

Arthur: I wouldn't think so. It doesn't take much remembering from Saturday to Monday, does it?
         (He walks towards the door. Sam follows him.)

Alice: What shall I tell him when he comes in?

Arthur: Tell him that we came to see him like we said we would.
         (He opens the door. We hear the sound of rain.)

Sam: Christ, look at it. It's raining twice.
         (They put on their caps, turn up their coat collars and prepare to leave.)

Alice: Why don't you stop a bit longer, till it eases off?

Arthur: We've no time. We've left it late as it is. Come on, Sam.
         (They leave the house.)

Sam: *(Turning round on the doorstep.)* Ta-ra, Mrs Hayes. Thanks for the tea. We might see you again some time.
         (They walk away. Alice watches them out of sight, then closes the door.)

Alice: Just wait till he gets in. I'll kill him! It's not fair of him! It's just not right! *(She looks round, wondering how she can get her own back on him.)* And if he thinks he's having his dinner in this house, he's another think coming. *(She takes his dinner out of the oven and scrapes it onto the fire.)* And he can get washed in cold water as well. *(She takes*

155

the pan of boiling water off the gas ring and pours it down the sink.) Football. I'll give him bloody football. Where's them boots? *(She goes to the cupboard by the fireplace, rummages around inside and takes out his football boots. They are stiff and caked with dried mud. She hurls them onto the fire one after the other. Because the fire has been damped down with food, the boots do not begin to burn immediately. She stands there watching them.)* Go on, burn, you buggers, burn. *(Then, when they start to smoke and she begins to realise the implications of what she has done, she panics, picks up the poker and knocks them into the hearth. She picks them up, runs to the sink and drops them into a bowl of water. After they have cooled off, she take them out, wipes them with a floor cloth and inspects them.)* They're not too bad. He'll never notice if I rub a bit of muck on them. *(She puts the boots back into the bottom cupboard and closes the door. Then she stands there, her energy spent, wondering what to do next.)* Well, this is not going to buy the baby a bonnet, standing here doing nothing. *(She takes a shirt out of a tub and puts it through the mangle.)* God, what a life . . .

The lights faded, leaving the stage in darkness, and the studio ringing with the eerie, clanking sound of Alice turning the wheel of the mangle.

The lights came up again and the cast took their bows holding hands at the front of the stage. Lucy applauded too from the wings, but she was less certain about the play now than when she had first read it. Perhaps Tanya was right when she said that it was defeatist, and that it would have been much stronger if Alice had left the boots on the fire. But could she have done that? Would it have been plausible? Of course it wouldn't! In the context of the play, the idea was ridiculous . . . But what if she had? What if she had let the boots burn? What would have happened then . . . ? The question troubled her, and she was still considering it when the cast withdrew and the house lights went up.

They held the party on the stage. Lucy could not understand why anyone would want to drink and dance surrounded by washtubs, rubbing boards and piles of damp clothes, but everyone else seemed to think it was a good idea. Phil was standing at the table looking for some beer. He shook all the cans but they were empty, so he picked up the first bottle at hand and poured himself some wine. Red, white, sweet or dry, it did not matter to him as long as he had something in his hand while he stood about nodding and smiling. For the first time in years, he felt a strong urge to smoke. Lucy had done her duty and introduced him to all the people she knew there; but she did not want to stay with him, she wanted to move around and share in the euphoria they were all feeling at the success of the show. Dave remembered Phil from their meeting at the bookshop. When he asked him if he had enjoyed the play, Phil said that it was better than he had expected. It reminded him of when he used to go to his grandmother's when he was little; her house used to be like that. The seats were hard though, he said. It took a bit of sitting through. Dave quickly excused himself and moved away. People were congratulating him all the time. Women kept putting their arms round him and kissing him and telling him how marvellous it was. Phil had not congratulated him. He would have done, but he was embarrassed by such extravagant gestures.

His introduction to Dr Halfyard, the Reader in English, was a masterpiece of incomprehension. 'A welder!' Dr Halfyard repeated, making it sound as improbable as the handbag in *The Importance of Being Earnest*. 'How fascinating.' But his fascination only extended to asking Phil where he worked, before wandering away to find a refuge in more familiar literary topics, preferably Wyatt and other poets of the English Renaissance.

Julie was enthroned in the armchair which Lucy had helped deliver from Tanya's house: an unlikely-looking queen in her stage costume of pinafore and turban. 'Hi, Phil,' she said, presenting her hand. 'I've heard a lot about you.' Lucy looked startled. Julie had not heard *anything* about him. But she was just being expansive, and Phil was flattered by her remark, even though it could have meant the opposite of what he thought. It never occurred to him that she might have heard anything derogatory. Julie was already drunk. Several quick glasses of wine while she was still highly charged from her performance had given her a flying start. Her eyes were unnaturally bright and she looked wild and feverish. Lucy wondered what she was going to say next. What if she mentioned Dave, and started to tease Phil about them going off together after rehearsals? It was possible. There was no telling what she might do in this mood. It was time to move on while she was still safe. She took Phil's arm, but she need not have worried, because Julie forgot all about them when Mr Millinchip from the Language Department approached to offer his congratulations. She held up her hand and Mr Millinchip unhesitatingly bent down and kissed it. As Lucy steered Phil away from them, she wished that he had had the wit to do that, instead of shaking it roughly as he had done.

What would Tanya make of him? What would he make of Tanya in her red beret and dungarees? What if she started to attack him and they had a public row?

'Tanya, this is Phil.'

They shook hands (there was no question of hand kissing this time), then Tanya took a tobacco tin out of her pocket and began to roll a cigarette. Lucy looked anxiously at Phil to see what his reaction would be. It seemed like deliberate provocation to her. Phil looked enthralled. (What a tale he would have to tell his mates on Monday morning . . . and there was this bird there in overalls rolling her own.)

'It's a bit since I've seen anybody do that. My dad used to roll his own.'

Tanya offered him the tin.

'No, thanks. I'd finish up with more on the floor than in the paper.'

'I'll roll you one if you like.'

Lucy was immediately suspicious. What was she trying to do, prove that women could even roll cigarettes better than men? Apparently not, because, when Phil refused her offer, she put away the tin and began to talk to him about his work, the children, gardening and home improvements. Lucy was amazed. Why was she doing it? She did not usually spend her time in polite conversation with men. Possibly because Lucy was her friend now, and she was doing it for her sake. But, whatever the reason, Lucy was grateful to her. Tanya was the first person who had shown any interest in him and not made him feel like an intruder. Lucy could have kissed her for it. What an enigma she was. Yes, she could be infuriating and strident in her arguments. What had she said to Chris when they were discussing rape? 'As a man, your opinions on the subject are irrelevant.' And later. 'All rapists are normal men.' But Lucy had grown to respect her. She did not agree with a lot of what she said, but she admired her courage. She was formidable. She was her own woman. Lucy did not know many women who she could say that about. She certainly could not say it about herself.

Later, when Lucy had drunk too much wine, and people were dancing to Reggae music between the furniture, she stood by the mangle and looked at Phil, who was standing in a group of students at the other side of the stage. He had to keep leaning forward and turning his head to catch what they were saying. Was the loud music making him deaf? None of the others appeared to be troubled by it. Perhaps he wasn't exaggerating about the noise at work after all. Perhaps it *was* affecting his hearing. The conversation went on around him and across him. Lucy saw him nod and smile and sometimes laugh, but she never saw him speak. Sometimes he looked as if he was going to. He licked his lips, swallowed, opened his mouth; but he was always too late and someone beat him to it.

Lucy knew the feeling. It often happened to her in seminars. She could not think fast enough. Odd words and disjointed sentences emerged laboriously from the mist, refused to take shape and died stillborn in the head. Phil continued to smile and nod. It was the only contribution he could make.

It was strange, seeing him here in such an unfamiliar setting, distanced by wine and Caribbean rhythms. Was he really her husband, that man over there in the baggy grey suit? It was so out of date that it would have been fashionable on one of the students. Perhaps they thought he *was* trying to be fashionable: an ageing punk in an Oxfam suit. Philip Downs. She heard his name afresh, hated it afresh. It was his mother's fault and her stupid reverence for the Royal Family! Still, it could have been worse, she might have called him Charles. He would have been known as Charlie then. (To everyone but his mother, that is.) Lucy rehearsed an introduction using his new name . . . This is my husband, Charlie. She laughed out. She couldn't help it. Charlie Downs! He sounded like a dustbin man! And what's wrong with that? she immediately objected, furious with herself. My uncle Harry was a dustbin man and there was nothing wrong with him. Perhaps Phil was right: she was becoming a snob. She would be disowning the whole family next, if she wasn't careful.

She poured herself another drink and listened to the music. Never mind the family; she was having a good time. She noticed Phil looking at his watch, closed her eyes, and began a little dance of her own. Bugger the time! Bugger the babysitter! Let Judith babysit for ever! She wouldn't mind. That was all she was good for anyway, babysitting and bringing up kids. Have you had a nice time? she would ask sanctimoniously when they arrived home. They've been ever so good. I haven't heard a sound from them all night; implying that she possessed somnific powers, and that if anyone else had been looking after them all hell would have been let loose.

Lucy danced on. She wasn't going home. Not yet anyway . . . When she opened her eyes, Dave was dancing in front of her. He smiled and took her hands. Lucy wanted to pull him close to her and kiss him, but she daren't, it was too risky. If Phil saw them, there would be trouble. She had seen it before, when he had once threatened a man in a pub just for *looking* at her. There would be no preliminaries: no demanding explanations. He would drag them apart, smack her across the face, then thump Dave. She squeezed his soft hands. Poor Dave, he wouldn't stand a chance. He had probably never had a fight in his life. He was so well bred that Lucy felt she could have taken him on herself. She wondered if the other husbands present would have reacted in the same way? Hardly. She could not imagine Professor Jupp swinging a right hook, or Dr Halfyard gripping anyone round the throat. Their reproaches would have come later, in the privacy of their own homes.

'Let's go somewhere, Lucy.'

Dave continued to smile as he said it, as if he was asking her if she was enjoying herself, or enquiring if she would like another drink. *Go somewhere?* What did he mean, a day out in the Christmas holidays or something like that? (Vac! She must get used to calling it the vac.) It would be difficult. But she might be able to get away for an afternoon. She could always say that she had to go into the library for some books.

'When?'

Dave looked puzzled at her question.

'Now, of course. This minute. When do you think?'

Now! Surely he didn't mean elope, or anything stupid like that? He *must* be drunk. Then she realised what he did mean, and for a few moments she was too frightened to speak.

'I can't, Dave, it's too risky.'

'No, it's not. I'll go down into the props store and you can follow me in a few minutes. Nobody's going to come in there. Unless they've got the same idea, that is.'

It was no joke. Lucy looked terrified.

'And what if Phil notices that I've gone, and comes looking for me?'

'Don't be ridiculous. Don't you ever go to the lavatory?'

'I can't, Dave. I daren't.'

She glanced round to see if anyone was listening, but the music was too loud to prevent even the nearest dancers overhearing their conversation.

'I'm going now. I'll see you shortly.'

Lucy tried to hold on to him, but he pulled away from her and went backstage. As she stood there, wondering whether to follow him or not, her heart was beating so forcefully that it made her short of breath. Her fear was palpable, like that of a wild bird held in the hand.

She still went though, trying desperately to convince herself that it wasn't worth the risk as she edged towards the side of the stage. Exit left: fast. She hurried down the steps and made for the cloakroom. Anybody watching her would have thought she was desperate for relief or about to be sick. She was neither; she was excited and scared, and she thought that a few minutes alone in the clinical neutrality of a cubicle might make her see sense and go back. It did nothing of the sort. It made her lustful and determined to go on. Now that she was out of Phil's sight, she had lost her fear, and she stood with her back to the lavatory door trembling with anticipation. She flushed the bowl even though she had not used it, and unlocked the door. Two girls, who Lucy had barely noticed when she rushed in, were standing by the wash basins drinking wine and smoking a joint together. (Three months ago, she would have thought they were so hard up that they were having to share one cigarette between them.) They smiled vaguely and raised their hands in distant greetings. Lucy smiled back and went out. She had an alibi now. She would tell Phil about the two girls anyway; she enjoyed teasing him with risqué stories of campus life. Like the time she had gone into the wrong room and discovered two boys with their arms around each other. She had been shocked by that too, and had hurriedly closed the door and retreated down the corridor in confusion. When she told Dave about it, he just laughed and said, 'How do you know it wasn't a couple of Russians who hadn't seen each other for a long time?' Phil said, 'Bloody poofters, they ought to be locked up.'

Lucy glanced into the dressing room, listened to make sure no one was coming, then opened the door of the props store and stepped quickly inside. It was in darkness. She saw Dave briefly by the light from the open door, then it went black again as she closed it.

'Let me lock it, Lucy.'

He fumbled behind her and turned the key.

'That's better. Let me have a feel at you now. God, I want you so much.'

'Quickly, Dave, I can't stay long.'

He did as he was told, nearly pulling the buttons off her blouse in his haste to unfasten it. She could feel herself opening up as his hand went up her skirt, and when his fingers slipped inside her, she unzipped his trousers and began to match the rhythm of his hand with her own. He wanted to fuck her, he said, but Lucy was too far gone to care about his needs, and she heard no more as the sweet waves flowed through her and exploded in her head.

She came round on the floor with Dave's thigh against her cheek. She sat there, weak and wondrously calm. She could hear his shallow breathing, feel the heat between his legs. It was his turn now. She knelt before him and, with no sense of guilt or shame, repaid him in the most intimate way she knew for the good feelings he had given her.

As Dave unlocked the door, Lucy said, 'That was marvellous.

'Yes, it was. I'm not sure what we ought to do about it though; the complications could be hideous.' He peeped outside. 'Perhaps it's a good job it's the end of term. It'll give us a bit of time to think things out.'

A bit of time: four weeks. It seemed like a long time to Lucy. It meant a whole month at home. It seemed like a long time to Phil too. But a month at home would have been paradise to him. He had so many jobs to do. He could have mended the front gate, decorated the bathroom, put up the new wall lights in the lounge . . . When Mathew asked him why his mummy was on holiday, and he was still at work, he said, 'Because their brains soon get tired at university and they need a long rest.' Lucy pulled out her tongue at him in the mirror and continued to brush her hair. She noticed the brand name of her lipstick standing on the mantelpiece and wondered if they were one of the cosmetic manufacturers listed on the WAAT (Women Against Animal Torture) leaflet which she had picked up in the students' union. She could not remember. Even making up was a moral issue these days.

They were getting ready to go and see Tracey in the Christmas concert at school. Mathew had failed his audition. 'Miss Crowther says I don't speak up loud enough,' he said when Lucy asked him why he wasn't taking part. 'Who doesn't speak loud enough?' Phil said, picking him up and tickling him. 'She ought to hear you at home. You make more noise than a lorryload of monkeys.' But Mathew was not amused this time. He struggled free, suddenly tearful at the memory of the rebuff. 'Anyway, I didn't want to speak. I wanted to be a reindeer with Robert Clay.'

Every seat in the school hall was occupied. Mathew had to sit on Phil's knee, and there were parents standing down the sides and at the back. It was the first time that Phil had attended a school concert, but Lucy had not been surprised when Tracey brought the letter home, and he had said that he would like to go this year too. How he had changed. Last year, Mathew would automatically have sat on her knee.

The theme of the concert was 'Winter', around which each class had devised a related sketch. Tracey was a snowflake in theirs. She scurried around the stage in white tights and vest to the accompaniment of the 'Dance of the Jugglers' from *The Snow Maiden*. Then, as the storm subsided, and the music slowed down, she sank to the floor with the other snowflakes and lay curled up in a ball. 'She looks more like a hailstone to me,' Phil whispered, as all the snowflakes jumped up and took their bows. Lucy nudged him to be quiet and applauded until her palms stung. She wanted an encore. She did not want Tracey to go off. How she loved her as she stood there curtsying and smiling shyly. She wanted to stand up and wave, to show her that she was there. Being anonymous in the audience did not seem to be enough. Mathew was clapping too and Phil was whispering something to him and making him laugh. How fiercely she loved them too, her husband and her son. This was how it should be, the four of them together surrounded by other loving families.

At the end of the concert, when the audience stood up and the performers crowded the stage to sing carols together, Lucy was so choked with emotion that she could barely join in. She kept her head down and followed the words in the programme to hide her tears; and, when she did sing, all she could manage was the occasional croaked line. What a fool she had been. What an idiot to think that there could be anything better than this. Mathew looked up at the funny noises she was making. She blew her nose and put her arm round him. No more doubts and dissatisfaction. She was going to be a good wife and mother again from now on.

*

163

But her old-year resolution did not last long. After a few days at home she felt restless again. She wanted to go somewhere. She wanted to see Dave again. He had gone straight to London at the end of term to stay with friends (who? Lucy had wondered), before travelling on to spend Christmas with his parents near Stratford. He did not know when he would be back. Lucy had agreed that it would be wise not to see each other during the vacation, but she wished she had asked him for a telephone number, so that she could have spoken to him occasionally. Just hearing his voice would have been some consolation.

Sometimes, when she was alone in the house, she thought about what had happened at the party. It excited her and made her want to do it again . . . It was more sensible to keep busy and try to think of something else.

And she did try. During the first week of her holiday she cleaned and tidied up the house, caught up with the ironing – Phil thought it was Christmas and his birthday all rolled into one when he opened the wardrobe door and saw a full rail of shirts – wrote cards, hung up the decorations and did most of the Christmas shopping. But sometimes, without realising it, she would stop work and find herself staring out of the window like someone in a trance. It happened one Saturday morning when she was washing up and Phil was digging the vegetable patch at the bottom of the garden. She was attracted by the thrust of the spade and repeated turning of the soil. It was as hypnotic as the sea, and she would have let the sink run over if Tracey had not noticed and shouted to her to turn off the tap.

It happened again a few days later, when she was cleaning the lounge window and a woman walked by with three small children. The two youngest were riding in a double pushchair while the eldest lagged behind. His mother kept turning round, and although Lucy could not hear what she was saying, she could guess. The boy was sulking; he probably wanted to ride too. One of the babies was crying. The other one kept throwing her doll onto the floor. The mother picked it up: once, twice, three times, tried to comfort the other one, turned on the eldest for taking his cap off. Lucy could see the stress and fatigue on her face. She guessed what was coming. She was right. The eldest got a smack. That meant that two of them were crying now and the third still throwing her doll onto the floor. The mother picked it up and stuffed it into the bulging shopping bag hanging from the handle of the pushchair. The third child began to cry . . . Lucy watched their halting, fractious progress until they were out of sight. What was it all for? She stood at the window for a long time trying to find a satisfactory answer.

She often asked herself the same question during the Christmas celebrations. *What was it all for?* She wasn't certain any more, and she felt slightly removed from the people around her, as if she was observing them through glass. But Phil and the children did not seem to notice anything different about her behaviour, and when they invited people in, or visited their relatives and friends, Lucy tried hard for their sakes to keep up the pretence that they were a happy family, enjoying a happy family Christmas together.

Sometimes she was happy, but in a frenzied kind of way, and usually after too much to drink. But her moods were so volatile that she could not sustain it, and often, without warning, she would feel desperately lonely and surprise one of the children with a fierce, possessive hug. Pop songs often caught her off guard too. Maudlin lyrics (the more banal they were, the more potent their effect), which she thought she had outgrown years ago, affected her deeply and increased her isolation. Once, when Mathew asked her why she was crying, she patted her chest and said that she wasn't crying; it was the drink that had gone down the wrong way.

Lucy was relieved when Christmas was over, and she was hanging up the new calendar which Tracey had made at school. One more week, that was all, and it would be the start of the new term. She could hardly wait for it to arrive.

Lucy felt sick with nerves as she walked down the corridor to Dave's room for her first tutorial of the new term. It seemed like such a long time ago since she had seen him, that it was hard to imagine that the play, and what had happened between them, had really taken place. She had even forgotten what he looked like properly. She wondered if he had missed her as much as she had missed him. What would she say to him? What would he say to her?

'Hi!' he said, smiling up at her from behind his desk. 'Happy new year. Take a seat.'

Lucy was disappointed. He could have been welcoming any other student back for the new term. She wanted more than that. She wanted him to jump up and put his arms round her and tell her how awful it had been without her, and that he had thought about her every single minute of every day . . . Well, for some of the time at least. She sat down on a chair against the wall and watched him search through the pile of essays on his desk. She looked forsaken sitting there on her own, like the last patient in a doctor's waiting room.

'Here we are.'

Before he could remark on her essay, Lucy said, 'Did you have a nice Christmas?'

Dave gave a few non-committal shrugs and looked out of the window.

'About the same, I guess, as the man said.'

'What man?'

Dave laughed but did not elaborate. It was obviously a private joke which he did not care to disclose. He turned the pages of Lucy's essay and read the comments at the end to refresh his memory. It was as if they were student and teacher and nothing more.

Lucy felt humiliated. She wanted to run out of the room. She did not want to discuss her essay. She wanted to discuss *them*.

'It's an excellent piece of work Lucy, concise, well argued. It was probably worth A-minus rather than B-plus. However . . .'

Lucy did not care if it was the best essay that had ever been written. She would not have cared if he had given her an E. She was hardly listening to him . . . So it was all over then? What an idiot she had been. All that anguish. All those dreams for nothing . . .

She noticed that Dave was wearing a new sweater. A Christmas present from a new girlfriend no doubt. The cow! But why shouldn't he have a new girlfriend? He could have a hundred girlfriends if he wanted to. He had no ties. He could 'play the field', as Phil called it. She was jealous, that was all. She would have to try and forget it now; her little fling was over. Work, that was the cure. Plenty of hard work, so she had little time to think of anything else.

Dave passed her essay over the desk and Lucy stood up. She did not know if he wanted to discuss it or not. She did not care; she just wanted to leave now. Dave walked round the desk and they converged at the door.

'It's good to see you again, Lucy.'

Lucy kept her eyes averted and watched his hand gently squeezing the door handle.

'Yes, it's good to see you.'

166

'Why don't we celebrate our reunion by going off somewhere?'

'Where to, the props store again?'

He was aware of the sarcasm in her voice.

'No, I was thinking more in terms of a weekend. We could have a really nice time together.'

Lucy's heart began to thump so violently that she was afraid it would show through her clothes.

'I don't know.'

'Don't you like the idea?'

'It's not that. You took me by surprise, that's all. I wasn't expecting it.'

Dave put his arms round her, but Lucy kept hers by her side. She could feel her heart in both of them now.

'I thought you'd gone off me.'

'Why, just because I didn't jump all over you when you walked into the room?'

'I suppose so. I was looking forward to seeing you so much that it seemed like a let-down.'

'I was looking forward to seeing you too. I wasn't sure what to do. I thought you might have had second thoughts during the vac. Anyway, if you were so keen, why didn't you come and jump all over me for a change? It would be good to be propositioned occasionally, instead of having to do all the work oneself. It's hard work being a man sometimes, you know.'

'Old habits die hard, I suppose.'

She held his arms and kissed him.

'That's more like it. Now then, what about this little trip together?'

'I'd love to. I can't see how I could get away though.'

'You've managed it before.'

'I know. But an evening's different to a weekend, isn't it? Where could I say I was going?'

'I don't know. We arrange excursions to the theatre sometimes. We could arrange a private trip and make it an obligatory part of the course.'

She did not notice his sly smile. She was too busy thinking.

'Yes, that's a possibility, as long as I warn Phil in good time. He'll grumble like mad, but if he thinks it's part of the course . . .'

'Have you ever been to the Royal Shakespeare at Stratford?'

Lucy shook her head.

'Right then. How about travelling down one Saturday morning, going to see a show, then staying the night somewhere?

You'd have a perfect alibi. You could show Phil the programme, tell him about the play. I could even set you an essay on it, if you liked.'

Lucy laughed and thumped him lightly on the chest.

'You cunning devil. You've got it all worked out, haven't you?'

'Well, I have given it a little preliminary thought, I must admit.'

But Lucy's smile soon faded and she looked worried again.

'It sounds lovely. I'll try, Dave, honest I will. It would be really nice to spend some time together.'

'Well, don't push it. See what happens at home, and if you think you can make it, we'll go.'

Lucy closed her eyes and rubbed her cheek against his shoulder.

'This feels nice and soft. Was it a Christmas present?'

'No, I bought it in the sales in London.'

'It's lovely.'

She raised her face from his chest and looked up at him.

'You've had a haircut as well since the last time I saw you.'

Dave laughed and instinctively touched his head.

'Mother insisted when I went home. She still treats me like a little boy. She said I would have to sleep in the stable block unless I had it cut.'

Lucy slid her essay into her bag and prepared to leave.

'I've got to go now, or I'll be late for my Politics lecture.'

Dave nodded but remained in front of the door.

'I hope we shall still be able to sneak a few evenings out together in the meantime. To keep our hand in, so to speak.'

'Don't be rude.'

She reached behind him for the door handle and Dave stepped aside.

'It's really good to see you again, Lucy.'

'Yes, it's good to see you.'

She leaned forward for a quick parting kiss, but Dave got hold of her and pulled her close.

Lucy missed her Politics lecture, and when she left his room an hour later, she was determined to go away with him.

But before that could be arranged, there was the problem of seeing Dave in the evenings now that she did not have the play as an excuse. She invented a series of lectures instead. They had to be at night, she told Phil, because all the speakers were from other universities.

And what good times they had together. It was like courting again, with the pleasure of each meeting intensified by the sadness of parting. Lucy visited places she had never been to before. One evening, Dave took her to a little cinema called the Tramshed, to see a French film. (One of them pictures that you have to read, as Phil would have described it.) Dave met someone he knew in the foyer, and they discussed the director, his previous films, and the reviews of this one. Lucy had never heard of him, but she did not care. She was just happy to be there with Dave. Inside, in the darkness, they held hands and touched knees and Dave squeezed her thighs through her skirt.

They went to a poetry reading in a room above a pub, where earnest young people recited obscure verse to indiscriminate applause. 'A load of crap,' Dave said as they came out. 'But good fun all the same.'

He took her to a club to see a band called Victorian Outcasts. Lucy had not heard them before, but the name sounded vaguely familiar. The room was hot and crowded and the music was so loud that it hurt her ears. But after a couple of quick drinks, she tuned in and began to enjoy herself. Hemmed in near the stage, she closed her eyes and climbed with the guitar: higher and higher on each soaring rift until she was there, at the pitch, ecstatic and invincible. With her head back and eyes shut tight, she looked as if she was going to start howling like a dog.

Another evening, in an Italian restaurant, where the patron greeted them like old friends, Dave surprised Lucy by ordering the meal in fluent Italian. '*Buono!*' he called to the amused waiter when he tasted the wine. Lucy thought it tasted good too. She smoothed her hand across the clean tablecloth and touched the flowers in the vase to see if they were real. What could be better than this, being here with Dave, sharing a meal and a bottle of wine together?

There were heavy snowfalls during the next few weeks, so they decided to postpone their trip to Stratford until the weather improved. Finally, it was arranged for the end of March. It would be better then, Lucy said, more springlike.

During the week beforehand, Lucy spent as much time as possible at home. She did not see Dave in the evening (the bogus lecture had been conveniently cancelled), and she only went into university when she had classes. It was as if she was trying to salve her conscience in advance.

On Friday morning, as she was sorting out her clothes for the trip, the telephone rang. It was Mrs Lockwood from school. She would like to have a chat about Tracey, she said. What about her? It would be better if Lucy could come up to school . . .

Mrs Lockwood poured two cups of coffee from an earthenware pot.

'Milk, Mrs Downs?'

'Yes, please.'

'Sugar?'

'No, thank you.

They stirred matching cups and Lucy waited for Mrs Lockwood to speak.

'I'm glad you've been able to come up, Mrs Downs. We're a little bit concerned about Tracey at the moment. I thought it might be a good idea if we could have a chat.'

'Why, what's the matter with her?'

'Would you like a biscuit?'

She pushed the plate across the coffee table. The biscuits had been arranged overlapping each other like tumbled dominoes. Lucy shook her head.

'No, thanks.'

A year ago, she would have felt uncomfortable sitting in the headmistress's office; now, she thought nothing of it.

'Did Tracey say anything when she got home yesterday? Did she seem upset about anything?'

'Not that I can remember. Why?'

'Well, yesterday afternoon she stole some money from one of the girls in her class . . .'

'Our Tracey! Never!' Lucy could not have been more outraged if she had been accused herself. 'She wouldn't do a thing like that. She doesn't need to steal from anybody. She gets everything she wants.' She leaned forward and took a biscuit. She would have preferred a cigarette.

'Well, she did, I'm afraid. She took fifty pence from Mandy Parson's pencil case. We found it in her coat pocket later.'

'How do you know it wasn't her own money?'

'When we tackled her about it, she just broke down and started to cry. She said that she'd found it and forgotten to hand it in.'

Lucy felt like crying too. She couldn't believe it. Her daughter stealing? It wasn't true!

'Anyway, Mandy got her money back and no one else knows anything about it except myself and Miss Pallister.'

At least that was some consolation. The thought of the whole school knowing, and all the mothers gossiping at the school gates, was unbearable.

'What's Tracey been like at home recently, Mrs Downs? Have you noticed anything different in her behaviour at all?'

Lucy hesitated. She had a sip of coffee.

'Not that I can think of. She seems all right. Why?'

'Well, she doesn't seem to have been herself at all just lately. She's usually a very outward-going, well-adjusted girl. But she seems to have become very withdrawn and aggressive all of a sudden. Obviously we're concerned about it, and when something like this does happen to a child, it often stems from something that's happened at home . . . Not that I'm trying to pry into anything personal, I hope you understand, but the more we do know about a child's home environment the more it helps us to understand when anything goes wrong at school.'

Lucy stared at the coffeepot. It was the same pattern as the tea service which her parents had bought her for a wedding present. She wanted to pick it up and look underneath to see if it was the same make.

'The only thing I can think of is me not being able to give her the same attention now that I'm doing my degree. Obviously I'm not at home as much now. And even when I am in, I've always got some work to do.'

'How's the course going?'

'Very well. It's hard work, but I'm enjoying it.'

'Yes, it must have been a big change for the whole family.'

'It was.' Lucy spoke defiantly, as if she was being attacked. 'Mathew seems to have adapted all right though.'

'Oh, he's all right at school. No trouble at all. Gets on like a house on fire with everybody. I suppose he's a bit too young to understand what's really happening. I think the younger they are the easier they find it to accept change.'

What did she mean, *really happening*? Did she know something? Perhaps *everybody* knew! Perhaps somebody had seen her in town with Dave, and it was all round the village. The thought made her blush and she had a drink to hide her face.

'More coffee, Mrs Downs?'

Lucy's hand trembled as she leaned forward, and she had to hold the cup steady on the saucer.

'It's difficult to know what to do about it though. I stay at home as much as I can.'

'Yes, it is difficult. I agree.'

'Anyway, it might be nothing to do with me being at university. She might be just going through a phase. Children are up and down all the time.'

'I agree with you, but in Tracey's case I think it's more serious than that. At the moment she is a very unhappy little girl.'

Lucy looked out of the window at the deserted playground while she searched for another spurious excuse. But she could no longer deceive herself. She knew the reasons for Tracey's unhappiness better than anyone.

'I suppose I shall have to try harder, that's all.'

'What about your husband, is he supportive? Conflict between husband and wife in situations like yours can often cause stress in children.'

'No, Phil's all right. He couldn't do any more really. It's amazing how he's come to terms with it all.'

'Well, that's the main thing. If the family is working together, children can overcome all kinds of difficulties. Tracey probably just needs a little extra attention, that's all. Children are great ones for routine and they're soon put out by any changes. She probably feels that you've deserted her in some way.'

When Lucy left the school, she was determined to go straight home and telephone Dave to tell him that she could not get away. How could she now that this had happened? Surely her daughter's welfare was more important than a furtive weekend in Stratford? No, she could not possibly go now. They would have to go some other time. Tracey must come first. Dave would be disappointed, obviously, but he would understand. But would he though? He did not seem to care about children. He never asked about Tracey or Mathew, or mentioned nephews or nieces, or children of friends. He never said anything about his own childhood unless Lucy asked him. He was still a mystery to her. He was 'close', as her mother would have said.

What a pity. And she had been looking forward to it so much. She had planned what she was going to wear, and had already packed an unused card of pills in case there was any late confusion and she forgot her current one. Dave had arranged the hotel and tickets for the theatre. He said he knew a nice little French restaurant where they could eat afterwards . . .

The tingle of anticipation returned, and instead of going

straight home to phone Dave as she had intended, Lucy found herself going the long way round, along Robin Mount and Chaffinch Drive. What would he say when she told him? It was hard to tell. He would probably think that she had lost her nerve at the last minute, and was making it all up to get out of going. Whatever his reaction, Lucy could not imagine him asking her to go again.

At least Phil would be pleased. He would probably celebrate her change of plan by treating them all to a visit to the caravan and camping exhibition that he had been talking about for the last couple of weeks.

Lucy unlocked the kitchen door and hung up her coat. She decided to have a cup of coffee to compose herself before phoning Dave. Then she would ring him. Yes: definitely . . .

As Lucy turned the corner by the senate building, she was relieved to see that Dave was already there. She would have felt conspicuous waiting on the pavement with her suitcase. Dave saw her coming and opened the car door. She passed him the case, then ducked quickly into the car. It was like making a getaway

Lucy was too nervous to speak as they drove through town. She was convinced that everyone was looking at her, and when they stopped at pedestrian crossings and traffic lights, she wanted to crawl under the seat and hide in case she saw anyone she knew. What if Phil had followed her? What if he had suspected something all the time and laid a trap? What if he suddenly drove up alongside and forced them off the road? She had to fight the urge to turn round and look. And why did Dave have to have a yellow car? Why couldn't he have chosen something more subdued like brown or blue? Lucy felt like baling out. She had only been travelling ten minutes and she was a nervous wreck already.

She began to relax when they left the familiar city roads behind and reached open country. At least the animals in the fields flanking the road could not tell on her. Dave sensed the change in her mood and patted her knee.

'Feeling better now?'

'A bit.'

'Did you have any second thoughts before you set off?'

'Not really.'

'I wondered if you might have changed your mind at the last minute.'

Lucy watched two lambs tugging hungrily at their mother's teats.

'Why should I?'

It seemed unnatural going on a journey without the children. She was used to having them behind her in the car. They would have been wanting a sandwich by this time if they had been here now. She would have given them an apple and told them they were saving the sandwiches for lunch. There would have been an argument then as to who had got the biggest apple, or the one with the most red on it. Questions, answers. Mathew's face at her ear. Phil telling them to sit still. One of them wanting to stop for a wee . . .

'I thought we might tootle along the ordinary roads, if that's all right with you. It's much more pleasant than travelling on the motorway.'

Lucy did not mind which way they went; she was still getting used to the novelty of being able to sit still and quiet and not having to keep turning round. But she was still nervous, and when they stopped at a pub at lunchtime, she sat at a table in the corner of the room while Dave ordered the food and drinks.

She could not finish her sandwich. Each bite stuck in her throat. She felt embarrassed leaving it, but Dave understood how she felt and he reached across the table and squeezed her hand.

'We don't have to go, Lucy, if you don't want to. We can always turn back, you know.'

Lucy nodded and tried to smile. She looked like a lost child being reassured that her mother would be along soon to collect her.

'I don't want to turn back. I want to go.'

'Are you sure?'

'Positive. Anyway, it's too late to turn back now. I'll be all right. Just be patient with me. I've never done anything like this before. It takes a bit of getting used to.'

'Would you like another drink?'

'No, thanks, I'd like to go now.'

Lucy felt better as soon as they arrived in Stratford. There was so much to see, so many quaint buildings and interesting shops to look at. Dave did not need a tourist guide; he obviously knew the town well. He took her to Shakespeare's birthplace and Anne Hathaway's cottage, and pointed out buildings of historical interest, as they walked about the streets. They shared some expensive hand-made chocolates, and visited an antique shop where Dave knew the owner. They held hands, and sometimes Dave would put his arm round her and kiss her on the cheek. She had never known such attention.

But she could not forget the children. They were with her all the time. She no longer felt guilty because she had left them, and she did not want to be at home. She wanted them here with her, sharing this new experience. She wanted to show them the half-timbered buildings, the theatre, the swans on the river. There was so much to show them, so much to share. When they went into a tea shop, she knew which cakes the children would have chosen: Tracey a vanilla slice, Mathew a chocolate eclair. Dave chose an eclair too. How would he have got on with them? Would they have liked him? As Lucy poured the tea, she realised that it was the first time she had spent a night away from the children since they were born. It was hardly surprising that she could not stop thinking about them.

They passed a toyshop on their way back to the car, and Lucy said that she was going in to buy presents for the children. Dave said he would wait for her in the bookshop down the street.

Lucy bought a little wooden lorry for Mathew and a rag doll for Tracey. What would Tanya have thought about such blatant sexual stereotyping? she wondered, as she paid for them at the counter. (What did she think of it herself?) For once, she did not care. She knew they would be thrilled by what she had bought them, and that was all that mattered to her just then. Anyway, what did Tanya know about bringing up children? It was all theory to her. 'That doesn't negate the principle of the argument,' she had once replied, when they were discussing the morality of buying children toy guns. 'Anyhow,' she had concluded, 'I wouldn't have any children. I think it's immoral bringing them into an already overcrowded world. The aim should be to reduce the population of this planet, not add to it.' Perhaps so, Lucy conceded, as she picked up the bag, and wondered what Phil was giving Tracey and Mathew for their tea.

Dave was still browsing in the bookshop when Lucy went in. She wondered whether to buy Phil a book. She knew that he wouldn't be expecting anything, but it seemed mean buying presents for the children and excluding him. But how could she with Dave there? She could always pretend that she was buying it for herself. But she did not want to look at cookery books, and she was afraid that his taste in war stories and thrillers would give a bad impression. She decided to buy him something from the newsagent's in the village when she arrived home.

Dave bought several paperbacks. Outside the shop, he opened the bag and took one out.

'Here you are, a little present for you.'

Lucy could not have looked more grateful if she had been given a gold watch.

'For me? Thank you.'

It would be her special book from now on. She would always treasure it.

'Do you know Margaret Atwood?'

'No, not at all.'

'I'll be interested to hear what you think.'

Lucy wanted to show him what she had bought for the children, but he did not ask to look, even when she opened the bag to put her book inside.

The hotel was in a village a few miles out of town. It stood back from the road and overlooked the green. As they got out of the car, Dave said that the building dated from the sixteenth century. Lucy would not have known. It just looked very old and very beautiful to her, like something on a country calendar. A gnarled wisteria framed the doorway, and in the late afternoon sunlight the stonework glowed warm and mellow.

'I can't believe it, Dave. It's lovely.'

'Yes, it is rather pretty. I've stayed here a couple of times before.'

Lucy wondered who with as she followed him inside, but she was too excited to let the question trouble her for long. She had never stayed in a hotel like this before. She had always considered such places out of her class. Dave approached the desk and rang for the receptionist as if he was resident.

The hallway opened out into a lounge with an ingle-nook fireplace, chintz-covered armchairs, and tripod tables containing magazines and vases of daffodils. A standard lamp in the corner helped the glow from the fire, and it looked so comfortable and warm that Lucy wanted to pull up a chair, kick off her shoes and put her feet up on the brass fender.

As they climbed the stairs, a grandfather clock chimed on the landing, the measured calm of each stroke matching perfectly the tranquil atmosphere. They walked along a low corridor with creaking floorboards, and as soon as Dave opened the door of their room, Lucy crossed to the window and looked out.

The view was from the back of the hotel towards a wood in the distance. Clusters of nests were visible in the bare branches, and the strident calls of circling rooks drifted across the intervening meadows.

'I'm glad we've got a view.'

'You won't have much chance to enjoy it, I'm afraid. It'll be dark soon.'

'That doesn't matter. As long as I know it's there, that's the main thing.'

'Do you like the room?'

'Yes, it's nice and cosy.'

She went round everything then like an inquisitive child: first the wardrobe (the rail was thick with wooden hangers), then the dressing-table drawers and mirror (two expressions, a smile and mocking grimace), the bed, the chair (how prominent her engagement and wedding rings looked when she gripped the arm), the taps in the bathroom and finally the lavatory. She wished she had closed the door when she heard the noise she was making, but she sat it out, blushing and determined not to be prudish.

When she came out, Dave said, 'Let's get undressed.'

'What now?'

'Yes, I want to look at you.'

Dave undressed quickly, then lay on the bed and watched Lucy take off her clothes. She felt embarrassed being scrutinised like that; she wanted to hurry up and hide herself against him. But she controlled herself, and arranged her skirt and jumper neatly on the armchair before crossing the room and climbing on top of him. It wasn't the first time she had undressed in front of him, but it was the first time she had done it so deliberately and in daylight. On previous occasions, she had always been protected by drawn curtains or poor light. Coming up for air, Dave said, 'You've got lovely tits, Lucy.'

Lucy shook her head. Her breasts shook too as if agreeing with her.

'No, not now. They've been spoiled by the ravages of child rearing.'

'I knew someone at Cambridge who was obsessed with tits. He used to hire a prostitute just to watch her take her bra off. All she had to do was keep taking it off and putting it back on again.'

'Sounds kinky to me.'

'Yes, I think he went into the church eventually.'

Lucy lay on her back while Dave, crouching beside her, began to kiss her body, working from her breasts downward. When he reached her stomach, she covered herself with her hands and turned away.

'What's the matter?'

'Nothing.'

'Come on. What have I done wrong?'

He persuaded her to turn over, but she still would not look at him.

'You haven't done anything wrong. I just feel ugly down there, that's all.'

'Well, you don't look ugly, I can assure you.'

He tried to remove her hands, but she pushed him off and stretched her skin to emphasise the blue lines marbling the flesh.

'Look at these awful stretch marks from being pregnant. And this spare tyre.' She pinched her waist. 'I've had that since Mathew was born six years ago, and it doesn't matter how hard I try, it never goes away.'

Suddenly, she thought of the slim, bronzed girl on the beach at Torquay and felt peeved at the sight of her own marred flesh. Dave soothed her by kissing her stomach, then aroused her by running the tip of his tongue along the offending seams. From above, he looked as if he was licking a cigarette paper. He nuzzled her, then dipped deeper as she opened her legs. What thin hips he had. What a slender back. She moved her hand up his spine and held his head. He looked so fragile, more like a boy than a man kneeling between her legs. She wanted to hurt him. She clenched her teeth and grasped his hair, and when the release came, and she cried out repeatedly, she dug her nails into his back and made him cry out too. He made a muffled sound, like somebody gagged.

Afterwards, lying on the bed together, Lucy said, 'I don't really understand what you see in me, Dave.'

'What do you mean?'

'Well, just think of all the women at university with no ties or domestic commitments. I don't know why you bother.'

'A lot of those women are still girls. They haven't done anything. They have nothing to say.'

'They've done more than me, that is a certainty.'

'Don't be silly. Most of them have come straight from school

178

from straight middle-class homes. Their ideas are utterly predictable.'

'They're no more predictable than mine: left school at sixteen, engaged at nineteen, married at twenty-one. What's so original about that?'

'Nothing. But it's experience, and look at you now. Look how far you've come. It takes courage to do what you're doing, Lucy, and I admire you for it. Anyway,' he pushed his knees between her thighs, 'I fancy you as well.'

Lucy gripped his leg to stop it going further.

'Do you know something? You're the only man I've ever been with since I met Phil.'

'Really!' He made her fidelity sound freakish. 'I wish you hadn't told me that.'

'Why?'

'It makes me feel a bit of a heel.'

'But not too much of one presumably . . . Dave?' Lucy moved her head back and looked at him seriously. 'I hope you're not using me. I mean, I hope I'm more to you than just a bit on the side.'

Dave looked her straight in the eyes when he answered.

'I'm using you no more than you're using me, Lucy. And as for being "a bit on the side", as you so charmingly put it, you're the one with the spouse and two children at home, you know, not me.'

'Yes, I know that. But I do mean something to you, don't I?'

She looked troubled and sounded desperate for reassurance.

'Of course you do. I've told you.' He pulled her close to him and stroked her back. 'There's one thing we've got to get clear though, Lucy. I'm not quite sure what you want from me, but I'm making no promises. No promises and no plans. Let's just try and have a good time together when we can. All right?'

Lucy nodded and smiled, but she did not look happy.

'Anyway, come on, we'd better get ready, or we're not going to have time for a drink before the show starts.'

He smacked her lightly on the buttocks and got off the bed.

'Run the bath for me, will you, Dave?'

While the bath was filling up, Lucy lay on the bed and listened to the distant clamour of the rooks across the fields. But after a while their discord disturbed her, and she went quickly into the bathroom, where the running water immediately drowned their noise.

*

Lucy's mood changed as soon as they entered the theatre, and she felt the buzz of expectation in the crowded foyer. She bought a programme, looked on the bookstalls, and studied the photographs of past productions on the walls. They had drinks in the bar, and finally, when the lights dimmed and Dave took her hand, Lucy felt so emotionally charged that she shivered and tears came to her eyes. She felt fierce and defiant and, despite all the guilt and anguish she had suffered, she was still glad that she was here, with Dave, and not at home with her family. It had all been worth it. Yes. It had. It had!

Next morning at breakfast she wasn't so sure. She had a headache. It was raining. She was going home. Dave poured her a cup of coffee.

'What time did you say you'd be back?'

'Teatime. About five or six.'

'That's great. It gives us another day almost. We could go somewhere. How about Warwick Castle? Or Coventry Cathedral perhaps? Do you know I've never seen it? I've been meaning to go for years, but it's the thought of the town that puts me off.'

Lucy had not seen it either, but she had never been troubled by the omission. She buttered a slice of toast and said nothing.

'You're very subdued this morning.'

'I feel a bit fragile, that's all. I must have had too much wine last night. I'll be all right.'

'Are you sure? We don't have to visit those places if you don't want to. They were just suggestions as they're on the way home. We can play it by ear if you like. Or perhaps you would like to suggest somewhere?'

Lucy did not know anywhere to suggest. She knew little of inland Britain: she was only familiar with places on the coast. But even if she could have suggested somewhere to go, she wasn't sure if she wanted to walk about hand in hand looking at historic buildings. Yesterday, she would have gone anywhere, looked at anything with him. But today she felt differently. She was still troubled by what had happened in the night . . .

She woke up sweating and confused. She had her arm around Dave, but she thought she was at home in bed with Phil. She listened for the children. Were they safe? She had just had a terrifying and vivid dream about them. The house was on fire and they were trapped in an upstairs window. She kept urging them to jump. But they just stood there staring down at her impassively as if unaware of the danger they were in. Something was banging, banging . . . She realised where she was. The wind had strengthened in the night, and the old sash window was rattling in its frame. She took her arm off Dave and turned over. What was she doing here? What had he meant by 'no promises'? She turned back again for comfort and reassurance, but Dave was asleep facing the other way.

'More toast?'

'No, thank you. I'd like some coffee though.'

After he had refilled both cups and ordered a fresh pot, Dave said, 'I know. How about calling in at my parents' house for lunch? It's only half an hour's drive from here. I'm sure they would love to meet you.'

Lucy began to stir her coffee as if it was full of sugar lumps.

'We can't do that, Dave. We can't just drop in.'

'I shall have to ring anyway. Mother will be furious if she discovers that I've been so near and not called.'

'But she might not have enough food in for us as well.'

Dave's laugh was loud enough to distract the other residents from their breakfasts, and Lucy blushed without realising what she had said wrong. Dave reached across the marmalade and patted her hand.

'I don't think you need worry about that. I think mother might manage to scrape a couple of crusts together for us.'

Dave made the telephone call in the hallway after he had settled the bill. He wanted to pay the full amount but Lucy insisted on sharing it. She stood by the luggage and watched him through the glass. He kept smiling into the receiver, and it was obvious that whoever he was speaking to was delighted to hear from him.

'First the good news,' he said, as he folded back the door and came out of the booth. 'They've already arranged to go out for lunch. Now the bad news. Mother would like us to call in for coffee.'

He picked up both bags before Lucy could reach for her own.

'The old hypocrite. She says she can't understand why we didn't stay the night.'

As they drove through the rich, well-ordered countryside, Lucy glimpsed large houses through gates and behind trees. She tried to work out their value by comparing them with her own house . . . Who owned them? How could they afford them? What did they do?

She soon found out who owned one of the houses, when they turned up a long drive flanked by rhododendrons, and stopped on a gravel forecourt in front of a double-fronted stone house.

'Here we are, home sweet home.'

He opened his door, but Lucy just sat there, gazing up at the house.

'It's big, isn't it?'

'I think it was a rectory originally,' as if this somehow explained its size. 'Father bought it for a song years ago. It was in terrible repair at the time.'

'How old is it?'

'Early. Queen Anne, I think.'

Queen Anne? Lucy did not know there had been one. Not wishing to display her ignorance any further, she left it at that and got out of the car.

The house looked even bigger from the bottom of the steps. It had two, full-length windows at each side of the door, corresponding upper windows and a window above the door. The effect was pleasingly symmetrical like the design of a doll's house. Lucy turned round and looked across a wide lawn towards a stand of pine trees, behind which a bank of daffodils coloured the spaces between their trunks.

Lucy hugged herself and inhaled the sharp, clean air.

'Oh, it's lovely, Dave. It's fantastic.'

'Yes, there are worse spots to live, I suppose.'

'Fancy being brought up in a place like this.'

'I wasn't brought up here. I was brought up at school. I only visited here during the holidays.'

Inside the house, the faint, continuous barking of a dog grew suddenly louder as it ran into the hall. Dave smiled in anticipation, but before he could reach the door, it was opened from inside and a black labrador squeezed out and nearly knocked him down the steps. Dave crouched down and fussed it while it licked his face and ears.

'That's enough, Bruno! Come along now! That's quite enough of that!'

But the woman in the doorway wasn't really concerned about the dog; she was too busy scrutinising Lucy.

'Come along, David. We'll all catch our death of cold standing out here.'

They entered the house. Dave kissed his mother's cheek and hugged her briefly before introducing her to Lucy.

'Pleased to meet you, my dear. Let me take your coat. Take Lucy into the drawing room to meet your father, David, while I make some coffee.'

She enclosed Lucy's hand between her own as if she had known her for years. The dog sniffed Lucy's coat as she took it off, and its claws scraped the marble tiles as it fussed around her legs.

'Come along, Bruno. You come and help me in the kitchen.'

The dog accompanied her halfway down the hall, then turned back and followed Dave and Lucy into the drawing room. Lucy saw the same view across the lawn to the pine trees, only this time a neater version, framed by the elegant windows. Mr Pybus was standing in front of a log fire reading a comic. As Lucy approached him, she felt as if she had stepped over the rope in a room of a stately home.

'Father, I'd like you to meet Lucy.'

Mr Pybus closed the comic and they shook hands.

'Delighted to meet you, Lucy! Please sit down!'

He indicated a variety of seats arranged about the room. Lucy chose a leather chesterfield by the fire and Mr Pybus sat down in a wing chair across the hearth from her. There's no wonder they've got such loud voices, Lucy thought, as she looked at him across several yards of Persian carpet. The rooms are so big that they have to shout to make themselves heard.

'This is not the usual level of my reading material, I can assure you,' Mr Pybus said, placing the comic on a tripod table in the corner.

Dave sat between them on the padded fender and grinned down at him.

'Oh, I don't know. It's about on a par with the *Telegraph* I would have thought.'

Mr Pybus stretched his legs, bringing his brogues close to his son's satin sneakers.

'You can scoff; but you'll return to the fold eventually, in spite of all that radical clap-trap which you subscribe to at the moment. It's the political equivalent of sowing your wild oats, that's all.'

Dave laughed but he did not deny it. He pointed at the comic on the table.

'As a matter of interest, why were you reading that?'

'We're thinking of making a bid for the company. I was just sampling the product, that was all.'

Mrs Pybus entered the room pushing a tea trolley and talking as she came. The labrador got up from Dave's feet and went to meet her, then, wagging its tail as if it hadn't seen her for months, accompanied her back to the group by the fire.

'. . . Here we are. I'm terribly sorry about lunch, but we couldn't really cancel at such short notice. If only David had let us know earlier . . .'

She addressed herself to Lucy while she arranged the cups and poured the coffee. Dave stood up from the fender and Mr Pybus leaned forward attentively in his chair, both of them giving the impression that they were helping, without actually doing anything.

'. . . He's such a forgetful boy sometimes. I told him on the telephone that you should have stayed here. It's ridiculous spending all that money on hotels, especially as they're so hideously expensive. Joan Bishop was telling me only the other day how much it had cost them when they went up to town recently for a few days. Thank God we have the flat, that's all I can say. Have a biscuit, Lucy.'

'No, thank you.'

'I can't say I blame you. They were a present from Fortnum and Mason, but I think they're pretty dreadful myself. Far too sweet for my liking. David will have one no doubt. He has a sweet tooth like his father . . .'

After she had served the coffee, Mrs Pybus pulled up a chair near her husband, while David resumed his seat on the fender. Lucy felt isolated on the chesterfield on her own. She wanted Dave to sit by her to even up the sides. There was a short silence between them while they drank their coffee, and the only sounds in the room were the chink of crockery and the crackle of burning logs. Mr Pybus placed his cup on the table and turned to Lucy.

'Did you enjoy the play last night, Lucy?'

'Yes, I thought it was a good production.'

That was what Dave had said about it, so she felt safe with her answer.

'Which one are they doing at the moment, by the way?'

For a second or two, Lucy could not remember. She was thinking about what Mrs Pybus had said about the biscuits, and the question took her by surprise. The others waited. Lucy could feel her colour beginning to rise.

'All's Well That Ends Well.'

'Ah yes.'

That nearly didn't though, Lucy thought, disguising her relief by leaning forward and taking a biscuit from the plate on the trolley. Mrs Pybus stood up and went round the cups again with the coffeepot.

'We went to see *Othello* just before Christmas. You know, it always worries me that play. I can never understand why Iago is so beastly to the poor fellow. There seems to be no reason for it at all as far as I can see . . . Talking of blacks, David. Did you know that Polly Hanstock is running around with a Nigerian? Very distinguished family, I understand, but all the same . . .'

Lucy noticed her teaspoon as she picked it up to stir her coffee. It had a faded crest on the handle, and the bowl was worn thin at the end from countless stirrings. It looked very old. She guessed it was silver.

Mr Pybus picked up a silver cigarette box from the tripod table and opened the lid.

'Would you like a cigarette, Lucy?'

She refused, even though she would have liked one just to see what kind they were.

'Do you mind if I smoke?'

'Not at all.'

Lucy was surprised that he should ask. After all, it was his house.

'Dave?'

'I'll have one of my own, thanks.'

He took a paper packet out of his jacket pocket and tapped out a cigarette.

'Good Lord! You're not still smoking that French muck, are you?'

Dave laughed and lit their cigarettes. The crumpled packet and disposable lighter seemed like deliberate provocation in the face of such pervasive good taste.

'You'll be killing yourself with those things, David. They really are dreadfully strong.'

Dave ignored his mother's warning and inhaled deeply, as if he was breathing mountain air. Mrs Pybus looked disgusted with him and turned to Lucy.

'He's always had a perverse streak. We wanted him to go to Oxford like his brother Tim, but he insisted on the other place. It's a wonder he didn't go the whole hog and choose somewhere ridiculous like Liverpool or Leeds.'

Dave crossed his arms, and the cigarette cocked in his fingers pointed to an oil painting on the wall above his mother's head.

'I did consider it briefly at school.'

'You didn't!' She made it sound like an admission of treason. 'You never mentioned it to us.'

'There was no need. Dr Noyes soon put the idea out of my head. He didn't even treat the question seriously. "We don't admit to the existence of any other universities outside Oxford and Cambridge at this school," he said.'

'Quite right too. You must have been insane.'

Mr Pybus agreed with her, and when they looked at Lucy to see what she thought, she began to nod vigorously too. She stopped, angry with herself. What did it matter to her which university he had gone to? And anyway, what was wrong with Liverpool and Leeds?

As she lifted her cup, she noticed the picture on the saucer. It depicted a hunt gathered on the lawn of a country house. One of the huntsmen was raising his top hat to two ladies, also on horseback. The hounds were milling about the horse's legs, and a servant girl was handing up a stirrup cup to another huntsman. She was the only person on the ground. Just her and the dogs.

'Pretty, aren't they?'

Lucy replaced her cup and looked across at Mrs Pybus.

'Yes, they are.'

'The set is called "Our Heritage". Judy, David's wife, bought them for me. Do you remember, David?' He wasn't listening, but when he heard his name he turned and nodded all the same. 'She got them at Harrod's sale. The most fearful scrimmage, she said, but you can pick up the most extraordinary bargains.'

A clock chimed faintly somewhere in the house. Lucy picked up the count after several strokes and she had only reached seven when they ended. She sneaked a look at her watch to see what the real time was. Mr Pybus said, 'I understand you're a member of the English Department too, Lucy.'

'Yes, I'm in my first year.'

'Are you enjoying it?'

'Very much. I'm finding it hard work though.'

'Yes, it always is hard settling into a new job. Where were you before?'

Before? What a funny question. Where did he think she was?

'I was at home looking after the children. When the youngest went off to school, I decided that I would like to take a degree.'

She smiled as if expecting praise for her enterprise, but no one spoke. Looks were exchanged between Dave's parents and Lucy realised that she had said something wrong. Mrs Pybus poured herself more coffee. It was so quiet in the room that it sounded as if she was running a bath.

'You're an undergraduate then?'

Lucy was bewildered. What did she think she was, a lollipop woman?

'Yes. Dave's one of my tutors.'

'I see.' Mrs Pybus tried to smile but it was a sickly effort, like someone trying to be brave while having a wound dressed. 'There appears to have been some misunderstanding. David led us to believe that you were on the staff of the English Department, not a *student* in it.'

She could not have been more disparaging if Lucy had admitted to being a cleaner. Dave slowly shook his head at her and smiled. He looked as if he was enjoying the confusion. Lucy wasn't. She felt humiliated. She wondered if he had set her up on purpose just to amuse himself.

'I said nothing of the kind. I told you that Lucy was a friend of mine from the department, that's all.'

'Yes, I know, David, but . . .'

'Anyway, what does it matter?'

'It doesn't matter at all. It's just that you're so infuriatingly elliptical at times, David.'

Lucy agreed with her. She was more annoyed with him than with his mother. She had got the measure of her now. She was nothing but a snob. Lucy knew what to expect from now on. But Dave? She never knew where she stood with him. It was like trying to nail jelly to a wall. Why had he brought her here at the last minute? Was he just amusing himself? Had he brought her to shock his parents? Their son going around with a married woman with two children *and* from a lower social class. Was she just another provocation, like his satin sneakers and French cigarettes?

'It must be tremendously hard work trying to study and rear a family at the same time. Tell me, do you get any help?'

Lucy did not allow Mrs Pybus to hunt for information. She told her straight out. Yes, it was hard work but her husband helped. What did her husband do? He was a welder. Ten minutes earlier she would have omitted his job and said that he worked for an engineering firm. Mr Pybus wanted to know who he worked for, and when she told him, he said, yes, he knew the company well. He looked as if he was going to say something else (something

187

important perhaps?), but decided against it and smiled at her, almost apologetically, she thought.

Lucy answered their questions honestly, with no ambiguity and no sense of shame. She kept looking at Dave as if he was doing the asking, until gradually he turned away, like a dog being outstared by its angry master.

When she had finished with Lucy, Mrs Pybus turned to her son.

'By the way, David, before I forget. Did you know that Judy called in to see us last week?'

She glanced across at Lucy to check her reaction. There wasn't one: nothing that Mrs Pybus could see anyway.

'Really? What was she doing in this part of the country?'

He tried to make his enquiry sound casual, but his real interest was revealed by the way that he watched his mother while he waited for an answer.

'She had been in Bath. She's doing a programme there on the recent excavations underneath the Pump Room. She seemed terribly thrilled by it. It's her first job as a producer, you know.'

'Yes . . .' Too late he realised his mistake. 'She told me about it when I saw her at Christmas.'

Lucy stared at him. She had never seen him blush before. If she had been standing in front of him, she would have pushed him over the fender into the fire.

She picked up her bag from the chesterfield and stood up.

'Could you tell me where the toilet is, please?'

'Of course.' Mrs Pybus pointed towards the door. 'There's a lavatory along the hall. Or a bathroom upstairs at the end of the first-floor landing, if you prefer to use that.'

Dave stood up and stepped towards her.

'I'll show you if you like.'

'No, it's all right. I'll find it on my own, thanks.'

She left the room and pulled the door shut behind her. It felt heavy, like the door of a church. She went upstairs to get as far away from them as possible, but she could still hear their voices when she reached the first floor. Dave said something. His parents laughed. Lucy hurried along the corridor, and even though some of the bedroom doors were open, she did not pause to peep inside.

She locked the bathroom door after her, then leaned back on it and looked round. It was the biggest bathroom she had ever seen. It was as big as the main bedroom at home. Everything was on a grand scale. There were twin wash basins, a massive cast-iron bath with ball and claw feet, and a radiator which reminded her of the 'pipes' at school. Even the lavatory bowl was on a pedestal. She walked across the room and sniffed the soaps and bath salts. She wanted to turn on the huge taps and wallow in deep water, then wrap herself in the white bath-sheet draped over the towel horse.

Instead, she rinsed her face with cold water and dabbed it dry with a hand towel. She automatically took out her lipstick and removed the cap. But as she raised it to her mouth, she suddenly changed her mind, and with a firm nod to herself in the mirror, replaced it in her bag and left the bathroom.

As she was going downstairs, Lucy paused on the half-landing and looked through a tall window into a paved courtyard sur-rounded by outbuildings. There was an oak tree growing in the middle of the yard and she could hear a missel thrush singing in its branches. She could not find it at first; then she saw it near the top of the tree. She was too far away to make out its markings, but it showed up in clear silhouette against the overcast sky. The wind shook its perch, but the thrush stood up straight, imper-vious to the elements, and its clear, solitary song rang like a challenge across the quiet countryside.

Lucy would have stayed longer at the window if Dave had not come into the hall and noticed her standing there. He walked to the bottom of the stairs and looked up.

'What are you doing there?'

Without waiting for an answer, he ran up the stairs to join her.

'Just looking out. And listening to that missel thrush over there.'

Dave stood behind her with his arms round her waist and listened too.

'Do you know what country people call the missel thrush?'

'The storm cock, don't they?'

'Do you know why?'

'They're supposed to be harbingers of stormy weather, aren't they?'

'Yes, something like that.'

Lucy hardly spoke on the way home. After one prolonged silence, Dave said, 'Are you all right?'

'Of course I am.'

'It's nothing I've said, is it?'

189

'Of course it isn't. Why should it be?'

Then, after several more miles of listening to the sweep of the windscreen wiper: 'I hope my mother didn't annoy you. She means no harm. She goes on a bit, that's all. They were really glad we'd called. Father was quite taken by you.'

'What does he do, your dad?'

'Nothing much now except shoot and fish. He's still on the boards of one or two companies; property mainly.'

'He seemed nice.'

Dave laughed.

'Yes, like a sleeping tiger's nice.'

'What do you mean?'

'Do you remember Lonrho and all that uproar over asset-stripping? The unacceptable face of capitalism, as Ted Heath called it.'

Lucy nodded. She had vague memories of the scandal, but she could not recall any of the details.

'Well, father had his snout well and truly in that trough. He made a fortune; in the process of which he closed down dozens of factories and put thousands of people out of work.'

Lucy stared out at the sodden fields and wondered if her father had been one of them.

Tracey laid the knives, Mathew the forks, and Phil had given them two spoons each so there would be no arguing. They usually ate in the kitchen, but tonight they were using the dining area in the lounge, as a special treat for Lucy when she arrived home.

After they had set the table, the children went back into the kitchen to see if there was anything else they could do to help. They were longing to see their mum again. She had only been away for one night, but it had seemed like ages to them. Mathew had cried for her when he went to bed and Tracey, who liked to tease him by calling him a baby, kept quiet this time, because she was nearly crying too. But they weren't crying now. She would soon be home, and setting a place for her at the table was proof of her impending return and made her real again.

Phil took two wine glasses out of the cupboard and gave them one each.

'Here you are, go and put these on the table. And be careful with them. No running, it's not a race.'

Mathew looked up at the wall clock again.

'How long will my mummy be now, daddy?'

Tracey looked at the clock too. If their sight had been tactile, they would have worn the numbers off its face.

'She'll not be long now. She said they'd get back about five o'clock.'

'That's not long, is it, daddy?'

Because Mathew only knew the halves and quarters, and the minute finger was pointing to four, he had phrased his question ambiguously to avoid any insulting remarks from Tracey. The least he could get was reassurance, the exact number of minutes would be a bonus.

'No, love, she'll not be long now.'

Phil was looking forward to seeing Lucy again too. Over the past months, he had gradually learned to accept the changes in his life. He had got used to looking after the children, doing housework, and seeing his wife less often. But this time, her absence had been different; and last night, when he was watching television with the children, the house had seemed incomplete without her. When he woke up in the morning, and she wasn't there beside him in bed, he panicked momentarily until he remembered where she was.

He remembered the wine. In one of his cookery books, he had read that you were supposed to open the bottle an hour before drinking to allow it to 'breathe'. He wouldn't have believed it if he hadn't read it. He thought it was like beer or Coca Cola, and would go flat if the top was left off. He wasn't interested in wine, but Lucy had acquired a taste for it since starting university, so he had bought it as a surprise to celebrate her return.

He uncorked the bottle and carried it through to the dining room himself to make sure that Tracey and Mathew had set the table correctly. They were both watching for Lucy out of the window so they did not notice him rearrange the cutlery. He went back into the kitchen and checked the potatoes in the oven. It was just a matter of waiting now. He had prepared the salad and mixed the dressing: all he had to do now was grill the steaks when she came in.

'She's here, daddy! She's here!'

Phil felt his heart bump. He glanced at the clock. She was early, and irrationally he imagined that she had told the coach driver to hurry up so that she could get back home. Tracey came running into the kitchen.

'Quick, daddy, the candle!'

Phil had the matches ready in his pocket. He hurried into the dining room, and while Tracey and Mathew fought to open the front door, he lit the candle which he had bought specially for the occasion. He watched the flame strengthen, then switched off the light and closed the door behind him just as Lucy came into the house. She smiled at him over the children. She looked pale and weary. She looked like someone who had travelled a long way. Tracey and Mathew kept jumping up at her. If she had patted their heads, it would have looked as if she was making them bounce. She hugged them to her, then crouched down and kissed them and stroked their cheeks against hers. 'Mummy! Mummy!' they kept shouting, as they vied for attention, and tried to tell her what they had done while she had been away. Lucy smiled and kept nodding. These are my children, she thought, as she watched their flushed, excited faces. That is my husband. This is my home. Gently, she disengaged herself and stood up. Phil put his arms round her and kissed her. They were all hugging her now.

'Have you had a nice time?'

'Yes, lovely, thanks.'

Tracey tugged Phil's trousers and they exchanged conspiratorial looks.

'Can we show her now, daddy?'

'Show me what?'

Mathew started to jump up and down again.

'It's a surprise! It's a surprise!'

They led her into the dining room, and when Lucy saw the white cloth, the bottle of wine and the flickering candle, the flame shattered into points of light, then went out as the tears flooded her eyes.

The following week, Lucy told Phil that she was leaving him. She had not meant to: not just then anyway. She wasn't even certain if that was what she wanted to do. She was trying to do some preparatory reading and make notes for an essay on Free Trade Imperialism, but she could not concentrate. She felt listless, and for no particular reason had been impatient with the children when she had put them to bed. She wanted something to eat even though she wasn't hungry. She wanted a drink, but definitely not beer, which was all there was in the house. (If she had been in a pub, she still wouldn't have known what to choose.) She wanted a cigarette, but she hadn't got any. Finally, to try to ease her restlessness, she went into the kitchen to make a cup of coffee.

Phil was cleaning the children's shoes at the table. He had spread a newspaper across the table top to catch the dirt and specks of polish, and as Lucy watched him while she waited for the kettle to boil, she became increasingly irritated at his absorption in what to her was an irksome task. He dabbed the polish with the brush as if he was frightened of hurting it, then applied it with little circular movements which caressed the leather. If the shoes had been dogs, they would have rolled over on their backs and panted in ecstasy. Working methodically from the front to the back, he covered every inch of leather, and the heels received the same loving attention as the toes. Lucy wanted to knock them out of his hands, screw up the newspaper and tip the polish onto the floor. Instead, she said, 'I'm leaving, Phil.'

It just came out. She was terrified. Her mouth dried up and she wanted to run to the lavatory. Phil went rigid, and with his arms up and brush poised, he looked like a waxwork of a valet.

'What do you mean?'

'It's not working, Phil. I think we ought to split up.'

'But why? What's wrong?'

He had a dazed, incredulous air about him, as if he had just been informed of her death.

'I need some time on my own, Phil, to sort things out a bit.'

'What things? I don't know what you mean.'

Lucy shook her head. She seemed irritated by the question. It wasn't as easy as that. She couldn't just reel off the reasons as if they were items on a shopping list. They were as complicated and inextricably knotted as a can of worms. The kettle boiled on the worktop behind her, sending up clouds of steam, and giving her an ethereal quality as if she was already being spirited away.

'Have you met somebody else?'

Again Lucy shook her head.

'Of course I haven't.'

'I don't want you to lie to me, Lucy. If you have, I want to know about it.'

He threw Mathew's shoe onto the table. Lucy winced as if he had thrown it at her.

'I'm not lying to you, Phil.'

'Of course you are. You've met somebody else and you're scared to tell me, aren't you?'

'No, I'm not. If that's all it was, it'd be simple.'

'Well, what the bloody hell is it then? What's the matter with you? What's wrong?'

'Don't shout, Phil.' She crossed the kitchen and closed the door which led into the hall. 'Things are bad enough without wakening the kids up as well.'

'I will shout in a minute if you don't tell me what's going on.'

'There's nothing going on. Not in that way that you mean anyway. I'm confused, Phil. I don't know what I want any more.'

'You want a bloody good hiding, that's what you want. It's university that's the cause of all this, you know that, don't you? I should never have let you go in the first place. We were all right before you went there.'

Lucy picked up a mug from the draining board. It had two pictures of Little Bo-Peep on it. On one side, she was crying because she had lost her sheep, on the other, she was laughing because she had found them.

'Do you want some coffee?'

Phil ignored the question.

'You know what's the matter with you, don't you?'

Lucy slowly unscrewed the lid of the coffee jar. She preferred to drink ground coffee now, but it would look as if she wasn't taking the matter seriously if she started emptying the coffeepot and measuring out the grains.

'I'm not good enough for you any more, am I?'

'Don't be silly.'

'I'm not being silly. It's true. You're not interested in me now. You're not interested in anybody but yourself . . .'

That hurt. But how could she deny it? She did not try. She made a mug of coffee instead and held it in both hands for comfort.

'. . . We never go out together. We never see any of our friends. When was the last time we saw Bob and Sue, or Christine and Ron? They must wonder what's happened to us.'

'I'm too busy, Phil. I don't have the time now . . .'

'You're not too busy to get involved in plays and suchlike, and going tripping off with your university friends. You can always find time for them.'

'But that's all part of my work.'

'Yes, and it's part of something else as well. You've become a right snob, do you know that, Lucy?'

He had accused her of this before, but never with such vehemence as now. Lucy was so upset that her hands trembled and her coffee threatened to spill.

'It's not true.'

'You could have fooled me.'

'Yes, I have changed. But I don't feel superior to anybody. It's nothing to do with that. I'm just different, that's all. I've developed different tastes . . .' She hesitated. How could she continue without sounding patronising? How could she begin to explain? She did not try. She knew that whatever she said would be misinterpreted by Phil. 'Don't think I wanted this to happen, Phil, because I didn't. I had no idea that it would turn out like this, honest.'

Phil picked up Mathew's shoe again and began to polish it, whistling swiftly and tunelessly in time to the brush strokes. Lucy remembered another time when she had heard him whistling in the same nervous way: they were driving to his mother's funeral, the monotone had got on her nerves and she told him to shut up. He did, and immediately started to cry over the steering wheel.

Lucy left the kitchen and went into the lounge in case he stopped whistling now.

Later, in bed, lying sleepless in the darkness with their backs to each other, Phil said, 'Where are you going to live?'

'I don't know. I suppose I'll try and get a flat somewhere.'

'You haven't got anywhere fixed up then?'

'No, not yet.'

'And what about the kids? I hope you've thought about them.'

'Of course I have. I'll take them with me.'

The radiator clanged as it cooled down. Outside, a car door slammed and someone called, 'Goodnight!'

'You'll not, Lucy. They're stopping with me.'

Lucy jerked her head round so quickly that she cricked her neck.

'Don't be ridiculous. You can't look after them. They're coming with me.'

Because they were having to speak quietly, Lucy's statement came out in a violent hiss, like steam being forced out of a pressure cooker. Phil lay still, facing the other way.

'They're not. If you do go, you're going on your own.'

'I'll take them with me. You can't stop me from having them.'

'Can't I? Just try it and see.'

His icy, unspecified threat frightened her. She started to sweat.

'Why, what will you do?'

'I'll take you to court if necessary and fight you for custody '

195

'You wouldn't do that, would you?'

'Yes, I would.'

She could tell he wasn't bluffing.

'You'd lose, you know that, don't you? They always give the mother custody of the children.'

'Not always they don't. It all depends on the circumstances. I'd have a good case.'

His quiet confidence alarmed her. He was too calm about it all. She wanted to shake him and make him mad. She did not like the tone of that disembodied voice in the dark.

'You're just trying to blackmail me, that's all. You're trying to take the children away from me to make me stay at home.'

'I'm not trying to take them anywhere. It's you that's wanting to take them away.'

'Because they belong with me, that's why. I'm their mother. They need me more than they need you.'

'Not now they don't.'

'Of course they do. You're just being awkward to spite me, that's all. You're trying to get your own back because you've been hurt.'

'Listen Lucy . . .' He half turned at last, and spoke in the direction of the ceiling instead of the wall. 'Yes, you're right, I have been hurt, and it'll get worse no doubt because it hasn't sunk in properly yet. It wouldn't be so bad if I could understand what you were going for. At least if it was another man I'd have something to fight against. I might feel like giving you both a good hiding, but at least I'd know where I stood. But this . . .' He shook his head and stared into the darkness. 'I don't get it at all. You must really hate me, Lucy, if you're willing to give everything up and take off on your own.'

'Of course I don't hate you. It's not you, Phil.'

'Well, what is it then? I can't understand you when you say that you don't know what you want any more. You've got a husband who loves you. You've got two lovely kids. You've got a nice home. What more *is there* to want? It's what most people are aiming for in their lives.'

'I know that. You're right, Phil. I know.'

She sounded as if she wanted desperately to be convinced.

'I know it's hard work for you being at university and having to cope at home as well. But you can't blame anybody for that. It was your own choice. Nobody made you go.'

'I know they didn't . . .'

'And don't forget that I've had to adapt as well, you know. It's been hard work for me.'

'I know it has.'

'But I'll tell you something, Lucy.' He turned his head slightly in her direction. 'In spite of everything, I'm still glad that you went to university now. It's changed me as well. It's made me get more involved at home for a start, and I enjoy the kids much more than I ever did before. I really look forward to coming home to them now and getting their teas ready, and I like reading to them and putting them to bed when you're not in. It's been good for me. You might be cleverer than me, Lucy, and what you do at university is miles above my head, but since you've gone there I've learned something as well.' Lucy wanted to reach out and touch him, to put her arms round him and comfort him. 'But if you are determined to leave, and I still can't believe that you will, then I think we've got to put the needs of our Tracey and Mathew first . . . What will it mean if you take them? A tatty flat somewhere in a strange place. And who's going to look after them when you're not in? It'll mean changing schools, making new friends. Their whole lives will be disrupted . . . No, this is their home and this is where they belong. I can cope now, and if I have to, I can give them a stable home life on my own . . .' He waited for Lucy to say something, but she felt too emotional to speak. 'Anyway, why should you have them just because you're their mother? It's not fair. If I lose you, you should lose them. That way, the pain will be shared out.'

Lucy had stopped listening to him. She was trying to imagine what it would be like living without the children . . The prospect was unbearable; she could not do it. She was their mother, they were inseparable, they were *hers*. And even if she did see them less often now, she still loved them as much. She did! She did! And they were *there*, that was the main thing, sharing the same house. They always knew she was coming home, and that she would be there next morning when they got up. And she always would be! She would take them with her in spite of what Phil had said. But where to? In some ways he was right. They did need a stable home. Perhaps she could get a flat first and then . . . No! When she went, they went with her. It would be new and exciting! They would love the change! What about babysitters though? He was right. And late afternoon lectures, who would look after them then . . . ? It was a conspiracy! That's what it was. They were conspiring to keep her at home!

*

For the next few weeks, Lucy did nothing about moving, except worry about it. She attended lectures and tutorials as usual, and conscientiously completed her essays on time. She was grateful for the work; it occasionally made her think about something else. But for most of the time, she carried the pain around inside her like a terrible weight; and one evening, when she was reading the story of *The Wolf and the Seven Little Kids* to the children, her sympathy went out to the wolf for a change. She knew just how he felt as he staggered across the grass for a drink, after the kids inside him had been replaced by six large stones. Perhaps that was the answer: to go and throw herself down a well and end it all.

She did not tell Dave that she was leaving home. She thought about it, and for a rare, mischievous moment, was tempted to tell him that Phil knew everything, that he had thrown her out onto the streets, and that he was coming up to the university to sort him out next. But no, that wasn't fair. She wasn't leaving because of him. She was leaving because of herself. She decided to wait until she had left and found a place of her own before she told him. She rehearsed the scene in her head: it took place in his room; but she experienced no sense of triumph after her revelation.

She told Tanya though. They met accidentally in the union snack bar one lunchtime, and Tanya asked her if she was going to help on the new production. Lucy said no, she had too much work to do; then she told her what was really wrong. It was such a relief to unburden herself. She was desperate to talk to someone about it; but had felt unable to tell her old friends, because she knew they would try to make her change her mind. The end of her marriage would constitute a threat to their own, and in the end, when all else failed, they would say, 'And what about the children, surely your first duty is to them?'

When Lucy put their arguments for them, Tanya said, 'Your first duty is to yourself. You don't have to possess somebody to love them, you know.' Then, 'Are you sure that it's the children who need you so badly, or you that needs them?'

Lucy had thought about this hard and often. It was both. But there was more dependency on her side than she liked to admit. Forthright as ever, Tanya said, 'It's like someone feigning a jail break by unlocking their handcuffs, but keeping the ball and chain on in the hope of being caught.' She finished her coffee and stood up. 'If you've nowhere to go, you can always come and stay with us until you get yourself sorted out. The attic's free. I'm sure the others won't mind.'

Lucy felt immense gratitude and relief as she watched Tanya walk away. She hadn't made her feel like a criminal or a lunatic. There had been no moralising and no sermon. She had listened sympathetically and offered practical help. Lucy smiled after her, and for a few minutes, sitting there eating a cheese roll, she saw again the possibilities of a new way of life.

But her old life dragged on. She could not make the final move. Sometimes, she looked in the local evening newspaper or on the university noticeboards for rented accommodation; but, without ever bothering to go and look at any of them, she decided that all the flats and rooms advertised were either too large or too small, too expensive or in the wrong district. She seriously considered Tanya's offer of the attic room. That might be the answer. She would have her own base, yet still be close to people she knew. She would be less lonely there; it would be an ideal halfway house before moving on to a place of her own.

But she decided against it. If she was going to leave, she wanted to do it cleanly, on her own. She wanted to find her own way. Or was her rejection of Tanya's offer just another excuse for inaction? The struggle went on . . .

They avoided the subject at home. Phil was afraid to ask Lucy when she was leaving in case she gave him a date. By saying nothing, and pretending that everything was normal, he hoped that she would eventually change her mind and decide to stay. But the matter was between them now, and although they were civil with each other, it had forced them apart.

Lucy was so immersed in her problem that she had hardly noticed the arrival of spring. The lengthening days, constant birdsong and fresh colours in the garden had given her little pleasure this time round. Then, one evening, while she was washing the teapots, she caught the smell of cut grass through the open window. The sudden scent took her by surprise and she paused and looked up. She inhaled again, deeply this time, then dried her hands and went outside.

The air was mild and still; Phil was cutting the lawn, the children were playing on the drive, and it was all so evocative of happier times that Lucy forgot her present troubles and remembered how it had once been. It was as if she had never heard of university, had never read a book or struggled with an essay in

199

her life. It was as if she had never worked on the play with Tanya, or been to Stratford with Dave. It was as if the clouds had suddenly shifted and let the sun come through.

Lucy walked across the patio to look at the silver birch which they had planted when they had first moved into the house. She examined the new leaves, then rubbed one of them affectionately between her finger and thumb as if it was the ear of a pet dog. It was the first time that she had looked at the garden properly all year. She was too late for the snowdrops and crocuses, and even the daffodils had shrivelled now. But the polyanthuses made vivid splashes in the borders and the tight heads of the tulips were gaining colour. Lucy bent down and scraped together a handful of grass cuttings. She squeezed them into a damp ball, sniffed it, then, releasing a few blades at a time, left an invisible trail across the lawn to the rabbit hutch at the bottom of the garden.

The rabbit came up to the wire netting to see if she had brought any food. As Lucy scratched his nose, she realised that she had not seen him since last autumn, when his hutch had been carried into the garden shed. She had not even noticed that he had been brought out again. What a lot had happened during his long dark winter under cover. She unfastened the door to give him a proper stroke, and as he flattened his ears, and she ran her hand over his silky white fur, she smiled and suddenly felt dangerously content.

The following morning, Lucy went straight to the noticeboard in the students' union to look for somewhere to live. There were several cards pinned up: one offering a large pleasant bedroom/ study with nice view in exchange for regular evening babysitting (no chance!), a few wanting people to share houses and flats (again she was tempted), and one for a single room with shared kitchen and toilet. Lucy wrote down the address and telephone number, then went to the booths outside the bar and rang the house. A woman answered. She sounded elderly and suspicious, as if she was used to receiving calls of a more dubious nature. Lucy asked her if the room was still vacant . . . When could she come to see it . . . ? Would twelve o'clock be all right?

As soon as she put down the receiver, she changed her mind. She wasn't going! It was a ridiculous idea. She snatched up her folder from the top of the coinbox and hurried away as if she had robbed it. She was so frightened by what she had done, that if anyone had called after her, she would have started to run.

That evening, Lucy could remember little of her visit to Askew Road, just a few gloomy impressions remained: dreary identical houses, antimacassars in cold front rooms, the monkey-puzzle tree in the garden, and Mrs Tyzack's brown dress merging with the front door when she let her in. She remembered the chest of drawers and wardrobe; it was the same kind of dark-stained, utilitarian bedroom furniture that she had known as a child. But what about the wallpaper? And was there a table and chair? She had taken the room after a quick look round from the doorway. She had not even walked across to the window to have a look at the view. She had asked no questions, and heard nothing of what Mrs Tyzack had said about gas and electricity. She had been in such a hurry to leave, that when she handed over the cheque for her first week's rent, Mrs Tyzack pointed out that she had forgotten to sign it.

Now, in a calmer mood, she was regretting her impetuosity and thinking of all the things she should have looked for, and all the questions she should have asked. Perhaps she should have looked at other places? Or considered sharing more seriously? Yes, she should have accepted Tanya's offer of the attic in their house, that cosy attic with the skylight . . . But it was too late for that now, she had done it, she had signed the cheque. And although she was terrified by what she had done, it was also a great relief. She had made a move at last. She was finally on her way.

At least the house was within walking distance of the university, and close to the bus route home. But was there a back garden for the children to play in when they visited her? And what would she do with them in that dismal room?

A few days later, Lucy decided to visit her parents. She wanted to talk to them and explain why she was leaving home. She had tried to tell her mother on the telephone, but she would not listen. She had started shouting at her and banged down the receiver

She caught a bus outside the university one lunchtime. It travelled out through the old industrial area, with its silent factories and attendant districts of decaying terraced houses. She stood up at the greyhound track – she had travelled this route so often that she did it automatically – and got off at the end of

Coleridge Street where her parents lived. (It wasn't until after she had left school that she realised who Coleridge was, and that all the adjoining streets were named after poets too.)

She walked down the entry into the back yard and opened the kitchen door. (She did that automatically too. She could not remember the front door being used all the years she had lived there.) Her mother was peeling potatoes at the sink. When she saw who it was, she carried on with her work without speaking. Lucy stood in the doorway and watched the peel unwinding in one long strip like a bandage.

'I thought I'd better come and see you.'

Lucy's mother rinsed the potato under the tap, then dropped it into a basin of clean water. It looked much smaller without its skin, like a sheep with no wool.

'I don't want to see you, Lucy. I'm disgusted with you.'

Lucy was startled by her vehemence.

'Aren't you going to give me a chance to explain?'

'Explain? There is nothing to explain, as far as I can see. You're running away from your responsibilities, it's as simple as that.'

And it was as simple as that as far as she was concerned: there was no point in trying to explain. Lucy watched her working. Whenever she thought of her mother, this was where she saw her, standing at the kitchen sink in a pinafore and shabby flat shoes. She thought of Dave's mother in her cashmere jumper and high heels. She had been wearing make-up and jewellery at eleven o'clock in the morning.

Two mothers, approximately the same age. Lucy's looked so old compared to Dave's.

'Aren't you going to offer me a cup of tea then?'

'If you want a cup of tea, Lucy, you can get it yourself. I'm busy.'

This was the most crushing rebuff of all. Not to be offered tea put her on a par with the police and bailiffs.

'Is my dad in?'

'No. He's down at the club.'

'What does he say about it?'

'What does your dad ever say about anything?'

Lucy remained unwelcome on the doormat. She was afraid to walk through into the living room in case her mother told her to come out.

'I think I'll pop down and see him then.'

That did it. Her mother's judgement of her was confirmed.

'You can't go in there on your own.'

'Why can't I?'

'Because you can't. It'll be full of men.'

'What difference does that make?'

Her mother thought she was being provocative. Lucy had never seen her so angry before.

'Look, Lucy, just go, will you. Just get out of my sight.'

Lucy hadn't been expecting the red carpet, but she wasn't prepared for this either.

'You're shameless. I'm disgusted with you.'

'But why?'

'Why? If you don't know now, you never will.'

It was hopeless. There was no talking to her. Lucy left the house, closing the door quietly behind her. As she passed the kitchen window, she glanced in, but her mother deliberately averted her eyes and reached for the kettle. It hurt, but she bit her lip and willed herself not to cry.

Lucy had never been in a workingmen's club before. When she walked in, most of the members turned and stared at her. There were no other women in the room. They made her feel like an enemy.

Trying hard to appear unconcerned, she scanned the room for her father. She felt sure that if she stayed in the doorway much longer, someone would approach her and challenge her right to be there. She knew from her father that the clubs were sticklers for correct procedure.

He was sitting behind the snooker table at the far end of the room. He looked a long way away. She felt as if she was running the gauntlet as she crossed the room, but she kept her head up and walked purposefully as if she had every right to be there.

Her father was watching racing on television and had not seen her come in. Now, looking up, and seeing her unexpectedly in such incongruous surroundings, he did not immediately recognise her. Then he jumped up, embarrassed and confused.

'Hello, love, what are you doing here?'

'I've come to see you.'

'Why, what's happened?'

He looked panic-stricken, ready to leave. Lucy laughed.

'Nothing's happened. I've just come to see you, that's all.'

'Well, in that case, you'd better sit down then.'

Lucy was glad to. She felt too conspicuous standing up.

Watching her father hurriedly pull out a chair for her, she realised that he felt the same way. She wondered if she had made a mistake, upsetting him like this. But it was important, she needed to talk to him.

'That's better. Now then, what would you like to drink?'

She was tempted to order a pint of beer to give the members something else to talk about, but out of respect for her father's feelings she ordered an orange juice instead.

When he returned from the bar, he said, 'You gave me quite a turn. You're the last person I expected to see in here.'

Now that Lucy had been placed as George Watt's daughter, everyone forgot about her and resumed their former activities.

'I've been home first. My mother said you were in here.'

'I bet she was glad to see you, wasn't she?'

He gave a wry smile at the thought of their meeting.

'Ecstatic.'

'She's taken it badly, you know, Lucy.'

'I know that.'

'She never slept a wink that night, you know, after you'd told her on the telephone.'

Lucy watched a man shuffling dominoes on the next table. They moved sluggishly, close together like a miniature log jam.

'What do you think about it?'

'I'm sorry. I'm bound to be, aren't I? But I'm not surprised. I could tell there was something in the air when we saw you at Christmas. You and Phil weren't right together even then.'

'Why didn't you ring me? I thought you'd taken the same attitude as my mother.'

'Well, I can't say I approve. But whatever I say's not going to make much difference, is it?' He had a sip of beer. 'What is it then, have you got another bloke?'

Lucy did not answer immediately. She was looking round the room and wondering if it was always as full as this at lunchtime. Then she realised why: most of the men were probably out of work.

'No, not really.'

'What do you mean, not really? You either have or you haven't. I can't see as there can be anything in between.'

'There was someone, but that's finished now.'

'So what are you leaving for then?'

Lucy looked up at the television, which was set on a high shelf on the wall. The horses were being led round the paddock watched by their owners and trainers, who were standing round in expensive-looking groups. The sun was shining. They all looked as if they were enjoying themselves.

'Because it isn't enough for me any more.'

'I would have thought that running a home and going to university was enough for anybody.'

'That's the trouble!' Her voice was loud enough to make the domino players at the next table look round. Lucy took no notice of them. 'I feel hemmed in by it all. I need to be on my own for a bit. I know that now. It's the only way.'

Her tone was so impassioned that her father glanced around nervously. He was afraid that she might get too excited and cause a scene.

'It sounds as if university's gone to your head to me.'

'It has, but not in the way that you mean. It's opened my eyes, that's all.'

'I suppose it has. But is there any need to go to such extremes? I mean, what about the kids, what's going to happen to them?'

'They're stopping with Phil for now.' She tried to sound positive as if the decision had been hers. 'I think it's best to keep things as normal as possible for them.'

Her father shook his head and watched the horses cantering down the course towards the starting stalls.

'It's a hell of a thing to do, Lucy. Still, it's your life. It's up to you what you do with it.'

Lucy felt like swiping his beer glass off the table. He seemed to be more interested in the racing than in her.

'You always say that, don't you?'

He turned sharply, surprised by the bitterness in her voice.

'That's what you said when you went up to school to see Mr Parkhouse, when he wanted to know why I wasn't stopping on.'

'Bloody hell, Lucy, it's a bit late in the day to be bringing that up, isn't it? You'd made your mind up. You were determined to leave.'

'But you shouldn't have let me! If I'd been a doctor's daughter or somebody like that, I wouldn't have left. I'd have stopped on and gone to university then. I think that's half the trouble. If I'd gone at nineteen instead of twenty-nine, I wouldn't be in the mess that I'm in now.'

'But you weren't a doctor's daughter. You were a steelworker's daughter working all three shifts to keep his family going, and too buggered to do anything else. I let you leave school because I

205

didn't know any better. Let's face it, at sixteen you were better educated than me! What the hell did I know about university and all that?'

It was a rare sight to see him so animated. The only times that Lucy could remember him getting worked up was when he had occasionally been close on the football pools. The things he would have done with one more draw . . .

'But can't you see, dad, that's what I'm trying to get away from now, that same kind of ignorance. I left school because I didn't know any better. I didn't know any better when I got engaged, got married and had children. It was as if the decisions had been made for me somehow, as if I had nothing to do with it. I feel as if I've been conned!'

She finished off her orange juice and surprised her father even further by asking him for a cigarette.

'I've had enough of being told what to do. I'm ready to make my own decisions now.'

'Yes, I can see that. But I still can't see why you need to leave home?'

The horses were at the starting line. Eight of the runners had entered their stalls quietly, but the ninth was refusing and two handlers were trying to shove her in.

'Because I know what would happen if I didn't. Things would just drift back to what they were before. As soon as I got my degree, Phil would expect me to revert to my old role as housewife and mother. He'd resent me starting a career, it would make him feel inferior, especially if I was paid more than him. He wouldn't be able to stand that . . . Mind you, he's been marvellous with the children, I'll say that for him. But even then I always have the feeling that he thinks I ought to be grateful to him for what he does, and that he's doing me a favour somehow . . . No, there's too much happened between us now for it ever to be right again.'

Her father watched the horse race on television. It was over five furlongs so it did not take long. When it had finished, he said, 'You've got a nerve, Lucy, I'll say that for you. I just hope you know what you're doing, that's all.'

'You're not the only one.'

Her father laughed and finished his beer.

'I suppose I admire you really. I'm not sure that I know what you're after, but I can see why you're doing it. There's no point in carrying on if you're not satisfied, you'll only regret it afterwards

. . . That's the trouble, there's too many people put up with things instead of doing something about them.'

Lucy wanted to reach out and take his hand, to lean across the table and kiss him. But she resisted the temptation because it would have embarrassed him, and his mates would have made fun of him afterwards.

'Would you like another drink, dad?'

'It's all right, I'll get them.'

He started to feel in his jacket pockets, but Lucy picked up her bag and stood up first.

'You sit still. Come on, what do you want?'

He hesitated. Lucy knew why, but she stood her ground. He looked as if he was going to make an issue of it, then, shaking his head slowly, he looked up at her and began to smile.

'You've turned out a rum bugger, I know that much, Lucy. Go on then, I'll try a pint.'

Lucy picked up his glass, then, ignoring a renewed outburst of staring, walked confidently across the room towards the bar.

Lucy wondered if Phil would say anything to her before he got up. Would he make a last whispered plea? Or attack her with bitter accusations? She lay still with her back to him, pretending to be asleep. Phil did neither. He slipped quietly out of bed like he always did, closed the bedroom door behind him and went into the bathroom next door. Lucy knew his routine. She listened to him shaving and wondered which razor he was using. He had three. Phil enjoyed electric razors like some men enjoyed pipes. He turned on the taps. She could see him washing his face, getting dressed. Was this it then? Was this *really* the end?

He went downstairs. She wanted to call him back, to say something; anything. Would he come back up before he left for work? She listened to him moving about downstairs, heard him turn on the radio. She wanted to go down to him, to make his breakfast; anything . . .

The kitchen door banged. Too late! He had gone! But there was still time! Time to . . . Time to do what? The car started first time (as it always did), and Lucy listened to it reversing slowly up the drive. She could see Phil's intent expression as he squeezed between the gateposts. Then he was gone, accelerating up the street until the sound of the engine merged with the distant morning hum.

Lucy got up straightaway. She did not want to doze off and find one of the children snuggled up beside her when she woke up. That would be too much to bear this morning.

At breakfast, she casually told them that she was going away for a few days. (She had agreed this with Phil.) Where to? On a course. What does 'a course' mean? Something to do with university. No, it wasn't far. Yes, she would bring them a present back. Mathew seemed happy enough with the arrangement; a dumper truck, that was what he wanted, he said. But Tracey went quiet, and when Lucy saw her slopping her cereal about and told her to eat it up, Tracey just stared at her reproachfully.

Lucy wanted to hold their hands all the way to school, but they might have suspected that something was wrong if she had insisted. Especially Tracey, who considered herself too grown up now, and would only hold hands if there were no other children present. Lucy tried to behave normally. She laughed and chatted and pointed out sights on the way: a cat up a tree, the vivid cherry blossoms and a thrush tugging a worm out of a lawn. But all the time, her heart was threatening to choke her, and when she showed them a pair of swallows darting in unison, and told them that they had come all the way from Africa to build their nests, she had to feign a coughing fit to explain the tears in her eyes.

Lucy kissed them goodbye at the school gates, gave them fierce little hugs, and told them she would see them soon and to be good for their daddy. They raced across the playground, then paused in the doorway and waved before going in. Lucy turned round and hurried away in case any of the other mothers tried to speak to her.

It did not take her long to pack: one case and a bag full of books. She would come back for the rest later. She wondered if Tanya would lend her the van? Perhaps Phil would lend her the car . . . ? It was no time for joking. She made the beds and washed the pots, then, after checking that all the gas rings were turned off, she picked up her bags and left the house. After she had locked the door, she stood there wondering what to do with the key. She decided to keep it: she might need it some time.

At the top of the drive she changed her mind, ran back and dropped it through the letter box. Finally, she tried the handle, to make sure that the door was locked.